M000286820

Delicious
Conversation
a novel

Delicious Conversation

a novel

Jennifer Stewart Griffith

spring creek
BOOK COMPANY
Provo, Utah

ISBN 978-1-932898-82-8
e. 1

Published by:
Spring Creek Book Company
P.O. Box 50355
Provo, Utah 84605-0355

www.springcreekbooks.com

Cover design © Spring Creek Book Company

Printed in the United States of America
10 9 8 7 6 5 4 3 2 1
Printed on acid-free paper

Library of Congress Cataloging-in-Publication Data

Griffith, Jennifer Stewart, 1971-
 Delicious conversation / by Jennifer Griffith.
    p. cm.
 ISBN 978-1-932898-82-8 (pbk. : acid-free paper)
 1. Confectioners--Fiction. 2. Salt Lake City (Utah)--Fiction. 3. Chick lit. I.
Title.

PS3607.R5487D46 2007
813'.6--dc22
                        2007032813

For Colleen
who cares about people and dessert
more than anyone I know

Many thanks to Adrienne, Donna, Tina,
Virginia, and, of course, Mom

"After about 20 years of marriage, I think I'm finally starting to scratch the surface of what women want. And I think the answer lies somewhere between conversation and chocolate."

Mel Gibson

Chocolate Meringues

*These light and frothy little numbers are fat-free,
cholesterol-free, practically nutritionally bankrupt.*

"Bankrupt? What do you mean, bankrupt?" Colette dropped her maple syrup-laden fork and stared at Susannah in shock. The fork clattered in the diner's thick air.

"I mean full-on Chapter 7. Not a gentle Chapter 11 restructuring. Just a cut-your-losses, take-your-toys-and-go-home bankruptcy." Susannah sighed and pictured an entire aircraft carrier sinking, with a million rats jumping out into the flotsam and foam. She herself was the ash blonde rat wishing for bicep floatie tubes.

"But, Susannah! Pointman Westerford is, like, the backbone of the whole finance world in Salt Lake—in the state of Utah—in the whole Intermountain West! And, besides—you've basically devoted your whole life to them." Colette was practically shouting. Luckily the diner was all but empty at this time of the morning.

"Tell me about it." Dejected, Susannah took another bite of pancakes. Colette was right. Susannah Hapsburg had given the past eight years (basically her entire employable life) to that tall building which could now be leaped in a single bound—by a one-legged man. Pitiful.

She tossed Colette a syrup packet and took another pumpkin walnut muffin for herself from the basket. Food did wonders for deadening dismay. It was sweet of Colette, the friend Susannah cherished but hadn't had time to visit with for ages, to get so worked up over the situation. She really was a good friend. Susannah kicked herself once again for allowing that place to take over her life, to make her bury her ostrichy head in its sand sixteen hours a day, six days a week. And for what? A great big crater, blasted to smithereens

1

by an asteroid known as "Derma Double Heal-X."

"I've never even worked anywhere else, except the tennis shack for summer camps. It was completely weird to pick up my potted plant and wander out to my car—forever." Susannah stared at her reflection in the chrome napkin dispenser. It made her nose look narrower and her dark brown eyes too close together. She brushed a stray strand of her fair, straight hair off her brow and frowned, then reminded herself to reapply lipstick after lunch. Her face, though generally considered pretty, required lipstick.

"Bankrupt! I'm still reeling. How did it happen?" Colette shook her head. The two women had known each other since college. Susannah had been the maid of honor when Colette married Blaine, the cute grad student who had taught their Econ 250 class.

"I guess I saw it coming a couple of months ago, not that anyone asked my opinion."

"And that was their big mistake, Suze. You've always had a good financial head on your shoulders. Why didn't they put you on the board?"

Flattery was nice, but Susannah didn't know of a single major financial corporation that let lowly Fund Management Team members make suggestions during top-level board meetings.

"You're sweet, Colette. Thanks for the vote of confidence. I think it all started when Mr. Harville convinced them to buy heavily into that Internet company selling skin cream according to people's DNA."

"That's actually a good idea."

"I know. But think about it: who among us knows enough about our DNA to buy skin care products according to it? The molecular-biologists-skin-care market is a mighty tight niche to squirm into." She looked out the big plate-glass window into the summer morning. The inversion over the Salt Lake Valley had settled the smog into a nice, thick brown blanket. It made her want to hold her breath or wear a protective mask or something.

"I guess you're right." Colette peeled the paper from a blueberry muffin. In pre-Blaine college days, Colette had been the girl with the daring hair who danced by herself in front of the speakers at dances and parties. Susannah liked her for her bold independence.

"So, the skin cream fiasco marked the beginning of the end." Susannah had sensed tremors of PW's demise beginning last fall. She could see why the DNA thing, and so many other recent additions to the firm's portfolio, had been big lures—what with those shiny, mesmerizing terms like health and beauty and cyberspace and burgeoning China trade. "Poor Mr. Harville. He took it pretty hard."

"Didn't you pet-sit for him once?"

"As a matter of fact, I did—while he was on that fact-finding trip to Beijing. Remember, though, I only did it because he said I'd be watching Beagle, so I naturally thought it was a dog."

"Naturally."

"Of course, I was wrong there. Tortoise named Beagle."

"Should have seen that one coming, Susannah. Really."

"I know, I know." It had been a terrible weekend. How was she supposed to know that huge beast was a "unique breed" that rears up on its two hind legs to reach food? When she had found the thing's head buried up over its eyes in her full bathtub, she feared the reptile was making a bizarre suicide attempt. Why on earth would she know that's how tortoises drink? Susannah shook off the memory with a shudder.

"Pass the butter, would you? Mercy, it's hot in here." Susannah fanned herself with a napkin. The clock had barely struck eleven, but the searing sun already heated up the whole establishment, and Susannah's legs were sticking to the vinyl seat. It was the first weekday she hadn't worn pantyhose in eons. Vinyl seating repulsed her. The only reason she and Colette came to this dive they called Spammy Lunch (besides the bread basket) was the view of the Wasatch mountains, and today even that came dimmed by sludgy haze. "Don't you wish there were somewhere a little nicer in this part of town to get a bite?"

"Yeah, but it's a long-established neighborhood, Blaine says, so there's nowhere to build without demolishing something historic. What I really want is dessert. Should we get the apple pie? I bet they use real lard in the crust at a place like this. Seriously, lard is the way forward when it comes to pie crusts. Down with Crisco."

"Don't they have anything chocolate? I need it to soothe my weary soul."

The waitress in the pink apron brought them each a slice of Mississippi Mud Pie, the perfect chaser to pancakes with syrup and the muffin basket for a total carbo-blast brunch. How many years had it been since Susannah had enjoyed a leisurely, mid-morning, caution-to-the-wind calorie smash with a friend? Too many to recall.

"I'm still weirded out, Suze. Good old PW—finito. So, that begs the question: what are you going to do now?" Colette leaned back in the booth and sipped her ice water, holding it to her lips with her right hand and patting her full tummy with her left. She snatched one last crumb of the Mud crust.

"Well, I've had about 24 hours to mull it over. Honestly, I don't know."

"You've got some money saved. Why not think about your next move while sipping frosty fruit drinks on the deck of some Caribbean cruise ship? Ooh. I drank something called Mango Granita over at Coral Hills last week. Tangy and delicious."

"That would be nice, except I don't have any leisure skills. I tried to sit in front of the TV last night, and I kept getting antsy. I ended up driving over to my little house in the Avenues and pulling dead weeds out of the flowerbed until it got too dark."

It had been a sad little weeding outing. The city still hadn't cooled at sunset last night, and with each handful of stubbly yellow straw Susannah yanked from the long-neglected dirt, she had expelled puffs of frustration—frustration at losing her job, frustration at the demise of a century-old institution, and mostly, frustration at the horrific lurch it left her in: single and unemployed with two mortgages.

Why did this sudden financial downturn have to rear its ugly head so soon after she closed the deal on her darling little dream cottage in the foothills below the Utah Capitol building? Especially since that dream cottage remained so much closer to a nightmare than a dream? Nearly every portion of it still required major surgery. And although she had long ago determined she was willing to perform that surgery, at whatever learning curve or sweat equity it would cost, Susannah also knew other, more tangible costs would have to be incurred in the form of cold, hard cash. Two mortgages plus fixer-uppering plus unemployment added up to financial insolvency.

"So, are you going to have to put that fixer-upper back on the market?"

"Could you see it in my eyes?"

"It's the look you get whenever I've heard you talk about that house."

"Oh, Colette. I don't know. Two mortgages? I'm unemployed. But I can't face losing it, not after all this time finding it and financing it and working on it." It wrenched her soul, but Susannah knew what practicality demanded.

Colette smiled, "It won't be long before you've got five offers."

"On the house? You think? It's a good zip code, but the condition it's in—"

"No, for employment. If you want, I'll tell Blaine, and it won't take fifteen minutes for your résumé to get from the business school to half the banking companies in the Salt Lake Valley." Colette's husband Blaine had, since their marriage, moved up to full-tenured professor in the business school at the University of Utah, and he now rested his finger on the pulse of Salt Lake's financial world.

"Tempting, but I'd better hold off." Susannah wasn't ready to jump back into the financial melee yet. Certainly the double mortgage monster gave her the creeps, big time. But when she got through with college she snapped up the Pointman Westerford position so quickly she'd hardly had time to consider her options. And since then, they'd kept her busy enough that she hadn't even had time to dream. Yesterday afternoon she'd played tennis for the first time in months. One thing she did know: she refused to take any new job unless it felt absolutely right.

"I want to take a week to figure out my next career move."

"Have you given any thought to abandoning terms like 'career move'?"

"Plenty. And no, I still haven't met anyone who fits the job description."

"Susannah, you've been so immersed in your work—you haven't even been advertising for the position."

"I date," she proclaimed, albeit hesitantly. "It's just that I don't have a steady boyfriend right now."

Colette raised an eyebrow at this, and Susannah knew she couldn't hide behind her façade here. They'd known each other too long.

"Okay. Whatever. But there isn't anyone in my immediate circle right now who even catches my eye."

Colette opened her mouth to protest, but Susannah cut her off. "And don't you dare mention the term 'single adult ward.' You'll be the third person this week, and I don't want to send you to three-strikes-and-you're-out-of-here zone." First it was Susannah's mother's e-mail message from Brazil, then it was her temp-mom, Barbara Russell, and now Colette? No. Susannah must ward off the impending conversation. "I'm perfectly content with my calling as Junior Primary chorister, so don't even go there."

"Are you through?" Colette rolled her eyes, and Susannah, satisfied, nodded. "I was simply going to gently suggest taking your mother's class ring off your left ring finger and at least getting out there a little. It's like—"

"Like what?"

Colette hesitated, twirling her platinum blonde highlights with her index finger. She was a compulsive self-highlighter and often shared her skills with her various friends and acquaintances. "It's like you were this dating queen back in college, and then after I got married, and you went on that weird outing to South America—"

"—Central America. Guatemala."

"Whatever. When you got back you were different. All dreamy-eyed for about a month and then, suddenly, mission! And, after that, basically the monastery."

"Don't you mean nunnery?"

"You see? You know exactly what I'm saying. What happened to you down there?"

It was more like what didn't happen to her on that humanitarian expedition a decade back. Susannah had never leveled with Colette about it, or with her parents. Even with Barbara, Susannah didn't discuss the full trauma of it. It was too tender at first, and then, by the time she got back from her mission to Austria, too scarred over. Reopening the old wound then didn't appeal, and he had left Salt Lake for who knows where. Susannah kept nearly all the harrowing details to herself, and with no fanfare, that whole chapter of her life had closed.

"Oh, my goodness. Look at the time. Blaine will be home for lunch in about five minutes. He doesn't know where the can opener is, so he could starve." Colette glanced at the check, plopped a few ones onto the table, and collected her stylish purse and highest-tech phone. As a wife but not yet a mom, Colette could afford toys and fashions and cooking hobbies many other women her age couldn't. Luckily, her good fortune didn't spoil her good personality. "I'm so glad we got together. Love that pie. Hey, can you come for dinner? I'm making Italian—homemade tortellini with parmesan and spinach filling. Oh! And chocolate chip meringues for dessert. Your old favorite."

Susannah smiled and thanked her but explained she had plans with herself tonight to rent a movie and order Thai.

"Ah, foray number two into the scary world of leisure skills. Good for you." Colette gave her the thumbs up. They hugged good-bye, and Susannah watched her friend walk out to her Camry and drive toward home in Federal Heights, which was across the north end of the Salt Lake Valley.

Susannah lingered in the diner, opening little packets of Sweet 'N Low and emptying them slowly into her glass of water. As the granules descended and dissolved, she thought about life. Today she pictured it as a river. She'd gone along for what seemed forever on the Mighty Mississippi—wide and smooth, no bends or rapids or snags, not even a Tom Sawyer Island in her path to break up the monotony of the view—simply going to her narrow, financial analysis job every day, reading her little pile of books and magazines at night, playing with her sister Carly's kids on Saturdays, and singing with the Junior Primary on Sundays. It felt like nothing would ever change—like nothing could ever change.

Now she suddenly found herself not on the Mississippi, but the Colorado River. Buying the cottage had been the first bend in the swifter-moving stream, and that decision sent her into the whitewater when Pointman Westerford went down. Now she was barreling through the narrows, smashing into rapid after rapid as she floated helplessly between the walls of the Grand Canyon with her two mortgages and no job. Then there were the other snags: having no husband (or prospects) and, therefore, no kids. The sharp, renegade branches of aloneness lurked below her raft, threatening to slash a hole in it. Some days those dangers themselves—loneliness and defeat—felt so menacing she considered climbing out and hauling portage, giving up on the whole thing and moving into her parents' basement, living off their food storage as a hermit until they came home from Brazil.

She picked up her spoon and stirred the water in the glass, then added a final few grains of the sweetener. They spun as they sank, and as she watched them, a premonition of sorts flashed in Susannah's mind.

You're not on the Colorado River, honey.

She wasn't? Then where was she?

You're on the Potomac.

That didn't seem too bad. The Potomac was a broad, lazy old river. So what?

Sweetheart, you're on the Maryland side, just upstream from Great Falls.

CHOCOLATE MERINGUES

2 egg whites
1/8 teaspoon cream of tartar
1/2 cup granulated sugar
1/3 cup cocoa
2/3 cup chocolate chips

Whip egg whites with cream of tartar until soft peaks form. Stir cocoa into sugar; then gradually add to egg whites, beating until stiff. Fold in chocolate chips. Drop by teaspoons onto cookie sheet. Bake 20 minutes at 300 degrees Fahrenheit. Serve on a napkin to catch the delicious crumbs. You won't want to lose a one.

♡
Flourless Chocolate Torte

*With each rich, buttery, chocolaty bite, you'll
realize there's no way around it: this impossibly
good torte is the best thing you've ever tasted.*

There was no way around it. Under current monetary trends, two mortgages were going to be impossible to swing. The darling little fixer-upper in the Avenues, with its nine layers of wallpaper and its leaky roof, would have to be jettisoned from her portfolio. With aching fingers, she dialed Joan the realtor's cell phone number and resigned herself to another five years in her middling condo, with its bleak white walls and its breathtaking view of . . . the parking lot.

The call finally connected, but Susannah entered the auto-answer-hold-void—press one if you want to strangle the person who designed this system. She sighed. How was she going to break it to her real estate agent that the house she'd scurried and bargained and practically begged for was going back on the market in such a short time? Could even a penny of equity have accrued? Not likely. More likely, she was out a cool seven thou' on closing costs instead. On the other hand, it was better than joining her bosses in bankruptcy court.

Finally the system spit her into Joan's voice mail, and Susannah left the dreaded message. "Joan. It's Susannah Hapsburg. Three months no see. You're not going to believe this, but I think I'm already ready to sell. Call me."

Then she gave her fridge a little punch with her clenched fist. It had taken her all day to get up the gumption to make the call. As self-punishment for her cowardice, she hadn't allowed herself to order the Thai for delivery until she mustered a bit of practical self-discipline. Now starving, she called and ordered takeout instead (which was a faster route from phone to gullet) and set out for the closest Blockbuster to snag her movie while Mr. Yan seasoned her Pad Thai noodles with that amazing, heady concoction of coconut, peanut oil, and Thai hot chili powder.

Her Jetta sputtered to a halt in front of movie heaven. Walking into the video store gave her the feeling she'd arrived in a foreign country. Nothing looked pop-culturally familiar as she emerged from her work-cave. She hadn't seen a single one of the new releases along the far wall. Shame on her for never making time to relax.

Tonight definitely called for comforting nostalgia. An Austrian folk song had played through her head all afternoon, which made her homesick for Salzburg and Vienna and Europe (or at least for the security of missionary life where every minute of every day was planned out for her), but none of the imported films appealed. Too foreign.

Aha. In the drama section she spied the perfect medicine: *Chocolat.* Oh! She loved that little flick with Juliet Binoche and Johnny Depp when she watched it years ago. Yes, a European-craving fix; foreign, but without subtitles; a beautiful heroine and delicious food as the main characters. Perfect. And her Pad Thai noodles should just be coming out of the pot. At last. A turn for the better.

As she entered the door to her condo, the telephone was ringing. She dropped her packages on the coffee table and raced to pick it up, hoping to hear from her realtor Joan pulling a late night.

"Susannah! It's Carly. Can you get over here quick?" Her older sister sounded desperate.

"Of course." Susannah glanced wistfully at her video and Pad Thai and hurried back out to her ailing red '94 Jetta, but she was thinking all the while, Carly's house had better be on fire.

♡ ♡ ♡

"Don't you absolutely love Ian's new barbecue grill? It doesn't even use charcoal—it's all electric!" Carly beamed as she bounced her three year-old, Poppy, on her hip. "We're searing the steaks and roasting the corn on the cob. That's it there in the tinfoil. See?"

Susannah saw. And she could vaguely smell her Pad Thai growing cold back at her condo. Grr. Oh, well. Couldn't takeout wait? These kids would only be 15, 11, 9, and 3 for a short time, right? Smothering her grumbling, Susannah took little Poppy from her mother's arms and hauled her off to the pool. The older kids, Perry and Piper, were splashing in the shallow end, playing keep-away from Polly.

"Aunt Zannie! Come play!" called Polly. Susannah stuck her toes in the shallow end and kept an eye on the swimmers.

Later, after a surprisingly delicious meal prepared entirely by her brother-in-law (men will cook if danger is involved), Susannah relaxed poolside with her older sister while the kids ran through the sprinklers and Ian scraped the spatulas.

"That's what I love about Ian. He may not be Mr. Attention-to-Details, but he sure makes me feel like a queen from time to time. Do you know, he made the most incredible-looking chocolate torte for dessert." Carly sighed. "You should get yourself one like him, sis."

"Ian's one of a kind, Carly. You know that."

"Yeah." Carly glanced over at him dreamily, then suddenly leaned forward, clapping her hands on her lap. "Guess who's back in town?"

Susannah had no idea. Carly, who never finished her sophomore year at the business college, still lived and breathed Sugarhouse gossip. The "suburb" of Sugarhouse sat practically dead center in the Salt Lake metro area but had a rumor mill like an isolated mountain village. Every life was an open book. Tonight Susannah found it impossible to rally enthusiasm for yet another old friend update.

"Come on, guess! Oh, you never will. John Wentworth."

John Wentworth? That was unexpected. John! It took every ounce of Susannah's will not to allow the shock of hearing his name to register on her face. But John had been gone for almost ten years—since the time she left for Austria.

"Yeah, John Wentworth. Oh, I bet you don't even remember

that charmer. He was all the rage and then, bammo! He, like, evaporated from the social scene here. Quite a few of my girlfriends wished they could take a crack at him. And where'd he desert us for? Alaska. And without even getting married before he left. Not likely a guy could get himself a wife up there. Do you know it's like a twenty-to-one guy to girl ratio in the tundra land? Hoowee."

Alaska! Susannah had never known where John went when he left. After Guatemala. After—

"But anyway, now he's back, and they say he's richer than Midas, and I bet he's in town to get married. He was never super handsome, his dreamboat days left the dock forever ago, but he sure had swagger. I like swagger. He bought a house—with cash!— in the Marmalade District, around the hill from your new place in the Avenues." Carly's ancient dog, a wrinkly shar pei named Mr. Lunch, came over to where the sisters sat and breathed his old dog breath on them. "It's so trendy and up-and-coming there. Remember how seedy Marmalade was five years ago? How is your little house, anyway?"

"Oh, uh, it's coming along." Susannah couldn't bring herself to reply intelligently to her sister's new topic, as she was cemented into the old one. Alaska? Never married? Not even after a decade? But, at eight years her senior, John would be nearly 40 by now. Fortunately, Carly's conversational thread required no responses, and Susannah was left to nod and say "uh-huh" at appropriate intervals while her thoughts ran madly through the past.

He was back. John Wentworth was back. It sent her heart racing, partly with hope—a hope she hadn't felt in ages, and partly with dread—dread that he was still as angry with her as he had been when . . .

"Which brings me back to John Wentworth." Carly wound her way back again. "He's down here during the off-season, doing who knows what, and buying up property, or at least that's what I'd be doing." Her conversation spiraled on about investment properties for a few blessed moments. It was a little disconcerting for Susannah to be bombarded with all this information from someone who had no idea how much it pained the listener to hear it.

"You can really make your fortune up there, especially on the crab boats. My girlfriend told me John started out plain old crab fishing but worked his way into part owner, then full owner of a crab boat and now makes more working three months a year than most of us make in five years. But crab fishing is no cake walk—they say it's one of the most dangerous jobs on earth. I think they even did a Discovery Channel thing on how scary it is. And Alaska's not a place to stay, to live forever. He's probably going to settle down in Salt Lake. His mother is still around here, I think. . . ."

Yes, Mrs. Wentworth still lived in the city, but John's father passed away the springtime before their summer in Guatemala. Susannah could never forget the feelings John confided in her about his father on that sweltering day, hauling buckets of concrete mix to the aqueduct project for the village. His words were engraved on her heart.

Just then, Perry pushed Piper into the grapevine, and tears ensued. Carly and Susannah both had to attend to the argument. But soon after, Susannah needed to be alone with her thoughts—enough to even beg off chocolate torte dessert.

At her condo, she found herself staring at the wall and hugging a sofa cushion tightly to her chest. He was back. Her first impulse was to rush out and find him, to get a good look at him, to let him know she was still here, still . . . still what? In love with him? Still available? Still desperately, hopelessly at his mercy? But why would he consider that a case of "still?" After all, she was the one who flat-out rejected him when he came home from CHOICE. Ha, ha. Wasn't that ironic, considering he spent the entire duration of the project basically fighting her off. Not that she was chasing him or making aggressive advances. Certainly not. Love on the trail was strictly verboten, and with his position as Project Director, a lot was at stake.

But by the fireside in the evenings, or during the grueling workdays, they naturally gravitated to one another, to each other's conversation and way of thinking. All the while he professed to be looking for a girl "with a few more years on her," but it was obvious to Susannah, if not to the whole crew, that John Wentworth was utterly smitten with his energetic protégé. He couldn't have hidden his longing for her behind the moon.

For Susannah, it was a fiercely intense three months abroad: backbreaking work, emotional peaks and valleys, the creation of the waterway to the village, and most of all meeting someone who opened her mind, and then her heart—someone courageous and idealistic, good to his very center. She was twenty, he was twenty-eight. The span of eight years seemed so great then. Initially it scared her, kept her from letting herself fall for him. But eventually, the pull of his charisma and character were too great, and she let herself be secretly, wholly in love.

And then there was the waterfall, where . . . But she didn't let herself think about that.

Susannah briefly nodded off on the couch with those memories rattling around in her head. She dreamed of his broad laugh, his wavy hair, his gentle way of speaking to the village leaders in their native tongue. Then, suddenly, the other visage appeared in her mind—his hurt and anger, and the way he turned from her, how his back looked as he stalked away. The image woke her with a start.

The pillow had fallen to the floor and she clutched it again. Chances were, John Wentworth had no desire to see Susannah Hapsburg again as long as he lived.

♥ ♥ ♥

Susannah spent a restless night on the sofa, going over dozens of scenarios in her mind, both regarding John and her economic life. Things had taken a serious downturn, and on her way home from Carly's, her Jetta had started making another suspicious sound. Not that she could have paid any attention to it under the circumstances. Her mind had been completely high-jacked by other anxieties.

She slouched around her apartment, bed-headed and pajamaed until nearly 8:00 a.m., and felt like a slacker loser, completely beset by the latest onslaught of negative circumstances.

Her mechanic didn't work weekends. Susannah had known for

a couple of years she needed to offload the Jetta, but as a savvy finance major, she also knew what a bad investment a new car always is. And as a transportation-risk-averse girl, she dreaded the task of finding a non-lemon used car. She needed her very mechanical and trustworthy dad in town for that process, and he was so not in town.

For now, what she really needed was a therapeutic outing to see Barbara Russell in her gated community on the East Bench. Barbara, her stand-in mom for now, was the only other person who knew—even partially—Susannah's former feelings for John Wentworth. She'd confided in Barbara, as always, as soon as she returned from Central America. Hesitantly at first, she let his name drop in a travel vignette or two. Then, when Barbara looked interested, Susannah more boldly mentioned some of her true feelings, but concealed a torrent of hopes. Barbara's responses governed what Susannah did next, and that decision had perhaps made all the difference.

Pulling a slice of Godiva cheesecake from her fridge, she sat down to look over the details of the job offers once again and let her mind percolate. Susannah longed to talk to her mentor and friend. Besides the John Wentworth disaster (Was it a disaster? Susannah felt like disaster incarnate herself, but she wasn't sure if the John Wentworth situation was a disaster or a cause for hope), she needed someone wise with whom to discuss her next career move. Two banks had contacted her directly, to her great surprise and delight, with offers she oughtn't refuse. Both places had impeccable reputations, and Susannah couldn't help but wonder whether Colette had pulled a string or two via Blaine's connections. But neither offer made her heart go pitter pat, so her confusion reigned. At last she came to an impasse and dialed her phone.

"Hi, Barbara—it's me, Susannah."

"Suzie! Have you gotten a job offer? Where is it?"

"A few, but none I'm sure about. What are you doing? Do you have time to come by and watch a movie with me? I'm working on my lounging skills."

"I'm just taking a peach cobbler out of the oven—my peach

tree runneth over. I'll bring us some. Do you have any vanilla ice cream?" Within an hour, the two ladies were ensconced in Susannah's sofas, savoring one of earth's ultimate comfort foods and setting up the DVD player.

"I haven't been to your apartment in ages. I like what you've done with the furniture."

Susannah hadn't done anything with it in four years, but she didn't want to bring up what a lousy friend she obviously was. Working nearly 100 hours a week of necessity made their visits rare, and Susannah was much more used to visiting at Barbara's fine home in the foothills on the east side of the valley, sharing good visits in her airy, walk-out basement, than entertaining Barbara—or anyone else—here.

"Tell me what's going on, Suze." Barbara sipped her lemon water, curling her feet up underneath her as she lounged. She was 15 years older than Susannah, and Susannah had been her babysitter when Madeleine and Matt were young. Now Barbara was a stylish grandmother to four of Madeleine's and one of Matt's, and Susannah couldn't believe Barbara was the age Susannah was now when they'd met.

"I got these two offers. One's at Carleton, the other is at Bonneville. They're both doing financial analysis, basically the same stuff I've been doing forever, but for more money. And they have an international presence, so there's a possibility of travel."

"So, what's the problem?" She made it sound like there shouldn't be any problem.

"Neither one calls to my soul." Susannah plopped her chin onto her palm for emphasis. "Besides, honestly? I'm not sure getting a job is the right thing to do."

"Hmm." Barbara chewed her bite of cobbler thoughtfully. "You're not saying you plan to stay jobless, with all that would entail."

"No. Heavens, no. I don't mean I'd stay unemployed, join the shopping cart living set. I mean, I feel like taking one of these jobs might be the wrong thing is all."

"What about house payments?" Barbara poured salt in the

sorest wound there, although Susannah knew it was unintentional. "Or do you have the condo paid off?"

"Not quite. Plus, the house in the Avenues is faaaaar from inhabitable." The very thought of the house sent a pang through Susannah's sad heart. Losing it was by far the most painful personal consequence of PW's bankruptcy.

"Too bad some rich, swarthy hero doesn't step into your life right about now and take you away from all these decisions."

"Ha. Wouldn't that be nice," Susannah nearly snorted. At that point she debated whether to share the information about John's return. Swarthy didn't exactly define him. She wasn't sure Barbara would even remember him as a blip on the radar screen. It would take too much explaining and make it seem more important that it was. Besides, there was basically no way on earth he'd be interested in being her hero—not after what had happened. "I'm afraid I'm going to have to work my way out of this financial downturn alone."

"Well, my dear, what are you going to do?"

"First things first: I'm going to shut off my worrying brain. Where's that movie?" She popped the disc in the player and sat back to soak in the movie's sienna-washed European ambience. Then, much to Susannah Hapsburg's surprise and delight, *Chocolat* did not have the mind-numbing effect on her worries she'd anticipated. Instead, it gave her inspirations that felt like the dews from heaven distilling.

FLOURLESS CHOCOLATE TORTE

12 squares semisweet chocolate, chopped
4 squares unsweetened chocolate, chopped
1 cup butter
9 large eggs
½ cup sugar
¼ teaspoon cream of tartar

Melt chocolates and butter together. Beat egg yolks and sugar until very thick and lemon colored. Fold into chocolate mixture. Beat egg whites and cream of tartar until soft peaks form. Gently fold chocolate/egg mixture (⅓ at a time) into whites, just until blended. Scrape into greased Springform pan. Bake 35 minutes at 300 degrees Fahrenheit. Cool completely. Refrigerate overnight in pan. Serve at room temperature, dusted with powdered sugar.

Red Devil Cake

*Put your best German Chocolate icing on this
amazing cake. One bite will transport you out of
this world—and you won't want to come back
to planet earth until the whole cake is gone.*

"Whoa! Welcome back to planet earth! Where have you been,
stranger?"

Susannah practically bounced from foot to foot as she stood on
Colette's front porch. She couldn't suppress her smile of excitement.
"Sorry, Colette. I've been completely swamped. And I have the
best news. Do you have a few minutes? I'm dying to show you
something. Oh. Any chance you could drive?"

"How did you get here? Where's your icky old Jetta?" The new
cherry red highlights in Colette's now-chestnut hair glinted in the
summer sun.

"My icky old Jetta's at her second home: the shop. Something
like the cataclysmic converter needs to be overhauled, which will
cost six times the value of the vehicle. I came on light rail."

"But you hate the light rail. Sure I'll drive. Let me take the soup
off the stove."

"Mm. Is that the asparagus soup with the lemon crème fraiche?"
She observed her friend's nod and wry smile. "Love that stuff. And
I love that you love food like I do."

"So does Blaine. He's getting to be a regular fatty. I don't
have anything until five. Highlights for Sasha. Again." Sasha.
Ugh. Sasha-take-two-Tylenol-and-call-me-when-she's-gone, their
other old roommate, still frequently sponged off Colette's skill for
highlights for her Channel 6 News helmet hair. Susannah followed
Colette to the garage and then guided her back downtown toward

Capitol Hill. It was nice to be out of the heat and into icy Camry air conditioning again. "You're not taking me to your decrepit old house, are you? You know how I feel about cobwebs."

"No. Look! It's right here. Pull over. I mean, pull in."

Colette wheeled her sedan into the driveway of a small brick house that looked completely outsized between two commercial buildings.

Susannah bubbled with glee. "You know how we were lamenting the lack of sidewalk cafés around here?"

"We were? Oh, yeah. When we were at Spammy Lunch. Sure."

"Well, it finally came to me. Perfect business venture, perfect location, perfect bill of fare. Come on!" She practically dragged Colette by the arm. "Isn't it great?"

"Wow! Great masonry! Cute house. It's all nestled back in there with maples and pines. Oh! Check out the sweet Tudor-style half-timbers." Colette gushed appropriately. The place was an utter charmer: brick, flagstone walk, lantern hanging over the covered porch.

"Yep. Loving it, and those are flower boxes. Picture them overflowing with geraniums. Think arbored walkway dripping with wisteria, ironwork chairs and tables under a shady lattice of vines there off to the side. I looked at this place when I was shopping for the dream cottage but hated the commercial zoning and high traffic. However, for this, it's great."

"For what? Don't you like your dream house on the hill anymore?"

"I do, but this place is my dream business. Look—it's right across the street from Temple Square, the Conference Center, Pioneer Park, and only a short walk from the Family History Library. Perfect location, other than the parking problem. And with all these shade trees!" Evergreens, aspen, a sprawling willow, and several Japanese maples now in full blazing red adorned the landscape.

"You're opening a business?"

"Over the past two weeks I've done some serious soul searching."

They stepped across the dappled driveway and wandered over to a wooden bench beside a terra cotta birdbath.

Colette relaxed onto the bench's slats. "Surprisingly comfortable." She patted its wooden rails and inhaled deeply. Susannah picked up a pinecone from beside her feet and toyed with it as she, too, breathed the musty scents of early autumn.

"This jolt—I'll call the death of my career a jolt—made me realize I'm ready for Plan C. Plan A was get married at 22 and have a passel of kids; Plan B, work my way up Pointman Westerford's corporate ladder. That leaves me with Plan C, like it or not. I don't want to work for someone else again, Colette. I'm ready to build something that will last . . . that might even outlast me. I recently witnessed a very respectable company going down in the flames of beauty and technology, and I thought, what I need is to create something wonderful for my fellow sisters. Something delicious. Something precious and delicious."

"Like what? What are you thinking?" A lilt in Colette's voice revealed she was beginning to catch the infectious excitement.

"Chocolate."

"Like in the movie?"

"Bingo. How did you know?"

"Because a place that serves precious and delicious chocolate to your individual taste is every woman's dream come true."

The distilling dews of this idea had fallen quickly into Susannah's brain. After viewing *Chocolat* with Barbara, a seed of an idea began to grow. She could picture herself at a café counter, smiling and dishing out relief, one refined cocoa bean at a time.

The seed germinated and sprouted, then stretched itself skyward throughout the evening as she soaked in the hot bath (for exactly four minutes, proving once again she had no leisure skills). The idea disturbed her thoughts until she sat down at her laptop and formulated an entire business model.

The seedling wouldn't let her rest until she'd driven up and down a dozen streets in downtown Salt Lake City when, at last, the little Tudor house sparkled out at her from its ideal location just off Temple Square in all its historic charm. At last, it took root.

Susannah scared up the funding and signed on the dotted line.

"What will you call it?" Colette asked vacantly, staring around, taken up in the dream.

"I'm thinking of . . . The Chocolate Bar." Warmth spread through her as she spoke it. "Let's peek in the window." Together they pressed their faces against one of the mullioned windowpanes, and Colette wiped a fine crust of dirt from hers.

"See that area?" Colette pointed toward the living room. "Can you imagine a huge, semi-circular bar, made of some warm honey wood with sweet little chairs all pulled up next to it?"

"Yep. There I am," Susannah mused, "standing behind it in a sporty apron. And all around that side are the chintz-covered booths. Barbara Russell told me she'll lend us some of her framed art and some lanterns from Madeleine's wedding reception. And there! That side! That's where the pastry case will be—with all the éclairs and chocolate almond mousses and hazelnut tarts in chocolate crumb crusts. I found the best china teacups on eBay today. It's right, isn't it? It's so right. And, Colette, I've settled on my perfect business partner."

"Who?" Colette looked surprised. "Me? Are you serious? I mean, Blaine doesn't mind letting me take on projects to keep me occupied, but—this is big."

It hadn't taken Susannah long to settle on Colette. Unlike Susannah, Colette wasn't a ball of energy, super woman in constant motion, but she had excellent instincts about people and food, and her laconic but precise style would put customers at ease. Colette's presence could make the atmosphere in the café.

"You're right. It is big. I'm just glad I know a few people in the money business, or I could never do it." The whole deal was contingent on offloading her second home loan, which was getting more and more frustrating, as Joan hadn't yet returned her calls. In another day or two, Susannah would have to abandon realtor loyalty and find someone else to list the dream cottage. The pressure was really on to sell now.

As awful as the prospect was of losing the fixer-upper, the excitement of the business venture outweighed it. She could already smell the cocoa and cream wafting on the air.

"Colette. You're the dessert goddess. You know and care more about food and people than anyone else I know. I need you."

"I cook, but I don't cook that much. Don't make me be your chef!"

"Oh, no. I need you there for business and moral support. We'll hire a pastry chef. I know a guy. You can be his sous chef, or just toss in a dessert entry when you feel like it." Susannah wanted Colette by her side at the bar to keep the clientele coming back.

"The Chocolate Bar." Colette ran her thumb thoughtfully along the curve of her jaw. "Hmm. Believe it or not, I can picture it. I can picture myself next to you in a sporty apron, serving up Powdered Sugar Dusted Dark Chocolate Waffles with vanilla ice cream and fudge sauce. Oh! Or Red Devil Cake—with German chocolate frosting." Colette paused to sigh. "Blaine won't believe it. He might freak momentarily, but yeah. *Vive le chocolat!*" She raised an upturned hand in the air and waved it in an Evita salute. "Let's be sure and put my Mousse-Topped Brownies somewhere on our well-written menu."

♡ ♡ ♡

With excitement brimming in her heart, Susannah took an afternoon run to her favorite tennis courts. She played a couple of pick-up matches against some teen enthusiasts and felt some of the old power returning to her backhand.

On her way home, she was so excited she began skipping down a steep-ish road and nearly twisted her ankle when she found herself in John Wentworth's old neighborhood. She'd forgotten. At least this route didn't take her directly past his mother's house. Wouldn't that be the most mortifying thing—being caught spying on him—and then not being able to escape with any speed but her two legs?

Her racquet banged against her ribcage as she jog-walked along the tree-lined street. It was a family neighborhood with kid bikes and Razor scooters and stray roller skates littering the shady, rosebed-filled yards. This part of town didn't have the historic appeal of the

Avenues, but it felt like middle America and quite homey. Her cell phone's ring broke into her thought patterns.

"Susannah!" It was realtor Joan. Finally, the moment of truth had come. Good-bye, dream home. Welcome back, condoville. "So, tell me quick. Are you loving your fixer upper? I know you are. And I hope you're really, really loving it with all the TLC it needs because you're never going to believe who just walked in here. Go ahead, guess."

Susannah couldn't guess.

"Brigham Talmage! Yes, *the* Brigham Talmage. From the TV commercials." What? Great. Joan was in love with him, too? Practically the whole body of single Mormon females was panting over the most eligible bachelor in Salt Lake City, Brigham Talmage, the devastatingly handsome, Harvard-educated attorney whose face on billboards had caused more accidents on I-15 than black ice. The Department of Transportation finally asked him to please switch to a different photo or use only text for the safety of the female driving population.

"That's nice." Susannah didn't know what else to say. She couldn't imagine what Counselor Heartthrob's appearance had to do with her, unless Joan had more matchmaking in mind than home to homeowner. Egad.

"Nice! Nice? Wait 'til you hear. He's here asking for a condo in your complex and has a cash offer of fifty over what yours appraised for last spring. Certainly you were calling to say yours is for sale, weren't you? Weren't you?"

Susannah tripped over a crack in the sidewalk, spilling the contents of her tote bag. "Actually, Joan, you won't believe this—"

♡ ♡ ♡

Closing the sale took less than two weeks, paperwork included, and Susannah giggled with glee as she lugged the final boxes from the U-Haul into her parents' garage and basement, while Brigham L. Talmage signed on the dotted line to become the proud owner of a brand-old condo on the less fashionable side of northern Salt Lake City. Good for him, she thought. And good for me.

Really good! With that completed, her own signature could slide onto the dotted line to make her the owner of the first and best chocolate restaurant in downtown Salt Lake.

With a last torch lamp and stray box of books, the U-Haul disgorged its final contents, and Susannah went inside to get a drink and take a breather in her mother's kitchen. The smell of the home where she grew up made Susannah long to talk to her mother. This week-long tale of job change, condo sale, and famous lawyers was exactly the kind of major upheaval that would make Sister Hapsburg cheer, and President Hapsburg would crack a smile at it as well. They'd been after their younger daughter to get out of her rut for a while now, and Susannah was banking on that fact for her assumption that they wouldn't mind her being a squatter in their vacant home for a bit—just until she could get her dream cottage off the nearly-condemned properties list. After all, they still had nearly a year and a half before their run as mission president and mission mom was up, which was when they'd need their home in Sugarhouse again.

Standing there in her parents' house, peace seemed to flow into Susannah's entire being, a peace so long absent she almost didn't recognize it. Ian had even offered to let her borrow his shiny chrome Vespa moped with the wide silver fenders and chrome helmet until she was set with the store and dared make another large financial outlay for transportation.

Opening her mother's spice cupboard, she found the recipe for chocolate chip cookies taped on the inside of the door. It was a butter-only recipe—no shortening or margarine—and Susannah thought once again of her mother's wisdom in many areas of life. It had been nearly two years since they'd had a heart-to-heart. Christmas calls and weekly e-mails didn't count.

Nearly every woman has a panel of advisers she consults on important decisions, and for Susannah, her mother sat on every panel. Her dad sat on most. Barbara joined them for the dating panel, and Colette was the one she called when she needed an idea for a pot-luck dish for a work party. Other unwitting friends sat in advisory positions as well. Now, here in this kitchen, despite all the other highly distracting events of recent life, Susannah longed to convene a panel discussion on the subject that filled every subconscious crevice of her mind: John Wentworth. Unfortunately, she realized as her bubble of misguided hope popped, there was nothing to discuss.

RED DEVIL CAKE

¾ cup shortening
2 cups sugar
2 eggs
½ cup cocoa
2 teaspoons soda
¾ teaspoon salt
2 ½ cup flour
1 teaspoon vanilla
1 cup sour milk (add 2 Tbsp of red vinegar to milk)
1 cup boiling water (added last)

Cream shortening and sugar; add eggs. Add dry ingredients and milk alternately. Add vanilla. Add boiling water. Batter will be very thin. Pour into greased and floured pans, and bake 25 to 30 minutes at 350 degrees. Frost with German Chocolate Icing and transport yourself to heaven.

Chocolate Velvet Ice Cream

One bite of this creamy dessert is like introducing your mouth to smooth, edible velvet.

Susannah smoothed the brown velvet apron tied at her waist as she surveyed the edibly rich scene, a fantasy made real. The past four months had been like a swirling dream of details and mayhem, but it was the happiest four months she'd spent in recent memory.

The view was shockingly close to the restaurant of her autumnal imagination. It was all there: chintz-upholstered booths, white lace at the mullioned windows, even Barbara's tin lanterns. She ran her fingers along the glossy wood surface of the bar that stretched halfway around the room. Golden honey stain for the tight-grained maple of the bar gave a glowing warmth to the hunk of gorgeous wood that anchored the restaurant, and the varnish made it shine. Her toe tapped to the hep-cat sounds of Frank Sinatra's liquid voice. His, Bobby Darin's, Nat King Cole's, and Dean Martin's crooning dominated the play list with a little Robbie Williams and Michael Bublé thrown in here and there for an updated version of the American Songbook: from "Summer Wind" to "Smoke Gets in Your Eyes."

The stone hearth in the corner blazed bright in February's stark chill today. Today—the day of their grand opening! Their press invitations described The Chocolate Bar as Salt Lake City's newest and first all-chocolate sit-down establishment. And it was, ideally and grandly, opening just in time for Valentine's Day, the biggest chocolate consumption day of the year.

Reporters from all the valley's newspapers, big and small, had RSVPed enthusiastically "yes" when she sent them invitations with a copy of the menu and an engraved coupon good for a dessert of their choice at the grand opening, so Susannah hoped for some good press to get things rolling. Only a few hours remained now. She nervously shined the counter and crossed her fingers and toes that her chef would show up in time for the press conference. At 2:00 sharp reporters began firing their questions.

"Tell us, how did you lure in Trevor Jardine as your chef?"

Less than a lure, it had been more like payback—and yet another bailout—for her former PW client. Trevor probably never could repay Susannah for the magic she worked on his finances after he slipped through culinary school with six figures of debt, and then took on that seven-figure signature loan to open his artisan bread company that tanked when the Krispy Kreme craze hit and everyone went for grease over quality, whole-grain carbs.

Not even Colette knew Susannah used her accounting wizardry to finagle a way for Trev to sell off the ovens, the buildings and property with indemnity and no tax liability, and hired him immediately as her chef. Susannah liked him too well to see him flounder. Besides, at 26 he was much too young and far too talented to waste on a grocery store bakery. Now it could appear he'd been lured away from his previous business rather than, well, running away.

"As you know, Chef Jardine has fantastic credentials, and we feel very fortunate to have him as our chef." When he showed up, that was. Susannah started sweating bullets over his disappearance on this, the day of days. "Two years ago he took first place in the international Coupe du Monde de la Boulangerie, a bread and pastry Olympics held every three years in Paris, with 11 countries competing. Chef Jardine had to bake 50 baguettes, including 25 decorated loaves of bread for the contest. The American team also was required to create several Hawaiian-inspired sandwiches: mahi-mahi on Kona bread, and roast suckling pig with papaya chipotle; as well as breakfast pastries made with blueberries, cranberries and dulce de leche."

She knew she was rambling here, but she was stalling for time, and the reporters scribbled madly. Still, there was no sign of the man of the hour.

"Other countries' contestants prepared their native cuisines, as well, but with Chef Jardine's expertise, the United States took first place. More recently, he spearheaded the opening of the Artisan Breads Emporium on Redwood Road. But, ah! Here he is." Susannah tried not to sound too relieved. "You can ask him about it yourselves."

Trevor stepped out of the kitchen, dressed for the part perfectly—poofy white chef hat, white tunic and spats, his broad grin stretching across his entire freckled brown face. He waved his wide hand to the twenty or so reporters who aimed their handheld voice recorders in his direction.

"Aloha. Thanks for being here." The Hawaiian's imposing figure loomed behind the wide circular bar, and his warm smile gave a glow to the room that even the golden honey of the wood couldn't compete with. The reporters asked several questions about his credentials, his specialties, his plans, and most of all they requested names and descriptions of the delectable-looking creations housed under the glass of the pastry case.

Susannah watched with interest. When she noticed two of the reporters whispering and pointing to the croissants, and another few fingering their "coupon" cards in their hands, she smiled to herself in satisfaction. Susannah herself had tested and approved each item in the display case, and they were all sure-fire wins. She waved her hand for the journalists' attention.

"Ladies," for today's group was, not surprisingly, all ladies, "Chef Jardine is needed in the kitchen to prepare for our customers. So, if you would like to find a place to sit, my dear friend Colette Coleman and I will pour you a cup of today's hot chocolate flavor, Orange Crème, and we can get on with the real reason that we're all here: to sample Chef Jardine's wares."

The Hot Chocolate Soufflés, served with Hot Chocolate Custard, were cleared out first, but the Cannolis and Colette's Mousse-Topped Brownies had a good run of things as well. Trevor stuck his head out of the kitchen to spy on progress. Susannah backed toward him.

"Where were you?" she whispered through her grin.

"Defensive driving school. Had to go or they'd take away my license."

"Nice." In her years of acquaintance with Trevor, she always found his pastry to be the flaky aspect, not his punctuality. Nevertheless, she mentally put him on probation.

Mint and chocolate was a favorite combination, particularly the Irish Mist Torte, along with its Emerald Isle companion Ballymaloe Chocolate Almond Cake. Everything with the word raspberry in its title disappeared like a snowflake on the tongue. When it was all over, the reporters left with a spring in their steps, many of them calling Susannah by her first name, and jotting down the hours of operation listed on the door. Susannah breathed a sigh of relief, and Colette joined her beside the blazing hearth, a cup of Orange Crème in her grip.

"Whew! I can't believe we survived that. Did you know the lady who writes for that paper in Murray has seven children? She does the food pages as a freelancer. I think she'll come back and bring her daughter. She said she would." Colette glanced up at the huge ironwork wall clock. "Look! It's already 3:00. We're officially open. Hey, someone's already here."

♡ ♡ ♡

At 7:00 that night, Susannah sank into the pink checkered booth and sighed in relief.

"How many customers did you say we served today, Colette?"

"Over 200. Can you believe it? And with only those two radio ads." Colette stopped wiping the bar and wheeled out the mop and bucket. Susannah pulled herself to her feet and took over the cleaning to let Colette sit for a minute. "That one girl came in right at the stroke of three. She was cute, wasn't she?"

"The brunette with the pretty face?" Susannah shined the glossy bar lovingly.

"Yeah. I think she said her name is Ivy. She hired a babysitter for her five kids and came down an hour early so she could be the first customer. When she saw the press corps leaving, she was crushed—almost turned back. Then she saw you flip over the Open sign and took courage."

This report from Colette confirmed the hunch on which Susannah had based her decision to rope Colette into the chocolate shop scheme. In all the years she'd known her, Susannah had never seen Colette meet someone she couldn't warm up with chitchat, especially on the topic of food, from the senator's wife to the paper boy. If The Chocolate Bar was going to develop a loyal clientele, it needed a good, sympathetic bartender. Susannah didn't mind visiting with the customers herself, but she knew she couldn't do it all on her own, and nobody pumped people for life details like Colette Coleman.

"You told her about the press conference, I hope."

"Yeah, but she kind of figured it out already. She's our age. From Idaho. She loved the Chocolate Shortcake Towers. Took two to go."

It was strange for Susannah to think of herself as the same age as another woman who had five kids, or to imagine either herself or Colette in the total mommy mode. Not that Colette would have minded, or Susannah either, for that matter. Simply put, life didn't seem to be working out that way for either of them.

Trevor emerged from the kitchen, wiping his hands on his generous torso and peeling off his flour-covered, cocoa-splattered apron. "Well, my wonder women, congrats. You did it."

"No, Trevor. You did it. The Black and White Cheesecake with Strawberry Coulis won over every single reporter. And the extremely critical food critic from the Tribune loved the Spicy Poached Pears with Hot Fudge Sauce. She called them 'wonderfully self-indulgent.' Yee-haw, eh? There wasn't a dissatisfied soul in the house. Bravo!" Susannah patted his shoulder.

"Thanks. Thank you very much." Trevor offered a respectable Elvis impression. "So. Do you want to come watch me arm wrestle for the championship at Gold's Gym tonight to celebrate?" He did an air smackdown to demonstrate.

Colette's head dropped heavily on her chest, and she snored loudly. "I have an appointment with Mr. Sandman. And Blaine, who, bless his heart, brought me a lovely lunch, is now probably getting wan and gaunt next to a full fridge. I'm outta here." She pulled her purse from beneath the bar and jingled her keys. "But, hey. Trevor. Good luck. Knock 'em dead with that Popeye arm of yours." She gave his Popeye forearm a happy squeeze and put her hand on the doorknob. "Suze, this was fun. Believe it or not, I can't wait to do it again tomorrow."

"What about it, Susannah? You want to watch the Trevorizer in action?" He flexed a bit and raised an eyebrow.

"Oh. You're so nice to ask. But the house that the owner forgot calls to me."

"You mean you're doing more remodeling tonight? In the chill of winter? Shouldn't you be exhausted after today?"

"Sure. But the best way I know to unwind is to cross a project or two off my to-do list. Besides, you should see the wallpaper. Hideous! My brother-in-law said he'd rent a steamer, but I'm going to see what vinegar and warm water will do for that ancient paste. Doesn't that sound like a riot?"

"A regular relaxation twelve-step. Have a good one."

♡ ♡ ♡

Just like the lyrics of the haunting theme from *Ice Castles*, which everyone learned to play the first six bars of on the piano in junior high, Susannah perceived this broken-down house while "looking through the eyes of love." Every aspect appeared as potential, not problem: the crumbling sidewalk became a red brick path lined with pansies; the rotting wooden porch swung high with hanging baskets of salmon pink petunias and a redwood swing; the squeaking door had a new finish and forest green paint with scrollwork at its edges. All that perfection floated before her—only about a trillion hours and a kabillion dollars away.

Once inside the frosty freeze box, she looked around and made an assessment. Today, the maize-colored shag carpet screamed for attention. It gave way to teal and black pile carpeting in the bedrooms and screeching orange and white linoleum in the kitchens and bathrooms. Tonight those gorgons would meet their match.

She pulled her crowbar and utility knife from the tool box and set to work. She had a strong hunch that . . . yes! As she pried up the metal stripping between the kitchen and living room and hoisted skyward the goldenrod rug, voilá! Beneath the utterly rotted and mashed carpet pad hibernated an absolutely fabulous wood floor!

With renewed energy and strength, she yanked and ripped and pulled and hauled those repulsive, musty stench traps out the back door and chucked them onto what would someday be her flagstone patio with container gardens. It was backbreaking work, and she frequently had to wield her trusty knife to slash the fleabitten masses into manageable chunks, but at last, she pulled the final remnant out into the pitch black of the night and stood back to survey the progress in the light of her dangling shop light. Glue randomly squirted in nasty patterns all around gave the hardwood a bit of a mar, but that was nothing a good sander and stain couldn't fix. Ah, hunch vindication felt like heaven! The cottage did have charm, after all, and she had the hardwood to prove it.

♡ ♡ ♡

"You'll never guess what I found under my carpet!" Susannah ran a cloth over the table near the hearth, chatting with Colette during a slow time the next afternoon. She loved the tabletops' wood grain and the slip covers over the upright chairs, tied with bunting-style bows at their backs.

"I'm not sure I want to have this conversation." Colette wiped fingerprints off the glass of the front door and straightened the sign in the cloakroom that read, "Seize pleasure now. –Jane Austen." It hung beside (creator of Charlie Brown) Charles Schultz's quote, "All you need is love. But a little chocolate now and then doesn't hurt," which hung right above John Belushi's bit-o-wisdom: "I owe it all to little chocolate donuts."

"Oh, it's nothing like that. Wood! Wood floors! They were there all along. I knew something good lurked in that house, beneath all the tackiness."

"And cobwebs." Their visit was cut short by a bevy of sister missionaries who came in to gawk at the pastry case. Proximity to Temple Square had its advantages.

One afternoon melted into another, like a fondue pot of extra creamy milk chocolate. The days were starting to thaw a bit as well, and more and more people were willing to venture out into nature instead of holing up in their caves like sleeping bears.

The bells on the front door jingled, and Susannah looked up from her Checkerboard Shortbread display. It was Ivy, their soft-spoken but friendly Thursday customer who arrived early on opening day, and who always ordered two items—one to eat and one to go. At her side stood an extremely handsome younger man. He had dark chestnut hair, like Ivy's, and in their soft conversation Susannah saw him flash Ivy a dashing smile. He was tall and lanky but in no way scrawny; and despite his good looks, his walk betrayed a slight embarrassment at being in what appeared to be such a female-oriented establishment.

Actually, Susannah was slightly surprised to see Ivy beside him. Didn't Colette say Ivy had a husband and five children whom she escaped the clutches of each Thursday afternoon?

"I'd like a Pine Nut Tartlet, and Cade needs to try one of those." She pointed to a slice of Chocolate Chiffon Pie. "It has the Brazil nut crust, right?" They seated themselves in a booth, not at Ivy's usual spot at the bar, which gave Susannah an opportunity to observe her discreetly. Her long dark hair was almost like silk, and it fell in large, loose curls over her shoulders and cascaded down her back. With fair skin and a demure smile, her only flaw, if it could be considered one, was a Julie Andrews nose, ski-jumping out at its end. She was soft-spoken and never ordered the same thing twice. Susannah had initially worried about that until Colette revealed that Ivy's intention was to try every single item on the menu before choosing a favorite.

Ivy and the so-called Cade occupied the booth for an hour and then left.

"Oh, Suzie! I love it! I absolutely adore it!" Barbara Russell soared in toting a large paper shopping bag. After taking in the scene, she followed Susannah back to the office and pulled a heavy Styrofoam clamshell box and a bottled water from the bag. "Just came from the Market Street Grill. They have great fish, but did you know they serve this, too?"

Opening the box, Barbara revealed a monstrous sandwich piled high with smoked turkey, brie cheese, lettuce, tomato, red onion, and dripping with honey mustard on a crisp French roll. "You need something besides the cocoa bean to sustain you if you're going to work day and night."

It tasted like heaven.

"Sorry I couldn't be here before today." She'd been out of town tending grandkids since the opening. "Forgive me?" Barbara pushed her smart bangs out of her barely wrinkling eyes.

They had a brief visit, Barbara took a Red Velvet Cake to go, and Susannah was able to take three whole bites of her delectable lunch before the customer slam demanded her presence.

The after-lunch crowd came, sighed over the pastry case, and went, little vellum goodie-bags in hand. Then, to Susannah's surprise, Ivy reappeared and reclaimed her traditional Thursday spot at the center of the bar.

"Oh, my brother is such a case!" Uncharacteristic animation filled her voice. Two ladies, sipping Minty Cocoa through tiny striped straws, turned to face Ivy as she continued her mini-rant. "The guy gave our mother's heirloom watch to a girl he met last week. He's taken her on two, *two*, dates, and he's granting her family jewelry ownership status. Why does he always do this?"

Colette's finger ran slowly down the menu, her lips counting softly, then she pulled a Phyllo Nest with Godiva Raspberry-White Chocolate Yogurt Mousse from the pastry case and placed it in front of Ivy, who hardly noticed the scrumptious decadence.

"Was that your brother you brought here earlier?" Colette asked nonchalantly.

"Yes. I wanted you to see him. He's a good-looking guy! He doesn't need to be so completely Jell-Oed by any girl who agrees to go out with him twice. It's not right. He doesn't believe me when I tell him he's got a lot to offer, and that he should hold off a bit and not fall for any girl who gives him the time of day. It's weird. It's like he's some needy teenage girl."

Susannah came over to listen. The other ladies at the bar swiveled their chairs toward Ivy.

"He was really good-looking—practically took my breath away," Colette interjected supportively. "You mean a guy like that doesn't ooze confidence?"

"None. He falls too hard too fast. As soon as a girl shows interest, he showers—nay, drowns—her with attention, calls her three times a day, gives her a big scare, and she has to run for her life. I've told him a million times, give a girl some room!"

Trevor's voice from the kitchen bellowed jovially, "Classic suffocation technique."

"Exactly! He's a suffocater. We used to call them that in college. And now it's my cute little brother." Ivy's eyes gleamed. "Please, what can I do to help him back off?" She took a bite of her phyllo nest dejectedly, and then suddenly took interest in her chocolate again. "It's totally a double dessert day. And this fruity, crispy, chocolaty mousse-y thing is delicious." Ivy sank into sugary oblivion amidst a murmur of consoling phrases.

Hearing about Cade's failed love life triggered Susannah's brainwaves, shooting them into thoughts of love and loss. Perhaps Cade was the type of person who couldn't ever be at peace during times of solitude.

That night, as she unlocked the door to her parents' big, empty house and walked through its hollow rooms, she felt an overwhelming sense of her own aloneness. Over and over she'd made this entry while living there the past few months, but it never got any easier. She always immediately flipped on either a radio or the television to create the sounds of companionship, although she knew they were artificial substitutes. She needed contact.

She checked her e-mail and found a note from her mother in Brazil, saying she and Dad would be touring the mission's backwater areas and be out of communication for several weeks. She tried to call Carly, but she only got three-year-old Poppy on the line and finally had to hang up. She knew Carly had never been much of a listener, and Susannah never intended to pour out her feelings over the phone. Nevertheless, Carly could chat up a storm, so at least maybe the feelings of aloneness might have been assuaged momentarily. No such luck.

Why did she have to feel this way? By 31, shouldn't Susannah be used to the situation? Usually, the loneliness didn't plague her, but occasionally it cut so deep it physically hurt. Like tonight. Most of the time her longings for love and friendship amounted to an irritation, a supreme annoyance, and she felt put upon by her emotions rather than angry or hurt. These annoying feelings contradicted her intellect. Logic insisted she should be able to be at peace, counting her myriad blessings, no matter what her marital status. If only she could locate the switch in her mind or heart or wherever to turn off that nagging need to give love—and receive it—if only for a few years until love could find her. It would certainly uncomplicate her life in the meantime.

Her thoughts slid to John Wentworth. Months had passed, flown by, really, and still she had yet to cross paths with him. There were definite pros and cons to that, but no relief, either. If she could only see him, perhaps she could get some kind of closure—or whatever those psychobabblers called it. She didn't want to tell Barbara about him yet, as there wasn't anything tangible to tell, and she'd feel like a silly goose making assumptions based on nothing. Susannah longed to unburden her soul somehow in this matter, but no cure presented itself.

♥ ♥ ♥

One frosty morning, Susannah sat at her desk trying to juggle bulk semi-sweet and unsweetened ordering along with catching up on some bookkeeping matters, when an unexpected rush of customers flowed in with the icy air of what Susannah called Indian winter, a late freeze. Among them was her sister Carly and a couple of girlfriends.

"So, this is the place, girls! Isn't it as splendid as I told you all? Look, Michelle. Here are the Swan-Necked Cream Puffs. Don't you love it?" Carly practically gushed with pride.

"Suzie! Come and say hi to my friends. We'll all have a dish of this Chocolate Velvet Ice Cream. Forget that snow! The calendar says it's spring."

Susannah spent a few moments with them and then had to tend to the other customers; however, she couldn't help overhearing the laughter and gossip coming from Carly's table. Suddenly her attention got hijacked by Carly's friend Michelle: "Did you hear who that one guy—John Wentworth—is dating? Cute Camie Kimball. You know—the one from the Olympic gymnastics team. Second string. No medals, but what a showing in Spain!"

Camie Kimball? The waif of all waifs? Everyone knew the little Olympian. She was from Sugarhouse—Susannah's home ward, to be exact. And wasn't Camie only about 21? Yes! Camie was 21—Susannah had taught her in Beehives the year after she got back from her mission. The very-late-thirties-John-Wentworth was egregiously cradle robbing! Almost two decades-worth.

Ghastly. Susannah's mind's ear heard the sickening crunch of her little rowboat of hope slamming into the rocks. Camie looked exactly like John's type, exactly like any guy's type: cute and happy and oh-so-fit. Drat! John was dating her former Beehive, a sweet one, sweet as the honey of the bee's hive, but wham-o! It struck her like a brick in the head. Or the heart.

"I'm putting my money on a June wedding. How about you?"

"Or May. May is a nice wedding month, too."

Her dire need to broach the topic with her parents or even with Barbara vanished as John's unattached status evaporated. Susannah's heart ripped a hole in the pit of her stomach where it fell.

CHOCOLATE VELVET ICE CREAM

4 cups heavy whipping cream
2 cups whole milk
⅓ cup sugar
1 can sweetened condensed milk
1 16-oz. can chocolate syrup
1 cup coarsely chopped cashews

Combine all ingredients well. Freeze in an ice cream maker. Serve in waffle cones immediately, drizzled with more chocolate syrup.

Raspberry Chocolate Croissants

These fruity, chocolaty, flaky breads can make even gloomy drear into a beautiful day and make everyone want to be your neighbor.

"It's a beautiful day in the neighborhood," Trevor sang in his rich baritone from his spot at the stainless steel stovetop. He was stirring a pot of boiling cream, soon to be poured over chocolate pieces and thereafter upon the croissants for today's Ganache-Topped Truffle Cakes and Raspberry Chocolate Croissants. "A beautiful day for a neighbor. Would you be mine?" Springtime had finally struck, and no one could resist it.

"I'd love to. But I don't think you want to be mine. My house is a gargantuan mess. It would lower your property value. The yard looks like some sort of missile hit it."

Susannah had spent every night the past week digging up the ancient lead-lined water lines and consulting over and over her do-it-yourself manuals. Once the yard pipes were done, she could get going on the indoor plumbing catastrophe. Her courage hadn't failed her yet, but it almost did when the roof over the back bedroom started leaking during a rainstorm the same day a mouse peeked out at her from behind some loose wiring in the kitchen, and the ceiling bulged, then burst, showering rainwater all over the big bedroom. The charm of the cottage hadn't faded, however, due to several recent discoveries, including a claw-foot tub embedded in the bathroom tile, and a thousand crocuses and grape hyacinths springing up beneath the eaves in the south side yard.

"You're in a chipper mood. Did you take down the reigning arm wrestling champ last night or something?"

"I'm only two slots away from top tier now. Invincible! Tomorrow night my opponent is some scrawny lightweight from Riverton. He's four-foot-twelve. I don't know how he even got on the roster. My arm is itching to take him down."

"Good luck there, Trev. Let us know how that turns out," the currently orange-highlighted Colette chirped. "You know, he's the closest thing I have to ESPN."

A few afternoons later, a bevy of sister missionaries from the Temple Square Visitors Center came twittering in. Colette had just worked deciphering magic on a genealogical document's spidery lines, illuminating the word "February" and the name "Chamois" for a woman from the Family History Center named Sister Shumway. Sister Shumway tripped out of the café with a relieved smile and a $70 Sachertorte, so Susannah was in an especially cheerful mood. She gave the missionaries a broad grin and noticed one of her favorite girls, Sister Havel.

"Susannah! My friend!" Sister Havel came from Warsaw. English was her second language, but food was her first. She studied cooking in her home country and offered to show Susannah and Trevor some of Eastern Europe's best-kept secrets of the bean.

"Sister Havel. Long time no see." She'd come from Temple Square herself a few minutes before, where she'd cut through to see some of the flowers on her way back to the café from the light rail stop. She'd greeted most of these very sisters along the way.

"You won't believe it." Sister Havel waved both her hands in excitement. "This guy, you know?" Her accent was heavy, but part of it was a put-on. She liked heralding her Polish heritage. In fact, most of the time she spoke English quickly, rattling away in excited animation every time Susannah talked to her. "He is coming up to us. On the Square. And he acts all weird, you know? Like he nervous or something. And it is right after we finish talking with you. He say, 'Does you know that lady there?' And then he point to you as you walking away. He is so good-looking! In an older man kind of way, and I am not now looking at good-looking guys, of course. I locks my heart." Sister Havel twisted an imaginary key into her heart to demonstrate.

"But anyhows. We say, yes, we knows you. And you walking away so fast. He look after you with the searching eyes. And he ask us, 'Is she is Susannah Hapsburg?' And we say, 'Yeah. She Susannah! She own the bar across the street.' And then, he get all funny-looking, and he say thanks and walk away. But not until he look at you walking around the corner, you know. I think you has an admirer. Who is this guy, Susannah? You has to tell us. We like how he look, althoughs of course we are not looking at the good-looking older guys now, right girls?" Sister Havel elicited nods of agreement from her fellow sisters, who all lifted eyebrows of suggestion at Susannah.

Susannah had no idea who this guy was shadowing her through the streets of Salt Lake. It made a cold shiver run down her spine. Yipes. Was someone actually following her around, traipsing after her, lurking in the background of her life?

Spooky thoughts reminded her she ought to make her way back over to the Nightmare On A Street she owned, and she determined to do so this very night. With the days getting longer, she could get in a few whacks with a sledgehammer before the pitch of night set in. She'd abandoned her plumbing plans for now, as she really wanted to get around to putting in the doorway to the kitchen between the bookshelf and the fireplace in the living room. Her internal Feng Shui demanded it.

Late that afternoon, a customer slipped in and sat quietly studying the menu. The past several days she'd been appearing like clockwork. Despite several attempts, not even Colette could figure her out or induce her to open up for a conversation. She was a sweet-faced girl of about 22, maybe a little on the over-chocolated side, but she always dressed to the nines in her Lane Bryant, smashingly professional style. Her makeup was immaculate, and her eyelashes batted like butterfly wings. She always sat in a booth facing the kitchen, not a very good seat, without even a view of the garden, and always ordered the special of the day.

One day last week, Trevor had daringly called his daily special

Mon Rêve, French for "my dream." It was a chocolate cloud made of smooth, cooled liquid custard with floating meringue islands and topped with sweetened whipping cream and slivered almonds. The stylish girl began to giggle when she saw it listed as such on the inserted card in the menu. It was a bubbling, infectious giggle that came from somewhere between the back of her throat and the bottom of her soul, and she had to take a deep breath before she ordered it. When Colette delivered it to her, she asked if she'd ever tasted a chocolate cloud before. The girl extinguished her smile and replied, "Never," in a soft, shy voice.

Today, back in the kitchen, Colette collared Trevor.

"I'm going to crack that nut."

"Is there a nut in here? Oh, it's you."

"Trevor. Thanks. I love you, too." Colette rolled her eyes at him for the fiftieth time that day. "No. I mean that pretty girl out front. She comes in here every afternoon, and she won't give any of us the time of day. All she does is ask for your special. Then she eats it in silence."

"My special? Every day?"

"Yeah. She'd probably order it if it were fried dirt on toast."

"I'll have to test her." He got a twinkle in his eye. "I'll make up a menu insert card just for her with something gross, like Deep Fried Little Debbie Swiss Cake Rolls. All that waxy chocolate. Tastes like the main ingredient is some petroleum byproduct. When you see her coming down the street, slide it in. We'll see what she does."

"Hey. I happen to like that waxy chocolate. And no, you won't." Susannah had come up without their noticing. "Are you talking about that quiet girl out front? She can probably hear you, you know. She sits as close to the kitchen as possible. And I don't want you doing anything to antagonize the clientele. Got that, Trrrrevor? My, but I think you've put on a couple of inches since we started this little Chocolate Bar experiment."

"I'm a growing boy. Have to be—if I'm going to get back in the running for arm wrestling champ."

"Back in the running? I thought you just had to take down scrawny Riverton boy to be ready to challenge for top arm."

Trevor's large face went hangdog. "Aw. It turned out he had freakish strength."

"Freakish strength?"

"Yeah. Short guys often do."

"I hope your brother didn't make fun of you."

"Yeah, Mike the Mechanic got his jollies for the day. He made me push the car around the parking lot three times to try and get me back into shape. But, hey, I'm not the only one around here with the escalating chin count." He passed his giant palm vaguely in their direction. "I haven't seen anything like you two since sumo days back in Hawaii in my grandma's hometown."

"Oh!" Colette clutched her throat.

"You're probably right. I need to get back to work on my cottage, or else cut back on the truffle inhalation." Susannah felt her hips for a bulge and decided Trevor was pulling his tormenting little brother act again. She promised herself she absolutely, definitely would spend more time on the tennis court soon. Very soon. Her office phone rang, and she made a dash to pick it up.

"Susannah! Best news!" Carly sounded breathless. "We're having a baby!"

"That's wonderful!" Susannah asked all the appropriate when-are-you-due questions, then added, "If there's any way I can help, let me know."

"I will, believe me. Babies after 35 are an automatic high-risk pregnancy." Carly bubbled on about her blessed event, and Susannah's heart sank at the thought that her own children (if she ever had any) wouldn't get to grow up with cousins their same ages. It looked like an utter impossibility now. Having children at all was beginning to look that way, too. All she could hope for was to be the best possible spinster aunt.

"I'll quiz Piper on her spelling bee words this Sunday, and tell Perry I promise to take him out for driving practice soon. A few spins around the church parking lot."

"That sounds great. He'll love that. He hates it when I ride with him, probably because I'm always clutching the dashboard and yelling, 'Jane! Stop this crazy thing!' like George Jetson flipping around on the out of control conveyor belt. It's better for our mother-son relationship if someone else teaches him to drive."

The dutiful aunt briefly took comfort in the fact that at least Perry liked Susannah, whether baby-kissing John Wentworth cared if she was alive or not.

RASPBERRY CHOCOLATE CROISSANTS

2 cups semisweet chocolate chips
2 cups whipping cream
½ teaspoon raspberry extract

Bring whipping cream just to a boil on stovetop. Pour over chips in a mixing bowl. Combine with an electric mixer until smooth. Add flavoring. Chill slightly. Slather onto a fresh croissant. Garnish with fresh raspberries and sigh with joy.

Little Lamingtons

This is what a yellow cake does on prom night. If only your own prom date had been this gorgeous.

"That Cary Grant is gorgeous, isn't he?" Susannah glanced at the projector's image and caught sight of him.

"Miss Hapsburg—can we pull these blinds down a bit more? The sun's putting a glinting glare on Katharine Hepburn."

Classic movie night Tuesday had pulled in quite a large crowd for tonight's showing of *Bringing Up Baby*. Susannah thought she was the only girl left alive with a perennial crush on Jimmy Stewart and Gregory Peck, but the weekly turnout was a pleasant surprise. She adjusted the blind from the final rays of the dipping sun and set about her cocoa-pouring duties afresh.

Evening customers differed vastly from the daytime crowd of sister missionaries and lady genealogists. The classic movie viewers were Susannah's favorite, although Colette preferred the fondue crew on Friday nights, and Trevor grudgingly admitted he liked the crêpe crowd on Thursdays. They appreciated his fillings most and gushed about his cuisine the loudest. The Chocolate Bar was a gigantic time vortex for all three of them, with its open hours from day to night, but fun still prevailed, and Susannah felt like they were on the cusp of making it a successful financial venture. Almost.

If only she'd had time for a lunch break this afternoon. Susannah's stomach growled. She daubed her brow and eyed the Little Lamingtons, Trevor's special of the day, chocolate-covered cupcakes rolled in flaked coconut and filled with raspberry jam and whipped cream. The movie ended, Katharine Hepburn made her true love choice, and everyone clapped. Tonight Trevor surprised everyone by bringing out his triumphant crêpes a couple of days early. Susannah gladly downed a couple of them behind the scenes of the crowded café, grateful for a moment's nourishment, however brief.

"I guess my wall project at the cottage has to wait until late evening," she sighed, shoveling a final forkful of Trevor's one-of-a-kind Chocolate Crêpes with Strawberries and Saffron Sauce into her happy mouth. In an instant she was back out front where she took in the café's conversations in impressionistic style as she cared for the guests.

From a booth: "I'm thinking about having my blood screened for Mad Cow disease. I can't seem to remember a thing these days, and I did eat that hamburger in London a few years back."

From a seat at the bar: "I don't want to break up, but I don't want to marry him, either. It's like the saggy part of the couch where you're not comfortable but you can't get up the gumption to squidge out of it, either."

From another booth: "She's more helicopter than mom. Hover, hover, hover."

From a table by the fire: "'Garlic goes straight to my feet.' He actually said that."

The most noise emanated from the center of the restaurant where four tables had been squared together to seat a group of twelve or thirteen women, all in their 30s and 40s, professional types. Susannah thought a few of them looked familiar, perhaps faces she'd seen in her Pointman Westerford days. Close to the end of the evening, when she'd filled their cocoa cups for the fifth time, one of them asked her, "Aren't you Susannah Hapsburg?" When Susannah affirmed, the woman said, "Oh, we were wondering who you were. We've heard so much—"

Just then, another customer hailed her, and she had to leave before she could figure out the connection. At closing time, the large group, minus three or four early exiters, gathered up their handbags and blazers and were heading out the door. As Susannah passed them in her bustle of clearing china and skewers, she distinctly heard the hushed expressions, "Well, no wonder Brigham Talmage said she was like hot buttered toast. She's very pretty." And then a reply, "Oh, only in an obvious, thin, smartly dressed, intellectual kind of way." And then a snorty, though not unkind, laugh.

The words were not intended for her ears, but they burned in them anyway. Were they talking about her? And why was her name connected with Brigham Talmage's? She'd never even met the Porsche-driving docket scrambler. She must have heard wrong.

♡ ♡ ♡

"Carly, I'm totally swamped with a project here. Can we make it tomorrow afternoon instead?" Susannah took another swing at the wall, and chunks of old plaster crumbled to the floor, followed by puffs of white powder. She wished she'd worn a dust mask in this asthma-inducing environment. "It's kind of late for driving practice, isn't it? Even in the K-Mart parking lot. Perry will understand, won't he?" She tried to help Perry whenever she could, but her arbitrary rules of self-preservation required daylight for driving practice with 16-year-old boys.

"Susannah, this has been bugging me, and I know here I am, calling to ask for your time, so it's weird, but I have to say this." What now? "Suze, you're the best. I appreciate what you're doing for Perry, and what you do for all of us, but I frankly find myself wishing you weren't so available."

Oh, great. The get-a-boyfriend lecture loomed again. Susannah gritted her teeth and swung the hammer, this time satisfyingly loosing a broad slab of the old plaster.

"There's got to be someone in your heart. You can't live like this." Carly meant well, Susannah told herself. She only wished for her little sister's happiness. Susannah thanked her and signed off, but Carly's words echoed in her head. There must be someone in your heart.

Kachonk. As she took another blow, she started to think about her life, her dating life, her so-called love life, chronologically. Obviously anyone from her days at Alta High was out. College days? All married. That one guy, Brett, he was divorced now, but she never really felt like they clicked intellectually, and the way to a woman's heart is not only through her stomach, it's through her brain, too. She needs conversation.

The guys from college after her mission left a lot to be desired. They were all so materialistic in the business department during those boom-time stock market days. All any of them could talk or think about was their portfolios, their money market accounts, their mutual fund picks. As much as she got cranked up about those things herself, she needed someone who had a little more perspective. At PW, the same. Nobody there, no one at church, no one. At least no one who was available all these years later.

It really stunk being 31 and single.

She looked a little deeper into her heart. Halloo! It echoed like Tigger's cry to the Jagular. Anybody there? It reverberated. In Mormon culture, sell-by dates expire early, and Susannah had long outlasted her shelf-life. With each passing month, the likelihood of someone dating her shrank significantly. Soon memories were all she would have. Of course, she would always have a soft spot, a relic of fond memories for John Wentworth, whether he was destined for a June wedding with his child bride or not.

She needed a break from the swinging, so she sat back on the lawn chair she'd strategically placed under the battery-powered lantern hanging on the coat hook beside the door. John Wentworth. Was there any harm in reminiscing? No. Nothing could be hurt by thinking back to that summer in Guatemala.

In her ultra-idealistic days she'd signed up for a six-week CHOICE expedition—the humanitarian organization that selected villages in remote areas and helped identify community needs, such as schoolhouses, health clinics, water storage systems, and such. The village she was assigned to was beautiful, and she was 20 and full of life and energy and enthusiasm. With the help of the villagers, she and ten Americans helped construct a small schoolhouse, then together they rerouted water from a natural spring in the mountains near the village.

It only took them a few short weeks, but she knew it changed their lives forever. Clean water would mean healthier children, longer life expectancies and, most of all, hope. She and ten other

Americans, one of whom was John Wentworth, had made a difference. It was the best, happiest summer of her life. She smiled thinking of it, and then laughed out loud when she thought of the scorpion incident.

"Be sure and dump out your shoes before you put them on," he'd warned her. "Scorpions sleep in there at night, and you put your foot in, and—" She didn't need to be told twice. John had given her every skin-crawl-inducing fact at his disposal as they sat around their campfire that night. "Smaller scorpions are more dangerous because their finite supply of poison has not depleted yet with years of stinging. They can stay in one place for up to six months without moving at all. They can live for nine months without eating anything. Their exoskeletons are so strong no pesticide can penetrate." He had a million factoids. "I keep a black light—a pen black light—in my pocket to shine down into my sleeping bag before I climb in for the night."

"What for? Do they glow or something? Disco scorpions?"

"As a matter of fact, they do."

"No way."

He pulled the pen light from his pocket, it was on his keychain, and waved it around in the pitch of the night.

"Look!" Susannah shrieked. There, crawling its venomous way toward them, was a huge scorpion, about the size of her fist. She stifled another shriek and silently but frantically waved her hand its direction. John trained his black light on it to make it glow until it crept its way into the legitimate light of their campfire. Then, Susannah watched in horror as the creepy beast tiptoed its sinister way across the scorching hot rocks that lined the fire pit, down into the ashes and cinders, through the fire, and out across the stones on the other side. Her eyes peeled back in wonderment. John turned toward her, and to her surprise he wore the same look as she did.

"Oh, my gosh! I didn't know one could do that." He put his pen light away in respect—and fear. Then they burst into laughter, uncontrollable laughter. She laughed so hard she couldn't hold up her head and had to rest it on his comfortable chest.

Susannah smiled again at the memory. A good memory. No,

Carly, she wasn't pining for a guy who lived for her only in the past. It was simply that no one since then had ever measured up to John. He was the standard. The standard of kindness, of warm-heartedness, of friendship, of feeling. Of goodness.

At night in her sleeping bag she'd stared at the stars, more stars than she'd ever seen before, and imagined different scenarios of what might occur when they both returned to Salt Lake. Could anything possibly be the same in the concrete jungle as it was in the steaming green jungle? Would he ask her to a baseball game? To go for a drive? All those trappings of civilization seemed so remote. There, that natural, splendid, sensory banquet was where reality lay.

Once home, she debated about whether to confide in anyone, parents, Carly, Barbara. But she wasn't sure what she'd say. The situation made her a giddy mess, and eventually she determined to vent—at least a little.

"Barbara, what's your opinion? Am I too young to think about marriage?" Susannah picked a dog-walking outing as the moment to consult her relationship advisor, Barbara Russell, about John Wentworth. However, she wasn't sure enough of herself to give Barbara full details. She decided to vaguely feel her out on the topic first.

"You're never too young to think about it. Thinking about it—as a future event, where you want it to take place, etc., is fine. But doing it—well. Let's see, you're six years older than Madeleine, right? Still 20?" The dogs were pulling the two women through the suburban yards of Barbara's posh gated community.

"Still 20. That's right."

"What a perfectly lovely age, if you can keep off that hideous 20-20."

"What's that?" Susannah pulled heavily on the leash of Carly and Ian's wrinkly shar pei, Mr. Lunch, to keep him from exploring a manicured yard.

"Oh, haven't you noticed? Most women automatically pack on 20 pounds when they're 20. Perhaps it's a natural function, getting her ready for the baby years. If the freshman 15 doesn't get you, the 20-20 will." Barbara pulled Brutus, her St. Bernard, out of a flowerbed. "Of course, you're lucky. With that tennis scholarship you've got exercise built in to your schedule. Most girls don't have that blessing."

"It's a mixed blessing. You should feel my shin splints, just for a split second."

"Oh, you poor thing." Barbara let Brutus's leash out dangerously far. It threatened to tangle with Mr. Lunch's leash.

"Thanks for the sympathy. I guess it's not that bad. There's the thrill of victory that occasionally makes up for it."

"Love how you smashed that UCLA girl all the way back to the beach, with her suntan glowing only half as bright as her humiliated blush." Barbara came to every home match Susannah played, and also helped her relive them. They rounded a corner onto another tree-lined street. "Oh, Susannah. You should make the most of this time of life. It's so brief. You only have another year left on your scholarship contract, and then you either go pro or you play only for your personal enjoyment after that."

Susannah wondered if there were another undercurrent to Barbara's comments, whether they referred back to her original question. She boldly ventured, "So, do you think marriage might interfere with my scholarship?"

Barbara paused thoughtfully while Brutus inspected a parked bicycle. "Hmm. The things that come along with marriage supposedly could. I'm not necessarily saying it would interfere, but a married woman naturally feels a need to start a family."

Start a family! Why—! This was the first time Susannah had ever in her life connected that phrase with herself. Oh, my stars. With all of her effort she tried to keep the alarm from showing on her face and replied calmly, "Oh, yes. And probably more so if her husband is several years older, like you and Walter."

"Exactly. That's exactly what I was thinking. But I'm not a bit sorry Madeleine and Marcus came to us so soon. Walter enjoyed them so much." If the Mormon culture encouraged the practice of wearing widow's weeds, Barbara might still be in black to this day, mourning the loss of her decade-gone husband. As it was, she spent a lot of time doing his family's genealogy instead.

As they and the dogs walked in the summer warmth, Susannah continued rolling her own situation around in her mind and giving her friend only the sketchiest of details. "So, you might say a major factor for a girl's marriage thoughts might be asking herself if she's ready for motherhood—to be a nurturer. A diaper changer. A spit-up wiper."

"Focus back on that 'nurturer' idea and you'll be happier." Brutus now wrapped around a tree, and Barbara began the task of extracting him and his impossible leash. "No one ever chose to start a family due to the allure of burp cloths and Huggies."

That was probably true. Barbara often shared her motherly wisdom, and Susannah appreciated it. She seemed to really understand Susannah without being too judgmental, although she made her high expectations for the girl known. It was only Barbara's encouragement that got Susannah the tennis scholarship in the first place.

"You might be getting your fill of baby screams as it is over at Carly's place."

"Oh, baby Piper makes her discontent known amply, but Perry is a scream in a different way. Do you know he started the lawnmower all by himself?"

"He's four." Barbara's eyes widened in fear and surprise.

"Yep." Laughter, and then a silent moment passed between them. They crossed the road to the shadier sidewalk.

"Susannah, is there something—or someone—on your mind?"

"Well, to be truthful, I met someone." Susannah pulled on Mr. Lunch's leash and cleared her throat. How much should she tell? How much should she conceal? The whole thing felt so scary. "In Guatemala. He's an American, from here in Salt Lake. We really hit it off over there."

"Tell me about him."

Where could Susannah begin? Should she mention the mudslide and her illness and the macaroni and cheese? Here and now it would sound weak to say, "He shared his only box of macaroni and cheese with me when I was sick." The significance couldn't possibly shine through in a place like here. What about the time he pulled the girl out of the stream? Or the way he let the local village leader do most of the direction for the project, building him up? It just wouldn't translate very well into . . . America.

"He's a little older. You might have heard of him—John Wentworth."

"John Wentworth. Leo Wentworth's son?"

"I think so."

"They were in our ward several years ago. I remember him. Nice fellow."

Susannah sensed a "but" in Barbara's silence, so she tried to fill the air. "He's been working as an outdoors guide and doing humanitarian expeditions for a few years."

Barbara didn't respond immediately. She was busy picking something from behind Brutus's ear. Susannah's mind concocted a hundred scenarios of what Barbara might be thinking. Before her friend could make any verbal objections, Susannah decided to ward them off.

"Honestly, I have to say I don't know him very well." It was true. Nevertheless, she'd felt she knew him better than she knew anyone else, ever.

"Has he called you?" Barbara asked at last.

"Not yet. He should be coming home in a few weeks." Susannah's stomach churned at the thought of the impending phone call. Her thoughts raced. She felt so young. Too young to make an adult decision, to decide on something she felt instinctively had such bearing on the rest of her life—of her eternity. Then again, nothing in Susannah's life experience so far had ever felt so inevitable. With horrendous force, this predicament pulled her in opposite directions. A riptide. From the neck up, she intended to stay afloat, happily bobbing along near the safety of shore. But from the heart down, the emotional undertow grabbed her, dragging her, helpless, into uncharted seas.

Being away from him these past few weeks hadn't afforded her the perspective or the levelheadedness in regard to him she'd anticipated. Rather, she felt a greater need for him. Uncertainties tore at her. She needed shelter! Peace! What could she do? At last, she clutched at a thought: The only safe way to play it was to give herself more time.

"No, he hasn't called. When he does, I'm thinking I'd love a way out of it."

Barbara stopped walking a moment, letting Brutus sniff a tree. "Out of what?"

The emotional danger, drowning in love, treacherous, fearsome life decisions, she thought, but didn't say aloud. "Oh, I don't know. It's just part of me wants a life with him," as his wife and his true love, raising his children, being his forever companion, "and part of me is way too scared," she replied, omitting the big details of her hopes.

Barbara paused a moment then offered, "Suze, your twenty-first birthday is just around the corner, isn't it?"

♡ ♡ ♡

And so Susannah turned in her mission papers, all the while noting the similarities between her situation and Fraulein Maria's as she ran back to the abbey; then, when the call came reading Austria Vienna, Susannah couldn't suppress an ironic laugh.

Three weeks later, sitting across from John at the Cinnabon in the mall, the table felt like a gulf separating them as wide as the Pacific. She knew he kept attempting to narrow the emotional gap between them, but with all her will she fended off his modest attacks on her heart. Frivolous nonsense flowed from her mouth, childish gibberish, until he began looking at her in dismay. She heard herself babbling things like, "And until I was five I thought the letters l, m, n, and o were a single letter: ellemeno," followed by a tinny laugh that hurt her stomach as well as her ears.

John opened his mouth as if to speak, and she quickly broke a crust off her cinnamon roll and popped it in his mouth. In doing so, her finger accidentally brushed his lip, and at that instant, all her pretentious defenses crumbled in the tingling earthquake that resulted. Suddenly quieted, they sat without speaking for a long moment, and he gazed at her hair, her hands, her shoulders, and into her eyes. She could feel traitorous tears welling in them and knew they grew red with emotion.

Ooh! This was exactly the moment she'd dreaded!

He spoke. Her mind longed to stop him from saying the words, but her heart longed to hear them more. Her heart won, momentarily.

"Suzie." He took a deep breath. "I told myself you were so young." Yes. That's right. She was too young. "Too young." Exactly! "I told myself every sleepless night in my wretched hammock, close enough to hear you breathe, far enough from you to make me grit my teeth. You must have seen my torture."

Maybe she hadn't witnessed his writhings clearly, but she felt her own. Now, too. She kept her eyes on the table's ironwork pattern.

"What I said to you, Susannah, that last day at the falls, it was wrong." Yes! she breathed. It was wrong. Exactly. He never should have said them, made her admit to them, either. Perhaps he would be making this easier for her, easier to tell him that— "Suzie, I never should have done it under those circumstances. It wasn't ethical. I was your boss. I knew better. We both could have been fired, could have left the project severely shorthanded, could have left the village without water. That was too much to jeopardize. My impatience—I should apologize."

Yes. He should. Maybe he would, and maybe the apology could serve to twist off the spigot of gushing love she felt for this unbelievably good man, who gave and gave of his time, energy, means, and love, without showiness, without hesitation, without fear. The words to the song "Longer" floated into her mind. "Longer than there've been fishes in the ocean, higher than any bird ever flew . . ." They resonated with the soft tones of John's voice when he'd sung them to her. For a moment she got lost in the memory of the falling water and the pool below. Oh! She felt her will slipping away, like mud on a hillside in a heavy rain. . . .

"I ought to," he continued, now looking directly into her face, tilting her chin up with his hand, "but my conscience won't let me. I meant what I said. No other woman even begins to compare with you." He called her a woman. She felt like a baby, a crying baby. Yes, she was far too young. Just a baby.

Exerting every last ounce of power from her head, she forced herself to interrupt him. "John, look!" Susannah forced a lilt into her voice as she produced the tri-folded letter that had arrived in the mail just that morning. "Before you say anything more, I have to show you this."

With a startled air, he took the letter, unfolded it, and scanned it, unspeaking.

"Austria?" he asked finally.

"Vienna. *Sehr gut!*" Her voice snagged in her throat as she said the words meaning "very good" in German, betraying her excess of feeling. But she regrouped quickly after dashing a tear from her cheek, hoping he wouldn't see. "I was talking with my good friend Barbara Russell, remember I told you about her? From my ward. I used to babysit her kids. Anyway, we decided, wow! How cool would it be for me to go on a mission? You can't believe how fast they're issuing calls these days. I've already accepted and everything." Her voice got slower, softer. "Signed on the dotted line." Smaller. "Committed."

He knit his brows. She couldn't read them.

"Signed." He paused. "You do know, Susannah, that the prophet and the brethren, and your stake president and everybody will understand perfectly if you tell them you've changed your mind. It is okay."

For a fleeting moment, Susannah did change her mind. Mentally she flung herself into John's arms and buried her face in his chest. Physically, though, she sat stonily in her iron chair, the whole world turning to milk around her. She recognized this moment: a moment of no return. She must choose. But she couldn't, her vocal chords immobilized.

Finally, his eyes pleading, John reached across the table and rested his hand on hers. Warmth rushed up her arm and through her frame. But she didn't hint at a response. If Susannah allowed herself even a twitch of a muscle, she knew she'd end up in his arms, acting out the flinging image she'd just conjured up in her mind. She clenched her teeth and steeled her will and pulled her hand away.

Eventually, John's eyes narrowed. He rubbed his rejected hand on his whiskers. A frown tugged all the lines of his face downward. Soon the silence got to her.

"Aren't you happy for me?" she attempted, knowing how hollow, how false she must sound. Unfortunately, he didn't follow her lead into shallower waters.

"No. I mean, honestly, Susannah." She didn't like hearing him call her by her full name, and his off-balance voice was stuttering mercilessly, throwing her even further off kilter, too. "It's just that— I thought. Well, I thought you understood. I thought we—"

Suddenly gathering himself, John surged to his feet. "Look. I'd better go. I can see that." She couldn't tell if it was anger or pain in his face, in his voice. A few awkward moments passed, and then he leaned down and kissed her lightly on her forehead. Oh! She'd waited all her days for a man to kiss her forehead! Then he stalked away.

With every atom of her heart she longed to call out to him, to stop him, but her mind restrained her. She watched him disappear around the corner, into the crowd, and out of her life.

"Austria! Think of it!" Barbara beamed later that day, oblivious of Susannah's heartache. "Now you'll get your first taste of Europe!"

And taste she did—mostly all the different varieties of European chocolate. Swiss had the richest flavor, Italy the sweetest, German the boldest, France the most variety. Every P-day was a smorgasbord of chocolate. She fell in love with it, and with the gospel, and together they filled her aching, empty heart.

♡ ♡ ♡

There's got to be someone in your heart. Carly's words echoed once again in Susannah's mind. The water in her Evian bottle was down to its last drop, and the battery in her lantern began to flicker. She should have shut it off during her rest, but darkness made the charm of the cottage morph into creaking creepiness. She'd better give the sledge a few swings before she packed it in for the night.

Blatt. Kashockle. The iron tool crumbled the plaster into shards that splayed onto the floor noisily. As Susannah lifted her now weak arm for another swing, her eye caught sight of something unexpected in the flickering lantern light. With gloved fingers she pulled carefully at the fibers and chicken wire that covered the wall, then pulled harder at their resistance. What was that? A door? A door! To her happy amazement, there was a door right where her mental architect demanded one. Jackpot! Now she wouldn't have to put one in. It could save her a tenth of a percent of her monthly Home Depot budget.

It was work that would require more light and more time than she possessed this evening. Oh, the cottage held a treasure trove of the sweet unexpected.

Just then, her lantern flickered and went out. Simultaneously a knock sounded at the door. The front door? Or was it the newfound door?

She knew in her mind it was the front door, but fear froze her feet in place. The hidden door appeared sinister in the dim light. She couldn't pry her eyes from it. Why was it walled up? Was this some freakish Edgar Allan Poe plot? What lay behind it? A cold chill ran down her spine. The knock rapped again. Who could be here in the dark of a 9:30 spring night?

With all her will, she wrenched her feet from their spot and crept toward the sound. There was no porch light, obviously. She pushed aside the flap over the peephole to peek through. If her night vision served her right as she viewed his silhouette in what there was of moonlight and streetlight illumination, a man, a dark crop-haired man in a shirt and tie, stood on her step, shifting his weight. She had a decision to make. As a lone woman, was it wise opening her door late at night, to an unexpected male visitor? Certainly not. With shaking hands she chained the lock. He knocked again, this time with force.

"Susannah Hapsburg?" Oh, dear. Night Stranger knew her name. How did anyone know she was here? Had she been followed? Suddenly, a flash of Sister Havel's story zinged into her mind. Someone had been watching her! Every detail of this moment combined to give her serious fright. "Susannah? Is that you?"

How should she answer? She needed to make it appear she was unalone.

"Just a minute," she called, trying to sound nonchalant. Perhaps pretending another male person was here with her might throw off whatever evil intentions this stranger held. Guido. That sounded masculine enough. "Guido, honey, would you get the door?" Then she clunked around in her steel-toed boots on the wood floors for a minute. "Never mind, I'll get it, hon." How ridiculous to be clunking around in the dark.

"Who's there?" she called through the doorframe. "What do you want?"

"Um. I'm sorry. I came by too late. You were already in bed. I'll, uh, come back another time." Through the peephole she saw him stumble slightly down the dark stair and nearly tumble into the pit of despair she called a front yard. Night Stranger then climbed into a suspicious-looking SUV and left. Whoever it was, she'd gotten rid of him.

Who was he?

She had to get out of there before anything else happened.

LITTLE LAMINGTONS

Cake Ingredients
    1⅔ cup self-rising flour *(sifted)*
    ½ teaspoon salt (sifted with flour)
    ¾ cup butter or margarine
    ¾ cup sugar
    3 eggs
    ¾ cup milk
    ½ teaspoon vanilla

Coating Ingredients
    1 cup sugar
    ¼ cup water
    1 heaping teaspoon cocoa
    sweetened flaked coconut

Cream butter and sugar in a large mixing bowl. Add the eggs one at a time, then add vanilla; mix well. Combine the butter mixture with about half of the flour and salt. Add the milk, mixing well, and add the remaining flour. Fill greased cup cake tins two-thirds full with the mixture and bake at 350 degrees for 15-20 minutes. Allow to cool.

Coating: Combine sugar, water, and cocoa in a saucepan. Bring to a boil, stirring constantly. Allow mixture to cool slightly. Dip each cake into the cocoa mixture, using a skewer, then roll in the coconut. Let stand on a wire rack. Slice horizontally and fill with raspberry jam and sweetened whipped cream.

Never-Fail Chocolate Chip Cookies

These are the cookies your grandma used to bake, and for you they'll turn out every time.

As it turned out, Susannah didn't go back to Chateau de Fright for some time. Not that she exerted a Herculean effort to make that happen, but with a growing clientele as well as family and church obligations, Susannah felt stretched as it was. Summer loomed.

One Thursday felt like the busiest afternoon in weeks. All their regular patrons ordered double desserts. The weather had been quite cloudy and hot without the relief of rain, and women everywhere were getting anxious—chocolate needy.

"You know, the cacao tree from which we derive chocolate has the botanical name Theobroma cacao, from the Greek for 'food of the gods,'" The Chocolate Bar's know-it-all Felicia Patterson announced for most to hear, at least those sitting near her on bar stools. "White chocolate isn't really chocolate at all but rather vanilla-flavored sweetened cocoa butter. Some mid-priced brands even substitute vegetable fat for the cocoa butter. Isn't that wrong?"

"I think white chocolate in general is wrong," another replied. Some disagreed, but a lively discussion ensued, and Felicia looked gratified to be the moderator of the conversation.

Shortly thereafter, the Thursday-reliable Ivy appeared. She fanned herself and ordered a cold-anything. Colette promptly appeared with a Chocolate Frappe and a Chocolate Chip Cookie Ice Cream Sandwich Drizzled with Hot Fudge.

After a long draft through the straw and a couple of refreshing bites of the ice cream, Ivy exhaled and shook her head. Colette, who currently sported black streaks in light brown hair, sidled up to hear Ivy's latest report on Suffo-Cade, now a Chocolate Bar soap opera hero.

"Please. Did she really need flowers every day?" Ivy recounted the fifteen-day saga of Cade's latest dumping catastrophe. "Whoever guessed two weeks wins."

"That was me!" Felicia Patterson gurgled. "I said two weeks."

"Okay, and there should also be an honorable mention for Rena Goodwin. Is she here today?" Rena wasn't. "She predicted one week, but she guessed well that Molly would use the phrase 'need a little air.' So, everyone congratulate Rena when you see her." Ivy then gave all the crash and burn details of the sad tale, while Felicia savored the prize truffle Colette had promised the winner.

"I, for one, think he's doing his best."

"Oh, we all know that."

"Surely there's some girl perfect for him out there."

Trevor smirked. "Yeah, like there's a perfect person out there for all of us."

"How come you haven't strong-armed your perfect girl out of hiding yet, Trev?"

"That would take freakish strength, Suze."

Felicia Patterson got Colette's attention and asked quietly, "Is Chef Jardine a Tongan or a Samoan? The guy's humongorgeous." It came out as both words, humongous and gorgeous. "He's half-Hawaiian, half-White," Colette replied matter-of-factly while she swabbed the bar's counter with a soft white cloth. "His dad was an offensive lineman on the BYU-Hawaii football team when he met Trev's mother."

Trevor walked up behind them and startled Colette. "Mom worked at the Polynesian Culture Center. She danced the Tahiti dance, even though she was Hawaiian."

"I've heard about that Tahiti dance," Felicia nodded knowingly.

"That was all it took for dad. Now he sells cars in West Valley City. Mom works at a custom drapery shop."

"How come you decided to become a chef?" another barstool sitter interjected.

"It was either that or truck driving school. I took a serious look at the women-to-men ratio of both places, and the decision was obvious."

Colette came and stood close by Susannah's side, elbowing her. "Check it out." Susannah almost couldn't hear the whisper or see Colette's pointing thumb, so it took a few seconds to discern the hint, but soon she caught it. A certain person was watching Trevor and Felicia's exchange with interest—the sweet-faced young woman in the booth near the kitchen. She blushed and ducked her head when Susannah glanced her way. Aha. Her mind already formulating a plan, Susannah returned to the other chattering patrons, barely noticing their delicious conversations.

"I love these little dark chocolate heart outlines on top of this Chocolate Cheese Mini-Pot. I almost hate sliding it out of the way to dip my strawberries and kiwi fruits in it. How do you think he makes them?"

"I bet it's with a pastry bag. I tried it once, but it all glopped out. Trevor's a wizard."

On her way to work the next morning, Susannah swung past Barbara's place. It was sort of on the way, and Barbara was an early morning flower gardener. Her hydrangeas rivaled those on the lawn of the Governor's mansion. Aha! Susannah could make out her great sombrero over the tops of the zinnias and pulled the Vespa in to surprise her friend.

"Susannah! What is this? How lovely to see you. I've been gone for days. Madeleine had a baby boy, you know." And Barbara gave her the laundry list of baby details, followed by Susannah's update on the shop.

"I'm absolutely stopping by the Chocolate Bar as soon as I get unpacked. I'm craving anything Black Forest. Does Trevor make cherry stuff? Save me one of your favorites." They visited a bit more about the café and the baby. "What is that you're driving?"

Susannah explained the demise of the Jetta and the magical appearance of the scooter.

"My goodness. I guess it's all right for summer, but, ah, let me figure out something else for you. Just until you get your financial footing for a replacement. My goodness."

Susannah hadn't realized the Vespa held so little charm for some people. Of course, the whipping wind wrecked her hairstyle regularly and deadened all feeling in her skin. Plus, it was summertime in Salt Lake, a place where the growing season could be as short as five months. Barbara was right. The Vespa couldn't serve as a long-term fix in the soon-slushy world of Utah's winter.

"Now, Susannah, forgive me. I have to ask it again. You know me. Broken record." Oh, no. Susannah could feel the tremors of it: the old singles ward speech again. No! She utterly refused to consider it. She suppressed an exasperated sigh. Sometimes exasperated sighs must surely be counted as sins. "But have you thought any more about attending the Capitol Hills Park Ward?" The Jurassic Park Ward, living proof that dinosaurs still roamed the earth? No, ma'am. She hadn't. And she never, ever, ever would.

"Not lately. Oh, my goodness. Look at the time!" Susannah's entire restaurant could self-destruct if she didn't get going this very instant. "Come by. There's a Cherry Chocolate Brioche Pudding with Cherry Crème Anglaise that's to die for this week. I'll save one for you—stash it in the fridge with your name on it." And she buzzed off to the safety of work.

"Somebody needs to set Ingrid straight next time she's in here." Colette called from behind the pastry counter. For the moment, there were no customers in the café, and she rearranged some Chocolate Chip Scones that had gotten off-center.

"Who's Ingrid?" Susannah asked, wishing she could pop a scone in her mouth, but stopping herself. The sumo wrestling ring was only a few scones away from her waistline.

"That LA Fitness chick—always wearing workout clothes, ponytail on top of her head."

"Oh, her. Yeah. The one with the triceps. Straight about what?"

"About the fact that a guy who proposes to her but who refuses to give her a ring or set a date is a gelatinous mass of red flags."

"Wrant! Wrant! Wrant! Eardrum shattering warning klaxon." Trevor made the emergency buzzer sound from his spot near the big mixer. "Red alert. Sounds like the guy is messing her over. I tell ya. If I ever propose, I'll make that deal solid from the get-go."

Ingrid's love life, and the love lives of a dozen other patrons and local social celebrities, surfaced as topics of discussion throughout the Saturday conversation. Fortunately for Susannah, the name of John Wentworth only came up once, and it sank away again quickly as no one seemed to have any viable information on him. All anyone offered was sketchy picture of a John-Wentworth-Camie-Kimball-sighting near the Pioneer Theater, but no firm information whether they were sighted as a twosome or with other people. Susannah remained, she hoped, stone-faced throughout the gossip, and busied herself with retying the gingham ribbons they were using for napkin rings these days.

All the gossip left her feeling a bit spongy that night—like a wrung-out sponge—and there was nothing to do but continue to desiccate. No one in her basically non-existent dating pool could quench her, and she didn't feel anyone in her life would sympathize enough for her to open up about the subject. Complainers: unwelcome.

She stared at the door to the pantry where her mom kept the collage of inspirational quotes all stuck in random patterns with pieces of masking tape and stickers from fresh fruit. At last, one caught her attention. "Life is mostly froth and bubble; two things stand like stone: kindness in another's trouble, courage in our own." It wasn't attributed to anyone, but it struck her mind and her heart simultaneously. Courage. And kindness. "Red is for courage to do what is right." The words from the Primary song marched through her mind, giving her courage to overcome her emotional inertia, to make a kind move—in a positive direction.

With courage bright she sallied forth to prepare something inspiring for her wonderful Primary kids—a.k.a. the hope of Israel—whom she loved so much. After a moment's thought she found of a spool of wide red ribbon to make a big thermometer poster to use as a singing gauge—the kind where she could pull up the ribbon as the children sang with more gusto. "Yellow for service from morn until night." She could serve, and that would give her courage.

The next afternoon, after a rousing round of "Head, Shoulders, Knees, and Toes," Susannah whipped out the new poster. Seeing the light come on in the Primary children's eyes made it worth the effort of coloring in all those lines. She'd been their chorister since the Senior Primary kids were Sunbeams, and she knew the routine like her own makeup case.

Primary came first in their three-hour block, and the best part was Zane. Despite all attempts to quell the five-year-old with the missing tooth, he sang (loudly) an additional, previously unwritten verse for "Book of Mormon Stories." Susannah had finally decided to wait out the kid-invention, when he stopped abruptly, saying, "Wait. Does Heavenly Father already know this song? He knows everything, right?"

Susannah gave him a super singer badge. And, then, during Sharing Time, when the Spirit swept across the room, she felt once again how glad she was to be serving other people's children, since it appeared none of her own were anywhere on the horizon. Service gave her courage. The words of the Primary song rang clear and free in her heart.

As Sacrament Meeting began, Zane waved to her again, and she gave him the thumbs up just as Bishop Winthrop stood to conduct the ward business. Suddenly, she felt the eyes of the congregation upon her and heard her name mentioned from the pulpit.

"And we'd like to extend a vote of thanks to Sister Susannah Hapsburg for her years of service as our Primary chorister." What? Thanks? Why now? What? Was she being released? Nobody told her! "All who can join me in this action, please raise your right hand." No! No! Stop raising your hands, everyone! She looked around frantically and forgot to raise her own hand. Or should she? Was she supposed to thank herself?

They were singing the sacrament hymn now. What just happened? Time sped up horribly. The song was over. The deacons were passing, and sitting, and the bishop was up again. Oh, dear.

Claustrophobia took hold of her. Little Zane turned around and gave her another thumbs up, and she couldn't hold back the flood of tears. She pulled her thermometer poster from under the pew. It made a paper thunder sound and interrupted the youth speaker's speedy speech delivery as Susannah floundered out of the chapel to her Vespa, where her eyes emptied the contents of the water bottle she'd downed before church.

♡ ♡ ♡

"It was like the big Donald Trump boss-man of the ward stood up there in front of everyone and hollered, 'You're fired!' It was so humiliating, Carly. They could have at least told me ahead of time so I wouldn't have looked like such a blubbering idiot."

"I once heard about a bishop getting released and his wife didn't find out until during sacrament meeting."

"Not helping, Ian." Carly frowned at her husband and ladled another scoop of hummus into her pita bread pocket. "Pass the sprouts, please." It was no wonder Carly's family was all thin. They called this Sunday dinner? Where were the potatoes and gravy?

"Suzie, bishops make mistakes, too. In a few weeks this will all seem funny, I'm sure. But for now, I can see why you're so upset." Carly passed 11-year-old Piper another napkin and gave her the mommy-sign-language command to use it.

"Yeah, I'm upset. I just got voted off the Primary island. Vote-of-thanks voted." And it had been such a fabulous day up until then, too. She'd immersed herself in service and been able to forget her trials through courage. Then this.

"I think you were a good song leader, Aunt Zannie," Polly interjected. "Remember when I came to church with you that one time, and you let me pick the apple off the tree? We sang 'Once There Was a Snowman' and it wasn't even winter. That was so funny, huh." See, even a nine-year-old knew Susannah had a magic touch in the chorister department. Her baton was really a magic wand.

Ian cleared his throat. "Listen, Susannah. I'm sure the bishop would never make you feel bad on purpose. He probably thought his counselor mentioned it. Maybe the bishop was being nice, knowing how swamped you are with your new business. Maybe he thought you'd moved. Didn't your records transfer when you sold your house?"

"I don't know. No one told me if they did." She fought to keep the shrill screaming anger out of her voice and to speak in a reasonable tone. "I'm not sure where they'd send them. It's not like the cottage is habitable at this point. Besides, that whole ward membership clerk thing is a mystery to me. It must be a nightmare—keeping track of everyone." Susannah expelled a huff of exasperation and took another pita from the stack. "Maybe you're right. It's probably simple human error." Or maybe it's a gross, unkind, mean oversight. "I know. I'll go tell him I'm staying put until further notice." But at that, both Ian and Carly raised an eyebrow. Susannah paused. "What? You think that won't work?"

"Well, all I know is they aren't too lenient about letting people pick and choose wards. It could get pretty confusing."

To which, Susannah didn't reply. Wasn't she the exception to this rule? What about her extenuating circumstances of being technically homeless? Couldn't the entire city be deemed her province at this point? Aha! She could park her car in that ward and list it as her address: 900 East North Temple. There was a Schlotsky's Deli parking lot there. She could receive visiting teachers and grab a tasty sandwich at the same time, her treat. But her car was in the shop.

"Well, at least they didn't sustain anyone else to the position today. I could just go in and beg for my calling back. They need someone. The kids have to sing."

Something told her it wasn't going to fly.

NEVER FAIL CHOCOLATE CHIP COOKIES

1 cup shortening
1 cup sugar
1 cup brown sugar
2 eggs
2 teaspoons vanilla
2 teaspoons soda
pinch salt
3 cup flour
1 cup nuts
1 cup chocolate chips

Cream together shortening, sugars, eggs, vanilla, soda and salt. Add flour. Fold in nuts and chocolate chips. Bake at 350 degrees for 10 minutes. Serve to your cutest grandkids.

♡
Chocolate Kilaueas

*The molten chocolate-orange lava flows deliciously
onto your fork and down your happy throat. Yes,
one bite will catapult you into the beyond.*

Beyond the wound she received upon being catapulted out of
Primary, additional pains were laid upon Susannah each Sunday
as she invariably got asked the same question: *Are you still in this
ward?* Finally, after a month of this, she decided to unearth the
real answer. During Sunday School, she strolled into the ward
membership clerk's office and bent his ear.

"So, how exactly does it work when people's membership
records get transferred? Do you notify the member that they're
getting booted? Or do they tell you?"

Brother Green cleared his very froggy throat and scratched his
goatee.

"Actually, it's at the discretion of the bishop and the, uh, clerk.
Lots of times I exercise my prerogative to ship them out when I
know a person moves."

"Oh, really." So, he was one of those bureaucrats who had a
little kingdom. She knew the type. There was no trespassing in
their realms. "And so how do I find out where my own records are?
Just to make sure I'm going where I'm supposed to be going."

"Wull, I can tell you that right now. I was given information
by your home teacher that you'd sold your home and moved to,
let's see—" He typed a few keystrokes into his computer, waited
a bit, and typed some more until a new screen came up. "It looks
like your new address is still in Salt Lake City, but not in these
boundaries, so I had your records shipped to the Capitol Hills Park
Ward—due to your, uh, age and station in life."

Her age and station in life? What was that supposed to mean? Wait. Capitol Hills Park? That was the single adult ward. The Over 31 Club! The very Jurassic Park Ward she'd vowed never to attend. She had flashbacks of her college days when one of the older Capitol Hills guys would show up at an Institute activity or dance. She and her super-mature sister buddies would warn each other that there was an escapee from the experimental island. Raptor alert, or some other bit of adolescent insensitivity. Now, she found herself in exactly that position! Exactly that age and station, as Brother Goaty Green dubbed it. How vile! How ironically vile.

She knew how righteously she deserved it, too, and it cut deep.

"I think this all took place three or four months ago. Haven't you been visited by home or visiting teachers from your new ward yet? Some places have such lax leadership . . ."

Susannah didn't stick around to hear Brother Goaty Green's diatribe on the evils of lazy visiting teachers. She couldn't even bring herself to thank him for his time.

Capitol Hills Park! She felt an involuntary dinosaurish bellow rise in her throat. She could feel her nylons beginning to bag at the backs of her knees. Her arms were shrinking to the size of the T-Rex's. She would no longer be able to reach her mouth to feed herself. And she certainly would look silly leading the Primary children in song.

But there was no Primary in that ward.

Capitol Hills Park. Jurassic Doom.

After church she found herself buzzing north on the Vespa. It was a nice afternoon for a spin in the cool wind; not exactly a Sunday drive per se, just the scenic route home on a late summer day. She hit Ninth East when a feeling came to her that she ought to keep going north . . . and keep heading around the bend and toward . . . Capitol Hills Park. The chapel loomed. Even though everything in her head screamed "no!" her heart and spirit had to squelch that scream.

She followed (albeit grumpily) that whispering toward her newly assigned ward. *I'm simply going in long enough to locate the membership jerk—I mean, clerk—and get my records straightened out.*

As she motored northward through the mostly empty Sunday afternoon streets of Salt Lake, the words of Brother Goaty Green replayed in her head. Age and station in life. She knew what the throat-clearer was implying. "Old maid" and "spinster" and "loser of life's social lottery" were probably on the tip of his tongue. Either that or he had a more sinister meaning: that she'd been too busy building a career to follow the prophet's counsel to marry—that she was too materialistic to fulfill her womanly destiny as wife and mother. Unfortunately, there had been several people in her life who had hinted as much.

But, as risky as she'd allowed herself to become financially of late, what with the café and the cottage and all that, she was still very unadventurous when it came to dating. When it came down to marriage, there was no buyout option, no selling short, no readjustment of the portfolio. It was an all-or-nothing venture.

So far, she'd opted for the "nothing."

She sighed and shook her head. A lot of times the only thing that gave her peace in the matter was her patriarchal blessing (which reminded her—she really needed to find that thing). It said some things about marriage and children in the Lord's due time, but it definitely pointed to those things happening during this lifetime, not during some millennial existence. Unfortunately, it didn't give down-to-the-details specific counsel. It didn't come right out and say, "Get to know Guy X better." Or even "Marry him!" Instead it said something like it was the most important decision she would make in her life and would have all bearing on her eternal happiness.

No wonder she was so cautious about it.

One last time, (honestly, the very last time) Susannah indulged in wondering *what if.* What if she had let John date her and things had met their logical end? Would she have finished college? What about all those years working at PW? And what about finishing (or starting) her MBA? What about The Chocolate Bar? One thing was certain: she wouldn't have gone to Austria and met those people—

none of them, not even Liesl, who listened and loved her and felt the Spirit and got baptized. Leisl now had three kids and a family wagon there in Salzburg, where her husband was serving as District President over all the Austrian branches.

Momentous decisions ripple like waves on a sea. One creates the next. All the repercussions are impossible to gauge. She closed her mental what-if book and pulled into the bumpy church parking lot.

Susannah cautiously entered the stately brick edifice. It was built before the standard architectural plan came about. A large staircase climbed to the left, and huge mirrors loomed before her. She saw herself from head to toe, and it surprised her how timid she appeared, even in her sharp Sunday suit with the tailored lines and her smart heels. A large clock graced the wall beside the doors to the chapel. This was the building with the stained glass windows from pioneer days, and nearly everyone in the Salt Lake Valley had heard of it, even if they hadn't been fortunate enough to be assigned to a ward that met there. The whole foyer glowed a goldenrod yellow, and she felt comfort flow through her.

Ooh! No! Wait! She tried to shake it off. The Capitol Hills Park Ward was the last place she wanted to get comfortable—she'd rather be comfortable in Ghana or Bahrain.

"Hello!" A perky voice rang out. "I'm Sister Upton, the Relief Society President. Don't tell me—you're Susannah Hapsburg. We've been so looking forward to meeting you. I love your shop! I came in a few weeks ago, but you were out on business. I ate half a pound of that Candy Bar Fudge and about had a coronary." She clapped her hand to her mouth in surprise. "Oh! But not in a bad way. I mean a coronary of joy!"

That was a new one. Susannah couldn't help but like this upbeat woman of about forty, with her hair in an up-twist and the edges of her mouth turning north as well. Upton was an appropriate name, and Susannah figured it would be easy to remember if she ever came into The Chocolate Bar again. She extended her hand.

"Thank you. It's very nice to meet you. I was hoping to get a minute with the ward membership clerk. Could you point me in that direction?" Susannah didn't want to lose sight of her purpose here this afternoon. She let Sister Upton lead the way down a long hall of highly varnished oak doors.

As they walked, Sister Upton kept bubbling. "Only sixty seconds with the ward clerk? Pish. We'd all like about sixty hours with him, or longer, if you know what I mean. He's so dreamy. But, natch, I wouldn't want him to know the whole RS thinks so. Don't want him to get a big head. Not that he would." Sister Upton knocked on the door. "Brother Wentworth? Sister Susannah Hapsburg was wondering if you have a minute to talk with her." The office door creaked open, and there at a computer with a pencil between his teeth sat . . . John.

"Wha—" The quasi-syllable was all that could escape Susannah's lips.

His face registered mute shock for a long moment as he stared her way. He stood and shook her hand, electrifying her with their first touch in a dozen trips around the sun. "Susannah, hello," he greeted her softly while Sister Upton slipped away. The youth of his face had faded and been replaced with weather-beaten lines. His wavy dark hair was cut shorter these days but thick as ever. He struck an imposing figure in his crisp suit, his square shoulders echoing his square jaw. However, it was his eyes that held Susannah captive. She desperately tried to determine whether they were steely or soft, angry or pitying. Some people, mostly in books, possess the gift to read eyes, but not Susannah, not his eyes, not this time.

Oh, what must he think of her? To find her here, in this desolate place, adrift socially and emotionally, without even the poise to greet a former friend. Graceless and timid, she must appear as feeble, as spineless as he perceived her a decade gone by—unable to think for herself, persuaded against him by others.

But that wasn't who she was anymore! Hadn't she become much more since then? Hadn't she matured into a woman self-assured, opinionated and strong? Where was her now self when she needed her? Elusive . . . self-confidence was so elusive when she looked in his eyes.

"I . . . I didn't expect to see you here today." His voice rang hollow, as though spiraling through a cavern of ice. His tone chilled any courage that had formed in her heart. Oh, why must he still be angry? Why, after so long? Perhaps years in Arctic waters had frozen his very soul.

Finally she recovered and spoke. "Neither did I. I mean—" Susannah coughed nervously. "I mean, I didn't expect to come here today. It's just—are you the ward clerk?"

"I am. Only for the past few months. How's your house coming?" When she gave him a double take, he explained. "Ward clerks know where everyone lives." John's ice face almost cracked a smile—she could see a crinkle near those crow's feet in the corners of his eyes. Hope sprang through her chest as her knees went wobbly. "A lot of those places in the Avenues were built with nooks and crannies and crawl spaces. My place in Marmalade has a dumb waiter. Ah, the days before cookie-cutter houses." His rambling helped her recover a modicum of poise.

"Oh, the house." She shook her head wearily. "I don't have the time to spend on it I'd like, but I know what you mean about built-ins. The other night I was working on a wall. I want to put in a door, see? And right where I wanted one, there was a plastered-over door. Actually, it kind of freaked me out." She didn't mention the creepy stalker-knocker following close on the door-discovery's heels. She already feared sounding melodramatic. "I still haven't found the nerve to go back and find out what's behind door number weird."

"Kind of like the 'Cask of Amontillado,' eh?"

"Exactly!" It was exactly the Edgar Allan Poe tale she thought of when she saw the door. "I could almost hear Fortunato's cries from where he gets walled up in the wine cellar by his wicked friend."

"I got my first taste of imaginary claustrophobia reading that story."

Susannah didn't expect her first conversation with John Wentworth to be here or to be about Poe or to be so strange and simple. So much yearned to be spoken, and this wasn't any of it. The mundane had supplanted her geyser of feeling. How every ounce of her longed to beg his forgiveness, not to ask him to take her back, but rather to not think so ill of her for her youthful decision.

She ached to request his pardon, his tolerance, his mercy. Certainly Susannah couldn't dream of his gathering her in his strong arms and hushing her with comforting words, but forcing the soft image from her longing mind took effort. Here he stood before her as hearty and wholesome as ever she saw him a lifetime ago.

"Susannah—" His voice gentled a tiny fraction as he said her name this time, and she had to remind herself about Camie. "Maybe I could help you out. I've been meaning to come by—"

A tap on her shoulder made her turn around.

"Susannah? Susannah Hapsburg?" The deep voice startled her. She spun on her spiky pump's heel and there, before her stood the indisputably most handsome man she'd ever seen, glittering in a $1000 suit and flashing her a killer smile.

"We finally get to meet face to face." Face. What a face. Jet hair, cut features, sultry eyes. Where had she seen that face? He smelled like cinnamon and laundry soap and a faint, zesty cologne—or maybe it was simply himself. She had no idea who he was, but his scent and smile made her a little faint, nearly forgetting about gymnast-dating Mr. Frosty Freeze in the clerk's office. Helpless to resist, she turned her attention to this viable, viable alternative.

"Yes. Face to face, Brother—?"

"Brigham Talmage," and the words of course hung in the air. The barrister bachelor flashed a billboard smile at her, and her internal car spun out. If only this lawyer did accident cases of the heart.

Out of the corner of her eye she saw John Wentworth shuffle a stack of papers on his desk. She turned back toward him briefly, but his telephone rang. He gave it a helpless look, and then Brigham Talmage commanded Susannah's attention.

"Sunday School?" She nodded yes. "Let's go." He steered her down the hall, resting his hand in the small of Susannah's back, and something melted nearby. She took one over-the-shoulder glance at John who looked engrossed in his clerking duties, clearly uninterested. A wisp of regret fluttered through her soul, but she didn't allow it to light anywhere.

As she floated down the hall beside this bachelor of legendary repute, it occurred to Susannah how odd it was that everyone she'd met so far already knew her by name and sight. Fortunately for normalcy's sake, it didn't continue. Brigham Talmage graciously took her as his project and introduced her around Sunday School, greasing the skids with the bishop as well.

"Bishop North, this is Susannah Hapsburg. You'd better get her a calling, pronto. Preferably something requiring organizational genius and financial wizardry. She's famous for those and many other talents."

It suddenly occurred to her that her name had likely been circulating on the ward rolls for weeks now, and she'd probably been the topic of some kind of ward council conversation, or worse, an activation effort. Shudder. She wanted to protest that she'd been faithfully attending the ward where she was voted off the Primary Chorister island and shipped out without her knowledge, but there wasn't any way to edge in a word with Brigham Talmage at her side. The famous attorney lived up to his reputation for persuasiveness and charm.

"Come with me—as soon as church is over," he said as he dropped her off in Relief Society on his way to priesthood meeting. "You have to see what I've done with your old place. You knew I bought it, didn't you? I'm sure Joan told you. You don't have plans, do you? Cancel them if you do. Here's my cell phone. Call whoever you need to call and tell them you'll catch them some other time."

She assured him she was free, and he finally left her in peace to attend Relief Society, where Sister Upton gave her a warm welcome and inadvertently plugged Susannah's restaurant. Susannah tried to wave it off, but when the lesson was over, a dozen women approached her to gush about how much they loved the Chocolate Kilaueas and the Deep Cocoa Ginger Trifle. She recognized two of them from fondue night—the ones who had used the term "hot buttered toast."

It was absolutely surreal to be standing here in the last place on earth she ever thought she'd be and to feel so comfortable and welcomed—and (she didn't want to admit it) envied. It had been ages since she felt like she had a life that anyone could covet. But here she was, the apparent apple of Brigham Talmage's eye, the owner of a shop that made women's mouths everywhere water, and comparatively young. Now, that was an utterly foreign sensation, indeed.

She didn't have long to savor it, though, because before she could respond to all the sweet sisters who accosted her, Brigham appeared with his twinkling eye and his Armani shoes and his suede scripture tote (monogrammed BLT—she wondered what the L stood for) and whisked her out to his car. No! It was a Porsche after all—exactly as she'd predicted. "Surrealism lives," she whispered to herself as she pinched her arm to see if she was awake.

"I'll bring you back to pick up your car later." The front bumper of his German sports car dipped dangerously close to the concrete as they crossed the gutter and gunned into the shady, tree-lined streets. The engine was actually quiet enough that two people could hold a civilized conversation while the vehicle was running—a situation Susannah hadn't experienced in ages. He pressed a button on the dash and a Peter Breinholt song, "So Here's To You," began mid-chorus. ". . . here's to knowing just who's without who. Lai-di-dai. " Peter! Her favorite local voice sang in his unique folk-pop style. She pinched herself again. The words "too good to be true" swooshed through her mind.

"Look, I know the Porsche is over the top. Don't judge me by it." He shifted down—silently. Another foreign concept. "I only have it because I got it as an in-kind payment from a client, not because I went out and bought it myself. I've got a guy coming to look at it this week, and I'm trading it for a plain old Audi." Plain old Audi? Those words didn't go together in her mind. An Audi was an up-market Volkswagen, and everything she'd ever driven herself was way down-market from that—her current Volkswagen Jetta on mechanic's blocks being a particularly down-market example.

"Did you like the ward? I bet you knew practically everyone, what with your shop and all. The women talk about almost nothing else—except when they talk about men, of course."

"It's funny you should say that." She decided to finally join the conversation and try to be pleasant and not merely like some limp, stun-gun victim. "That reminds me of this thing that happened on my mission."

"To Austria?"

"Yeah, Austria." How did he know? It was like suddenly *The Life of Susannah Hapsburg* was being broadcast on reality TV while she bumbled through unawares. "One day the elders in our district accused my companion and me of sitting around on P-day talking about them. My Austrian comp laughed a big, in-your-dreams 'ha!' and they asked, 'So what do you talk about then?' It took less than a nanosecond for my companion to answer, 'Food.' I'm here to tell you, that German girl was so totally on. Since then, I've noticed that ninety percent of my conversations with other women have basically centered around food. In fact, once my friend Colette and I were driving back from Moab, and I realized we'd talked about nothing but recipes for the whole three-and-a-half hour trip."

"I remember Colette. From college. Her sister dated my roommate." Then Brigham went about peeling back the layers of their lives' previous intersections, discovering ties she never knew they had until she found herself at the door of her old condo, fidgeting in her pocket for the key that wasn't there but in his hand instead. It was a slight jar to her system, going home but to Brigham Talmage's home. Very weird. He pushed open the door, and a whoosh of dry, cool air blew her way. It still smelled like home, but with an added cinnamon and Tide appeal.

"I hope you don't hate the changes." He led her inside. New carpet squished beneath her feet. The paint, now a taupe with ivory molding and trim, felt odd but fabulously updated. His furniture was nice, all manly: dark leathers and huge loungeable throw pillows. A TV that would give any guy screen envy filled the entire center space in the mahogany entertainment center.

"Would you like a drink? I've got Coke, Sprite, orange juice. There's ice water." She accepted some water and sat down on the wide leather chair with matching wide leather ottoman. It was tempting to put her feet up, lean her head against the squashy pillow and let the sandbags on her eyelids take her into some kind of renegade Sunday afternoon nap. Something about the afternoon sunlight filtering through the curtains, and about being in this alternate Trading Spaces version of her old home felt like a huge soul-exhale, and sleep became irresistible.

When she jerked awake some time later, Brigham Talmage was leaning on a pillow on the long sofa, his feet up and thumbing through a book.

"Oh, hello, Sleeping Beauty."

Oh. My. Gosh. Did she doze off in Brigham Talmage's home? What time was it? Had she drooled? Her lapel felt wet. Oh! No, it was only the spillage over the lip of the water bottle she clutched to her chest. Weird. This was all very weird.

"Have I been asleep for long?" It looked like there was still daylight.

"Only an hour or so. You must be running on fumes. It was like you sat down for the first time in your life or something." He smiled warmly, revealing his teeth almost back to his molars on the left side of his mouth, reminding her of the incomparably dashing Errol Flynn's smile. She inhaled deeply to try to get the oxygen going to her brain again. "I've got some leftover Olive Garden takeout if you want some. Are you hungry?" he offered. She was starving but too confused and out of sorts to eat. "At least have an apple," he called from the kitchen.

"Sure. An apple sounds good." It was a tart Granny Smith he tossed her way, followed by a salt shaker. He sauntered in, an apple and a salt shaker of his own in hand.

"Try it this way." He bit out a large chunk without chewing it, then dropped it from his teeth into his hand, salted it and put it back in his mouth. She watched the strange ritual skeptically. "Come on. It's really good. Anyone who can live off Austrian food for 18 months can surely try Granny Smiths with salt." Then he bit one (carefully and without excess saliva—she was sure) and salted it for her to try. "I should have cut it, but you don't mind too much, do you?" No. Secretly and surprisingly she felt delighted.

Susannah placed the piece of fruit on her tongue, and the perfect balance of tart and sweet and salty hit her like a wake-up call. Her eyelids sprang open and her blood started flowing again.

It was delicious and refreshing and very good.

"Delicious. Refreshing. Very good."

"Wakes you up, doesn't it?" He smiled, and she created and ate a bite of her own salted apple, returning his grin.

"I'm sorry I fell asleep. You have to forgive me."

"Was it my company, or was it just the comfort of being home again?"

"Please. I do like what you've done to it. Very soothing." She laughed, only a little nervously, and rolled her eyes at her foolish sleep. "Why did you want to live here, anyway? I mean, it's a nice neighborhood, and the condos keep their value really well for condos, but what made you ask Joan for it specifically?"

"You."

"Me?"

"You. I wanted to meet you."

"You've got to be kidding."

"No. The only thing was, it backfired. I didn't know I would end up buying your condo, and that you'd be moving out so I couldn't come by to innocently borrow a cup of sugar or the *Deseret Morning News* or whatever. It took me until the mortgage signing to figure out how badly I'd botched my plan, but oh, well. I still laugh at myself about it sometimes."

She smiled his direction but shook her head in disbelief, feeling even more disbelief than she showed. "What are you talking about? How could you even know who I was to want to meet me?" She was a Pointman Westerford work hermit. A nobody.

"Oh, I knew of you from plenty of people. I'd seen you back at the U, and like we were saying, our paths have crossed a few times since then, although you obviously don't remember. I knew you were one of the sharpest financial minds operating at PW before its demise, and that you were nice, funny, and, of course, one of the most beautiful eligible women in the whole Salt Lake Valley. That's no secret in any of the social circles. You saw how everyone you met today practically drooled all over you like you were a celebrity. You can't deny it's who you are: 'Susannah Hapsburg, owner of that hot little chocolate café;' 'Susannah Hapsburg, the girl who could have saved Pointman Westerford if they had let her;' 'Susannah Hapsburg, who turned down the financial reporterette job at Channel 6—even with the six-figure raise;' 'Susannah—'"

"Whoa, there. That's enough. Look. I don't know where you're mining all these tales from, and I'm flattered as all get-out here." She was. But she knew about flattery, that she shouldn't put much stock in it or it would leave her . . . flat. "And you're sweeter than Viennetta." And better looking than Errol Flynn, Cary Grant, and Antonio Banderas combined. And as rich as those stars and triple fudge brownies combined. And nicer. And . . . here, in her old apartment, confessing a semi-obsession with her. What was a girl to do?

She yawned.

"Vienetta? I've got one in the freezer now if you'd like a slice, but I can see I'd better get you home." He pulled her to her feet. "I'd like to take you to dinner Thursday night. Could I?"

He certainly could.

CHOCOLATE KILAUEAS

6 oz bittersweet chocolate
2 oz semisweet chocolate
10 tablespoons butter, cut up
½ cup flour
1½ cup powdered sugar
3 eggs
3 egg yolks
1 teaspoon vanilla
1 tablespoon orange extract

Chop chocolates and melt together with butter in microwave, stirring to combine. Add flour and sugar to chocolate mixture. Lightly beat eggs and yolks, then stir into flour-sugar mixture until smooth. Stir in vanilla and orange extracts. Divide evenly into six 6-ounce greased custard cups. Bake at 425 degrees for 14 minutes. Edges should be firm but the center will be runny. Run a knife around the edge and invert onto dessert plates. A dash of sweetened whipped cream completes these little volcanoes of flavor.

♡
Bombshell Brownies

Baked thick, these brownies melt in your mouth. Slather them with rich chocolate frosting, and Bombshell Brownies become a chocoholic's dream date.

"So you've got your dreamy date tonight." Colette mopped up one of Trevor's spills beside the mixer while Susannah piled dishes into the sink.

"You remember too well." Susannah's heart thumped in anxiety when she remembered her evening plans. After years of living in a complete social Land of Desolation, wasting time on bizarre love triangles, blind dates from blazing places, and her eternal unrequited crush on John, perhaps this was her chance to finally break out of the dismal pattern.

"It's my gift. Like an elephant," Colette grinned. They returned to their customers out front. "So tonight I'll lock up and stuff. You go home early, give that sleek fair hair of yours a hot oil treatment—make it even shinier. Have fun. Blaine and I are going to the new superhero flick at the late show. Oh, look. Here comes Ivy. Do you think Suffo-Cade's still dating Gracie?"

"No, remember? Felicia won the bet on that with the two weeks guess." Colette, who had sleek fair hair (but with deep blue highlights) herself these days, went over to take Ivy's order. Felicia Patterson was prattling on about European history, when a group of sister missionaries came in and sat down at the bar beside Susannah. Sister Havel, the perkiest among them (and that was saying a lot), wore a broad grin.

"Guess what, Susannah. I getting transferred."

A wave of sadness washed over Susannah. She'd come to enjoy

and love this cute Polish girl. "Where?" She almost choked it out.

"Gotcha! Don't worry. It's just to the morning shift, and to a different companion. But I have to move my apartment to down the hallway. Temple Square—it is a unique mission, no? So anyways, I will not be coming into this shop anymore in the mornings before my lunch. I will have to wait to eat my chocolate until right before my dinner at night. Don't you think that will be a more healthy schedule for me, or what, Susannah?" Sister Havel gave her a playful pinch on the upper arm, and Susannah gave her a warm hug back.

"You never guess, Susannah, who we see on Temple Square today." Oh, dear. Not another stalker. Fortunately, the answer was simpler. "Elder Perry! He likes walking past the flowers, you know. He doesn't go in the tunnels under the ground so much. But I got to go. We having lunch at the COB today. Thanks for the Sweet Chocolate Sorbet. Tell that big lug Trevor I say hello, okay? Bye." The COB was the Church Office Building, and the sister missionaries ate in the cafeteria there. Of course, dessert for a few of them was always at The Chocolate Bar. They loved to joke about going to "the bar" before lunch.

"Susannah." Colette motioned her over to where Ivy sat. "You have to hear this." What now? Had Suffo-Cade proposed to a girl he saw one time on a bus?

Ivy sipped her Mint Chocolate Freeze. "Okay. So a new girl, Heidi, dumped Cade like a sack for D.I. Her reign as queen of his world was too short to even wager for—four days."

"So, how did he lose her this time?" Susannah rested her chin on her hand as she listened. It felt good to sit here at the booth for a moment. These pumps were burning her feet.

"Truly odd circumstance," Ivy sighed, taking a dainty bite of her cream cheese-laden Bombshell Brownie. "Cade was flat broke this week—probably from all that flower-buying—so he took a dare from a guy up at school to shave his head for a hundred bucks. Maybe the fact that it included his eyebrows pushed Heidi over the edge and out of his life."

"I see." It might push any girl away. Poor bloke.

"Poor bloke," a Tuesday-Thursday regular chimed in. In fact, everyone in the café was getting much chummier, with group conversations forming, especially among Thursday's crowd. The Suffo-Cade saga kept everyone stringing along like a miniseries. "I feel sorry for him."

"Me, too. My brother once wore the same shirt to high school every day for a month. He wasn't allowed to wash it. If he powered through, he got a hundred bucks. It's weird the things a guy will do for a hundred dollars."

"My husband might even mow our lawn."

"What would you do for a hundred dollars?"

"I'd eat a hundred of Chef Jenkins' truffles in less than a minute."

"Who wouldn't?"

"Honestly," Ivy continued, "I can't figure Cade out. He's still young enough to want to be out doing single life, getting his single guy stuff like Peace Corps and rock climbing of the way before he settles down with a wife and family."

"Some people," Colette mused, "feel their singleness acutely. Some people, self included, are in abject misery when they're alone."

"It's as if they're ashamed of their solitude." Another patron pointed her spoon into the conversational air.

"It's like Cade viscerally needs someone." Ivy shook her head. "Thank goodness he got that heirloom jewelry back from Juliet. Remember her? Five girls ago. Now he's cooking up a special date in the woods for this new girl—Naomi, I think. She's from Duchesne. Great." There was more to the woods date, about locating a necklace under a rock, following a string or something. Then Ivy got to the meat of her Cade quandary du jour.

"So, now my dilemma is: do I lend him the $178 to buy her the silver-dipped rose, or not? He says she's the one. He's finally met her, after all his searching. She was a good sport about the whole kayaking thing, but, I don't know if it's wise to finance his neurosis."

Everything in money-savvy Susannah wanted to scream, Don't

do it! Bad financial risk!, but the sole proprietor in her squelched it. Instead, she responded, "I don't know, Ivy. What do you think?" but she felt fake, like a droll psychiatrist as she did so.

"I told him to sell his plasma to earn money to buy it, but he says he needs the silver-dipped rose for her birthday in three days, and his body won't produce $178 worth of plasma in that short of a time." It sounded like Ivy was letting herself get suckered into it, so Susannah decided not to interfere. Not a betting woman herself, she didn't wager anything on how long it would take this Naomi gal to get out of there, but she couldn't imagine this scenario turning out to be more than eleven days at the outside. Poor guy. Susannah wasn't exactly the guru of love, but she did know a few things about life, and silver-dipped roses did not fit into the eternal scheme of very many things.

Colette had gone over to wait on the cute blonde seated at the bar. Susannah remembered Ingrid—the engaged LA Fitness girl with triceps and ponytail but no ring and no date. The two were in deep discussion. Susannah swished by with her water pitcher, and Ingrid called out.

"Susannah, what do you think? Is he serious, or is he about to break up with me? Keep in mind I've been dating him three years, and we've been engaged for two. Now this week he says in the same conversation that he's 'getting closer' to being able to marry me, whatever that means, and that he can't see me anymore except on weekends. I don't get it."

"Does he have a responsible job? He's not secretly unemployed, is he?"

"Not a chance. Totally responsible. He's practically a public figure. I'd know." Ingrid detailed the woes of committing to the noncommittal, and Susannah did her best not to glaze over. Yeah, it was unfortunate, but wasn't the "dump his sorry self" solution obvious? Ingrid's fiancé must be something utterly tops not to get the boot from this Scandinavian bombshell.

"He claims he'll buy me my own personal gym when he gets things worked out. But I don't need all that. I just want to be a family."

Susannah bit her lip to avoid saying, "Read the tea leaves here, baby doll! He's working you over. He's got another girl." Or he at least didn't have the same priorities as this super-fit beauty. Instead she simply shrugged and gave Ingrid's muscular shoulder a soft pat.

♡ ♡ ♡

"Look, I know you claim to have this hottest of all hot dates tonight, with a Mr. BLT. But I want to remind you mystery boy isn't the only tuna sandwich in the sea. Before you go hook line and sinker, do me a favor, okay?" Colette was babbling now, sitting at the café's office computer and staring blankly into the screen. "Take a look at this."

Susannah glanced over Colette's shoulder to view, what? The LatterdaySingles.com dating website. Great. The screen showed thumbnails of "GUYS in SLC, ages 30-40."

"No. Colette, absolutely not."

"Oh! You're like those stubborn Israelites who wouldn't look at the serpent on the stick to save their lives."

"No, I'm like the non-pillar-of-salt members of Lot's family who knew better."

"Take Harold Angell here. He's from Murray. Age 33. Computer programmer." Colette chewed her nail and glanced up at Susannah hopefully. "He's never been married, but yes, he does already own a minivan. Here's his blurb: 'I think that diamonds, flowers, and fur coats are no longer the symbol of a man's deepest love for a woman. True, ego-sacrificing, heartfelt love can be seen in the proliferation of minivans dotting the American landscape.' That's insightful. And look." She clicked on an icon that brought up a picture of Harold, age 33. "Here's a photo of him beside his blue Ford Windstar. Looks like he's got it all decked out with bumper stickers already. Ew. Does that one say, 'Got Breast Milk?' Okay, well not Harold. But I'm sure other nice fellows are on this site. Take a look."

"Colette. You're awesome. But, no, thanks." Susannah backed away and pulled her purse from its spot on the office coat rack.

"You're super sweet, but I'll take my chances with Bacon Lettuce Tomato for now."

"I love the code name, but you've got to tell me who sandwich man is."

"Not until I see how things go."

"Fine." Colette got up and hugged her. Susannah knew her friend simply didn't want to see her get hurt again and was reminding her not to pin all her hopes on this date. "Have a good time. And you absolutely have to tell me his name if you kiss him."

"Deal." Susannah had no intention whatsoever of kissing him on their first (and possibly only) date. As soon as he found out she was plain old Susannah Hapsburg of Sugarhouse, Utah, he'd drop her like a hot potato and go back to his world of wealthy socialites and supermodels.

"Ugh. You're leaving, and guess who just walked in. Sasha."

"Ugh." Sasha Perrier, their old roommate. The Channel 6 morning show Sasha. Chronic engage-o-path Sasha. Viper in Donna Karan's clothing Sasha. Before Susannah could duck out, she heard the familiar tones of the . . . voice. Like fingernails on a chalkboard.

"So, Barclay Barnes gave me the hugest most gorgeousest diamond. It's a trillion. Want to see? No, sweetie. It didn't cost a trillion dollars. It's a trillion shape. That means it's a triangle. Three sides, see?" Her laugh had a penetrating sound, like a train going through a tunnel.

"Colette, have you noticed that being in her presence is akin to having thousands of tiny spiders crawling all over your skin? I'm gone." Susannah escaped out the side door, leaving her dear friend Colette, dearer today than ever, to the ravening wolves. As she buzzed through the late summer streets of the city on Ian's Vespa, it reminded her of Audrey Hepburn in *Roman Holiday*, who took her first solo Vespa ride through the streets of Rome. And while the blocky stone fountain in front of the Wallace F. Bennett Federal Building on State Street was no Trevi Fountain, something about knowing she had a date with the world's most eligible Mormon bachelor gave her heart wings.

♡ ♡ ♡

"Wow, Susannah. You look like a—like a dream."

"Thanks, Brigham. You're looking quite charming yourself. Love the necktie. Fabulous."

"You like it?" He fingered the tie tack, then straightened his pocket square nervously. "I hope you're into the symphony."

"Into it? I love it." She hadn't been in years, but something about crossing the plaza to Symphony Hall with its fountains and bronzy lighting always made Susannah think romantic thoughts. He didn't disappoint. When they arrived downtown, he sprang for valet parking and gently lifted her from her side of the car, then confidently took her arm and linked it through his. The tap-tap of his dress shoes echoed alternately with her click-clicking four-inch heels. She liked a tall guy. She liked being able to wear high, high heels and not have a man be threatened by her height. She liked to be well-dressed beside him and have him be well-dressed, too.

"I'm glad you wore that black dress," he whispered as they waited in the will-call line for their tickets. "I figured you would."

"How did you know about my wardrobe?" she teased. "Were you peeking in my closets when you did the walk through of my condo before you bought it?"

"Oh, no." He laughed heartily. "Maybe I should have." He dropped his hand to wrap it around hers. It was warm. "No, I just imagined you'd wear a smart black dress like that, so I dressed to try to be an accessory to you. Everyone's looking at you, have you noticed?"

Susannah figured everyone was looking at the highly recognizable Brigham Talmage. But maybe he was right—they could have been looking at her. Of course, she knew the lookers were all wondering what on earth made him pick a plain girl like Susannah Hapsburg to take to the pinnacle show of the Utah Symphony's summer season.

The concert was heavenly, and she sat through much of it with her eyes closed, just letting the music wash over her. If she happened to open them, Brigham seemed always to be looking her way. It unsettled and satisfied her at the same time.

"Where would you like to eat? I have reservations at both Maharajah's and at Kuchendeutche. What will it be? Indian or German food tonight?"

"Ooh, tough call. I'm in a curry mood, though. Take me to the Maharajah."

He smiled. "I like a lady who can make up her mind." And he whisked her off to the heady scents of curry and ginger and saffron. She'd forgotten the place was so informal, with only large cushions on the floor for seating, which made for initial awkwardness in her fluttery Little Black Dress. But he didn't allow her much time for discomfort. Within no time he'd engaged her in enticing conversation about food and travel and history.

"When I was in Jordan, I visited Petra. Have you been to the Middle East?"

"Not yet. Someday. But Petra is in my top three must-see places for my life."

"Oh, you'd love it then. It's much better than in pictures. More imposing." Brigham went on to describe the city carved in the red sandstone walls of the desert, including theories of its history. "You know the place you see in Indiana Jones that looks like a temple?"

"Yes! It's gorgeous," Susannah gushed. "In fact, I thought it was a movie set or a painting until I saw it pop up on the cover of *National Geographic*. When I realized it was a real place, I knew I had to go."

"They call it the Treasury."

"So it was a bank?" It looked kind of like her bank, with its Hellenic pillars.

"No." He chuckled and ripped another corner of flatbread off the loaf. "It's actually a tomb. But legend says it's where Moses stored the treasures of Egypt on his way through to the promised land with the children of Israel." He gave her other details of the Wadi Valley and took another pita.

"Don't get me wrong, I love this place. It's a hotspot for Salt Lake, but nobody anywhere does anything like the spiced hummus I ate in Jordan." He then described the mixture of mashed chickpeas and olive oils spiced with garlic. Susannah could almost taste it, which was quite a feat considering the powerful, exotic flavors of India already mixing in her mouth. "That hummus was—almost—the best thing I've ever tasted." He breathed deeply, and she watched him as he sighed at the apparently pleasant memory.

She sighed inwardly as well. Ah. She liked a man who appreciated good food. She wasn't sure she *loved* a man who appreciated good food. Not yet, anyway. But she was pretty sure that was her heart she could hear singing.

BOMBSHELL BROWNIES

1½ cup flour
2 cups sugar
4 eggs
5 tablespoon cocoa
½ teaspoon salt
1 cup oil
1 cup chopped pecans

Mix all of the above together and pour into a greased 9x13 pan. Bake at 350 degrees for 35 minutes. When you take the brownies out, start the frosting. In a pan melt: ½ c butter, 6 T milk, and 4 T cocoa. Bring to a gentle boil while whisking constantly and let roll for 1-2 minutes. Then add 1 box powdered sugar, 1 T vanilla, 1 c chopped pecans. Stir together until well combined and spread over warm brownies. Cool and then cut, if you can wait that long.

Quick Mexican Pork Molé

Served over rice with a savory flair, this chocolate-tinged dish will fill your heart and your tummy, leaving no corner of your soul empty.

The next morning, no corner of the shop was empty. A group of genealogy ladies noisily discussed their scrawled printouts. Susannah busied herself with taking orders and updating the menu for fall while Colette wrapped to-go orders and examined ancient handwriting samples.

"I think," Colette hemmed and hawed, "this one reads Corsica."

"That's what I said. Italy! I'm Italian! No wonder I love these Cannolis."

A pair of young women stared furtively at the fervent genealogists, and Susannah heard their complaints as she glided past. One began in a conspiratorial whisper, "Chuh. There's nothing more tedious than other people's genealogy."

To which the other replied, "What about Kabuki? That Japanese mime drama thing?"

"Okay, fine. So there's something."

Cannoli. That had been her dessert choice last night. He took her to Coral Hills for dessert after the Maharajah. None of their sweet Indian offerings appealed to either of them, and he said dessert was the capstone of the meal. She couldn't help but feel a warm rush of agreement with his way of thinking.

The ladies' voices faded into the background of Susannah's thoughts. Her date with Brigham Talmage was almost too much to believe. Her first date in forever, and it was absolutely heaven. She pondered the root words inherent in the Disney term "twitterpated," *pate* meaning "head." Twittering definitely described her thoughts. She was looking at his amazing smile picture file in her mind's memory banks when the jingle bells on the door rang and a new customer entered. It brought her down to the floor again with a huge thunk.

"Suzers!" Sasha Perrier. Again. Twice in two days forced to hear the grating tones. They'd lived with her the semester Colette got married. Sasha herself had been through seven almost-husbands and now sported another shiny rock. Sasha was the one person on earth who could make Susannah feel small with a single word. The word "Suzers" did it today.

"Oh. Sasha. How are you?"

"Great. Ooh! Pardon my fur." She hung a mink fur sash on the coat rack. "It's from Barclay. He's so—" She expelled a contented sigh. "He gave me Yo-yo here." A toy poodle peeked its frightened, shivering head out of her Louis Vuitton bag. Yo-yo looked like it received high-dosage caffeine injections on an hourly basis. Poor thing. "I can't believe it's finally happening. We absolutely need Trevor Jardine to do our cake."

"I don't do wedding cakes," Trev hollered from the kitchen. He wasn't kidding. "No wedding cakes" was his mantra. What he really didn't do was brides. Bridezillas or their mothers. He kept them all at a distance so he could continue to have faith in womankind.

"Oh. But he'd do it for me, Suze. Wouldn't he? I mean, I'm one of your oldest friends." That was a stretch. Sasha was looking old, for certain, without the TV makeup, but the term 'friend' took truth to its outer limits. "And I only want a teeny weenie little three-tier with rolled fondant and a white chocolate fountain inside it."

"We can rent you the fountain, but Trevor is serious about not doing wedding cakes. It was a stipulation in his contract when he took the position as chef here." That might not have been one hundred percent true, but Sasha always brought out the worst in Susannah. She rationalized that she needed to protect Trevor (and herself) from Sasha who, as a seventh-time fiancée, would be a septuple-threat bridezilla. She made a mental note to write it into his contract this evening. He'd appreciate it.

"Oh, phoo. I guess I'll have to get Mario from Cakes of Bountiful to make it. He's always so booked, but I guess I'll pay the extra to get him to squeeze me in." She flipped her flipped hair and chose a stool at the bar, calling to Colette, "I'll take one of those. And could you cut it in half for me?" Sasha treated her like she'd never met her or didn't recognize her in this setting. It was all par for the Sasha course. Susannah turned her back and allowed herself one huge eye-rolling.

"By the bye, I heard about you, Susannah Hapsburg."

"What about me?" Why did she always take that bait? Ugh! Now she could actually feel the hook going into her lip and the painful tug of Sasha's pole reeling it in. Was Sasha cackling with delight, or was that only Susannah's imagination?

"About you and that torrid Brigham Talmage. He's not exactly chump change, if you know what I mean." Susannah didn't know, but she left it alone. Safer that way. "We all know he's out to wive it wealthily in Padua." Sasha was forever quoting Broadway musicals when she was off screen, and for once Susannah recognized a line, from *Kiss Me Kate*. "He must have seen your stock portfolio and developed an affection for you."

Oh? Couldn't he simply like her for, what did he say, her sharp financial mind? That she was nice, and funny, and because she was—she replayed these words in her mind like a great Top 40 mix CD—one of the most beautiful, eligible women in the Salt Lake Valley? Why did she always have to undermine Susannah? Sasha proved herself once again a toxic friend. That was the only context where Susannah could use the word "friend" with this barracuda.

"Rumor can go around the world twice before truth can get its boots on, Sash."

"Seriously, Suzers. Don't let this one get away. You've let quite a few slip out of your grasp." Sasha blew on her manicured nails. "You never should have turned down Wes Rowan."

Wes Rowan? He proposed to her via e-mail. He was one of the shortest blips on her memory blipper. Sure, he turned out to be a nice, normal individual with a good personality, but Wes Rowan was definitely not for Susannah, no matter what Sasha thought.

"I really thought you and Wes would have made a good couple." She dropped the other half of her scone into her purse for Yo-yo, who yelped faintly. "I'm the one who convinced him to ask you out, you know. He needed to bounce back after a bad break up. Climb every mountain, ford every stream." So Sasha had dated Wes first, dumped him, then told him to ask out Susannah? Girls do the weirdest, most insensitive things sometimes. Oh, it was so long ago.

"Brig will be a catch, that's for sure. Every girl I know has tried to get their claws into him, but he's been so slippery. He's a guy who knows what he wants, and he doesn't let anything stop him." That sounded a lot like what she'd seen so far. The thought gave Susannah a strange chill. She wasn't sure if it was a good chill or a bad chill.

"Colette, look at you. So fuzzy and cute!" Sasha commented on Colette's angora sweater under her apron. "It's so brave of you to wear that sweater. You always were one to take the risk, do the tough thing, like back in college when you married Blaine and dropped out. Talk about taking the road less traveled. Wow." Sasha's cuts made Susannah seethe. Colette dropped out because of a high-risk pregnancy, which she subsequently lost, but Sasha would naturally forget. "It's so great you went ahead and got your beautician's license to have a degree of some sort."

"How are things at Channel 6?" Susannah needed to eighty-six this conversation, so she turned it to the one sure-fire topic: Sasha herself. "Are you doing any good featurettes these days?" It was small of her (of course, Sasha always made her feel small), but she had to make it clear that she didn't watch Sasha's features, even though they were highlighted at the top of every hour. It swiftly shifted the subject for the remainder of her stay in the café, and Susannah didn't have to revisit any other conversations regarding her own personal life. An involuntary shudder shook her as the poison one stalked out the door, purse dog and fur cloak in hand. "Come on, Yo-yo. Mommy has to go now. Think of me, think of me fondly, Suzers!" Colette gave Susannah a sideways glance. They both simultaneously rolled their eyes.

"That's the one bad thing about customer relations. We can't deny anyone service due to annoying personality. What a shame."

"Ditto," Trevor chimed in. "And thanks for saving me on that one. That chick couldn't have been more plastic if she'd had Mattel stamped on her back. Definitely not the bride to bend my rules for. I owe you one."

"Yes, you do. You'd better come bash in a wall at my house. I need you to help me find out if a dead body is buried in there. Or at least follow me up there and make sure I'm okay."

"A la maison de money-sucking-black-hole?" Trevor flaunted his high school French. "I'd be honored."

"Splendid." Nothing was bigger than Trev, and it gave her courage.

A few more customers entered, and they had obviously met Yo-yo on the walk.

"I heard chocolate is lethal to dogs."

"That might be why I like it so much."

"I had a boyfriend once who thought a puppy was a good gift."

"What happened?"

"I married Roy instead."

"Good move."

In the kitchen, Trevor pulled Susannah aside. "I need to leave early Tuesday afternoon." He re-poofed his chef hat. "Defensive driving school."

"Not again."

"I have to go. This time it really wasn't my fault, but the cop didn't believe me. They're going to revoke my license if I don't go."

Of course, she didn't love the idea that her prize chef was going to defensive driving school again, for the second time this year, but what could Susannah do? "Can you just be sure and pre-make enough of those orange sherbet thingies with the chocolate igloos over them before you take off?"

He assured her he would. Those igloos, titled Siberian Citrus on their menu, were elegant, sophisticated, refreshing, and they were selling like water to a thirsty desert nomad these days.

"And can you make a few with lime sherbet, too?" Susannah loved watching the seasonal trends in the restaurant. Hot chocolate sales, naturally, dropped off when the weather warmed up, so they replaced them with Black Cows—a drink that would probably not go over in any other location in the country except maybe Wisconsin. However, Salt Lakers were drinking them like there was no tomorrow in this Indian Summer. Something about the chocolate ice cream and root beer combo mysteriously beguiled the populace, although the thought churned her own stomach.

Owning her own business forced Susannah to learn a novel concept. She always assumed she'd impose her own likings on all her patrons, like some kind of good-taste-enforcer, and that everyone would eventually come around to her way of thinking. But financial reality demanded otherwise, and she now joyously made Black Cows, as well as fudge with walnuts instead of pecans, and pumpkin muffins with chocolate chunks, and a savory dish called Mexican Pork Molé—all recipes she would never have dreamed of perpetuating a year ago. But the customer was always right, even when they were dead wrong.

At this point, their cash was what was right.

And by being as responsive (even against her will, if not against her culinary ethics from time to time) as she was to their wishes, The Chocolate Bar looked like it might very soon move from the red into the black. Maybe. And when it did, she knew the exact orange-cart big box store where she'd spend her first thousand-dollar surplus. It was time to start getting back to her major project, but tonight was fondue festivities, and it would be dark before she could get up there. She should at least make a trip to the hardware store and replace the nine-volt battery in her shop light and lantern. There. That was a resolution in the right direction.

"Did I hear the Devil Wearing Prada mention the name Brigham Talmage associated with yours?" Colette hissed as she wandered back into the cooking area and peeked into an oven full of dessert shells. "Mmm. These smell like butter." She needn't hiss, as the café was now empty but for the three of them. "Is he the Bacon Lettuce and Tomato of your dating life?"

"Bingo."

"Ooh!" Colette cooed. "How did you ever manage that?"

"Honestly, I don't know. But we're playing tennis next week."

"Not bad, dearie." Colette fanned herself dramatically. "Wow, I can't believe I was foisting Harold the Minivan Man on you when your social calendar listed Talmage the Sportscar Stallion. Shazam."

"Don't worry about it." The two ladies stole into Susannah's office and shut the door, where Susannah dished the details of their symphony and feast for Colette's hungry ears.

"You had Mango Granita, too? Excellent choice!" Colette sighed. "Maharajah's good, but I love Coral Hills. Blaine took me there for our anniversary. I ate the most succulent lobster. I think it was boiled in butter."

The lilt in Susannah's step and voice couldn't be concealed. Whether she decidedly reciprocated Brigham's crush or not, she had to admit being pursued so vigorously by someone—someone so suave, so self-assured—infused a huge dynamo of energy into her humdrum life. The next morning, on the doorknob of the café, in a little gift bag hung a fantastic freshwater pearl and stone bracelet with Susannah's name on it. "But you're more beautiful," was all the note read. She sighed in bliss.

A few evenings later, Trevor followed Susannah's Vespa on his mountain bike to the sad and creepy cottage. Orange crackly plastic sack banging against her leg, Susannah and Trevor climbed the creaking step of the sagging porch.

"This place looks like Hiroshima," he whispered.

To Susannah's surprise, the door was slightly ajar. "See what I mean? Spooky! Someone's lurking here!" When would the ghoulishness end? Was this house actually haunted? Wait. Was it being robbed? Her expensive tools!

An erratic flashlight waggled across the ceiling and floor of the living room and then straight into her face. She screamed against her will and turned to run, but sprawled down across the sloping, decayed porch and clunked over the crumbling cement step into one of her numerous gopher holes in the lawn. It was too bad to be true. So this was how death looked: dark and lumpy and painful.

"Susannah! Get a hold of yourself. It's only me." The man's voice was raised, slightly louder than her screams, and she finally caught her breath well enough to get a grip on reality. There, standing over her was John Wentworth. Of all people!

"John. What in the world—?" She almost wanted to hit him. "Never shine your flashlight in someone's face like that."

"You know this guy, Susannah?" Trevor's voice took on a protective tone.

"Yeah. Uh. This is John Wentworth." Trevor pulled her out of the mini pit and then extended his hand to shake John's.

"And this must be . . . Guido, your—?" The word boyfriend hung in the air.

Guido? "Uh, no. Forgive my manners. This is Trevor Jardine. He works with me."

"She's a slave drivin' woman," Trevor interjected. "She beats us and give us no food."

"I thought I heard voices. I had to see who you were—thought you were some kind of burglar."

"It's my house. I should be able to go in without being scared out of my wits. Just once."

"That's what I came for."

"To scare me out of my wits? Thanks a lot. Mission accomplished." She was acting more annoyed than she felt. Secretly her knees were too weak to stand at the sight of him, and she was having a hard time keeping her breathing even.

"No. No. Not at all." He sounded flustered, too, now. She finally reestablished personal control when she heard him stuttering, "I meant, I came to see what the thing was you told me about—the mystery door of, what did you say? Door of death? I can't remember."

"Something like that. You're the one who said Cask of Amontillado."

"Right, so I thought I'd check it out. I knew you were freaked out by it. I wanted to come by when it was light to see for myself, but I've had a few late nights."

Oh. With Camie, Tiny Wonder. Susannah filled in those blanks and scraped up all the energy in her soul not to look crestfallen. Brushing herself off, she tried to pretend this freakish, falling, screaming behavior never happened. She felt like a gawky teen around him and couldn't understand why she was badgering him like he was her brother and not like her lost love.

Trevor shifted his enormous weight and interjected, "Looks like you're taken care of here, Suze. I'll jet now, okay?" She hardly noticed as Trevor lumbered away.

"I saw your ceiling. It has a fifteen-degree slope." John cautiously wandered inside the so-called structure beside her.

"You could say it sags." She shrugged and nodded as she glanced up at it.

"You could. I measured. It slopes four inches from one side to the other."

"Is that significant?"

"It is. You could definitely say it's significant. And, I noticed there's something slightly off about the whole tilt of the place. Do you ever feel off balance when you're in there?"

"Only when people shine their flashlights in my eyes and make me fall into lawn crevasses."

"Well, the bad news is, from what I can tell with my trusty Maglite and my level, you may have to right the house itself. The decaying porch is masking the real problem. In fact, I'd say this house was built right near the fault line and has been shaken to its core by one too many small tremors."

"The fault line?"

"Yeah. Didn't you know there's a huge earthquake fault that runs right under the Capitol building straight down underneath the temple? You're close to the line. This place was built to code for some other kind of land, probably long before seismologists even knew about the area. If you ask me, the city should condemn all these places and make a nice hilly park from here over about three streets in either direction. It would save them a ton of money in the long run. But if you're sure you want to make a go of this potential disaster area, no offense intended—"

"None taken."

"—if you're sure, then the best way to go about it is to break the big problems down into little problems, and then attack the little problems."

"Oh. Like good project management."

"Exactly." He smiled. She saw it under the moonlight filtering in through the living room window and unplanned skylights of the holey roof. His friendly smile. She felt so comfortable in it. Like that nice squashy couch over at Barbara's. Oh. Wait. The Camie factor. Never mind. This whole warming toward her? A non-issue.

Back to the task at hand. Project management was right up her alley. She took courage at the thought, and the two of them explored all the rooms. What precisely were the big problems to be broken down? The sloping ceiling. The crooked frame. The deteriorating porch, the decayed roof shingles, the lead paint and rotting wood in the walls. Oh, the walls.

"I think I know which problem we should attack first," she said, hands on her hips as they stood in the pale lantern light of the front room.

"Tell Tale Heart behind door number weird?"

"You got it. In fact, John, would you wield the sledgehammer for the first blow of the night?"

"I'd be honored."

She located the tool, and he started in on the plaster. It didn't take long before his steady arm had the bulk of the door revealed.

"You're right. It's weird. There's a big space between here and the kitchen. Is there a basement in the home plan? Another coat closet?" He whacked away at the wall.

"No, there isn't. Okay. I'm getting creeped out again. You're not, are you?" She hung her lantern flashlight on its hook. He swung again and the last large chunk of dusty wall fell. It made them both cough as it billowed in the light of her now-lit lantern. They knelt together and cleared away the remaining smaller pieces and then started in on the protective chicken wire.

"How did you like the ward?" He asked this rather timidly. She didn't understand why, but thought maybe it was because he saw her traipse off with Brigham Talmage. She'd gone to church with Carly these past couple of weekends to help with the kids.

"Not bad. Everyone seemed quite friendly. Sister Upton is pretty fun."

"I like Gretchen. She's a widow."

"I didn't know." Why did a shooting pain sear through her when John mentioned another woman, even in passing? Why couldn't it be easy to let him go? After all, he'd been gone for eleven years. She pulled out her wire cutters and made quick work of the old honeycomb of metal that had shielded the door from their blows with the hammer.

"Are you ready for this?"

"If you are," he said. She couldn't tell if he was nervous or not. "Here goes." John twisted the old, ornate doorknob, which she figured had to be worth a fortune on e-Bay, and pulled the stubborn door toward him. More plaster crumbled to the floor. She stood back like the coward she was and shined the lantern into the dark recess.

"Shelves. It has deep shelves," she reported, although he could see them as plainly as she could. "What are those jars?" Formaldehyde! Oh, no! Preserved . . . icky . . . stuff! Her imagination ran wild.

"It looks solid." He picked one up, dust and cobwebs' resistance notwithstanding. To her horror, he screwed off the rusty lid, stuck his finger into the crusty mass, dug out a lump, and tasted it. She thought she might faint dead away. "Mm. Honey. Crystallized honey. Says 1953."

"And you ate it?" Her heart went into palpitations, her neck into spasms. "You tasted that unknown substance? You tasted something labeled 1953? I can't believe you."

"These are old food storage jars, Susannah. This is honey."

"Yeah, so? Even if it is food storage, it's from 1953. What were you thinking? It could be toxic by now."

He chuckled. "Look. They found honey in some tombs in the pyramids and it was fine. Edible. As good as the day the bee made it. Taste for yourself." He held out the heavy jar.

It was a crisis moment. Should she take her life in her hands to be a good sport, or should she run away screaming like she wanted to?

"Trust me, Suzie. I know this kind of stuff. Emergency management hobby guy here, remember?"

She was about to have an emergency of her own, but she swallowed hard, looked up at the heavens, and gathered every ounce of her good sportsmanship. It tasted like . . . honey. John smiled at her and screwed the lid back on.

"Do you know how much this is worth these days?"

"Honey appreciates with age?"

"Um, no. There's no Antiques Roadshow surprise value for old honey. But the price has inflated for domestic honey an enormous amount in the past few years as wild bee colonies have turned into Africanized killer bees. There are hardly any Italian honey bees left. It's tragic."

Susannah knew nothing about the recent demise of honeybee colonies in the United States, and she listened with interest while John explained the various ways professional beekeepers were trying to combat the onslaught of killer bees as well as the wicked bee-killing varroa mite.

"You mean the mite sucks the blood of the unborn baby bee in its egg?" Susannah received her dose of the macabre after all. Meanwhile they'd discovered what appeared to be 400 pounds of old wheat, some ammunition for a rusty shotgun, a pile of dollar bills from the 1950s, and some stinky candles. John swung the mysterious closet door closed on its arthritic hinges.

"Wait. What's that?" She pointed at the lowest shelf and shined the lantern that way. John squatted down beside her. Simultaneously, they both stretched their arms toward the back of the recessed area, and his elbow brushed hers. Her breath caught. But then his hand caught a tin handle, and he dragged a heavy metal box into the foreground.

"It's a safe." With an inch of rust on it, there was no way either of them would be able to open it tonight, if ever. Together they lugged it out to his Jeep Cherokee, and they agreed he would take it to his locksmith buddy to decide what to do with it next.

"So, how did you like the way your Edgar Allan Poe moment turned out?" he asked as she leaned up against a tree in the moonlight. Was he leaning toward her, or did it just look that way because of the slant of the hillside? She glanced at the now-dark windows of the cottage. It looked so empty and sad. It needed her to fix it up, to make it right, to give it an occupant again. Or, she reasoned, to tear it down and let it rest in peace.

"Frankly, I'm just glad we didn't find any mummified remains in there with our ancient Egyptian honey. Wheat was enough."

"They found wheat in the pharaohs' tombs, too, you know."

"No. Don't tell me it was still good as well."

"As a matter of fact—" He raised his eyebrows and nodded. She wasn't sure whether to believe him.

"Well, I'm glad I didn't have to gnaw on the loaf of bread made from that bushel."

"Amen."

Then the awkward moment came. It was time for both of them to go home. The pause in the conversation left a hole for him to fill with a question, with the obvious question, but he didn't. The hole sat silent and empty. Eventually she couldn't take the rejection any longer.

"Thanks a lot, John. I can't tell you how much I value your help. And friendship." She hoped she put the appropriate emphasis on the word "friendship." If he wanted her, he would have asked, asked her out, asked her about the past, asked her anything. But he didn't, and Susannah couldn't in good conscience let herself fall into this trap of liking him more than he liked her. She valued her heart too much.

"I guess I'll see you at church." He stared at the driveway and kicked a tuft of weeds with the toe of his boot.

"Uh, yeah." She gave him a quick handshake, climbed aboard her ridiculous Vespa with a hollered thanks, and roared away before her pounding heart could be heard by the entire historic neighborhood.

QUICK MEXICAN PORK MOLÉ

1 cup chopped onion
2 cloves garlic, pressed or minced
2 pounds pork tenderloin, cut into chunks
1 cup barbecue sauce
½ teaspoon red pepper flakes
1 teaspoon cumin
2 squares unsweetened chocolate, finely chopped

Cook and stir onion and garlic in 2 Tablespoons of oil on medium heat until tender. Add pork; cook and stir on high heat for 5 min or until golden brown on all sides. Add ½ cup water and remaining ingredients; bring to a boil. Cover; reduce heat; simmer 10 minutes. Serve over rice.

World's Best Hot Fudge

You'll be the talk of the ice cream social when you show up with this killer hot fudge sauce.

"Killer bees. He talked to you about killer bees. For an hour? No wonder the guy's like forty and not married." Trevor unloaded another paper bag of fresh baking supplies into the stainless steel refrigerator, including a gallon jug of heavy cream.

"Psst. Look who's talking, Suze. Mr. Female expert. Put that vat of butter over here. I need it for the puff pastry I'm rolling out." Colette threw her own pastry skills into the chef's kitchen now and then. Trev didn't mind. He preferred creating the cream-based wares anyway.

"It was interesting. Seriously. And it was contextual. We had just found about a thousand pounds of honey. Did you know Africanized killer bees are taking over all the hives practically everywhere?" Susannah flipped through her recipe file and pulled several late summer fruit possibilities for daily specials. She tossed them Trevor's way.

"Killer . . . bees." Trevor selected the two best—Grilled Tropical Fruit Kabobs with Glossy Chocolate Dip, and Pineapple Rings on Chocolate Wafers—and donned his white smock.

"Seriously. It was very good information. The keeper pinches the head off the old queen to put in a young queen and keep her from swarming away with her workers, because if the old one just died then a new queen would take over and most likely mate with a killer."

"That sounds eerily like a soap opera I watched last year when I was down with the flu." Colette pulled the pre-made Colettes, creamy orange-chocolate filling in white chocolate cups, from the freezer and put them on the counter to thaw.

"Please. Think about it. What if there were no bees? Ask yourself that. It's a real problem facing our nation."

"Okay." Trevor sounded unconvinced and began sorting through his paint brushes to begin making the day's chocolate leaves for garnishes. He had a pile of lemon and mint leaves ready to be painted with milk or dark chocolate.

"But I'm wondering. I can't help but wonder. Why do you think that door was walled up? It's kind of weird." Susannah put up the recipe file and leaned against the granite countertop.

"Oh, I know," Trevor said. "If you wanted to keep something long term, and you didn't need ready access to it, but you definitely wanted it there for an emergency, it's perfect." He began painting the mint leaves with chocolate and setting them on waxed paper to cool. "Who's going to expect you to have your cash behind a plaster wall? It's a stroke of genius, I say."

"I'd keep mine in the freezer. Or in my sock drawer." Colette pushed back through the swinging doors with her empty pastry tray, ready for another load for the case out front.

"You and every other deep thinker alive," Trevor guffawed. "Do you know that's one of the first places thieves look for stashes of cash? The freezer. And it's where the cops go to find people's stashes of other stuff when they have search warrants."

"You've been hanging out in defensive driving too much." Colette called over her shoulder as she toted a platter of various cheesecakes to the front.

"Speaking of that, guess who was at driving school with me— that girl who comes in and never talks. She sat by me." Trevor's voice registered mild disbelief. "She didn't talk, of course, never does, but I talked to her anyway. I think she thought I was funny because she laughed at everything I said."

"I like that. Blaine gives me the requisite chuckle now and then. He's a good husband." He was a good husband, all right. He came in with dinner for Colette every night—he'd learned to open soup cans in her recent absence, and it had blossomed into a passion for boxed-meal cooking. She'd dined on fresh Hamburger Helper twice this week already.

"Yeah. I was thinking about it." Trevor wiped his hands on the towel and put the leaves in the fridge to set. "I used to think I wanted to marry someone who was funny, but now I think I'd like to marry someone who thinks I'm funny. Then I feel good about myself all the time."

Suddenly, the effort of putting up a non-anxious façade drained Susannah. With the morning plans in place, she retreated to the dim office, drew her blind and flipped on her warm yellow lantern light to think. Swiveling in her chair, she rested her chin on her hand and allowed her thoughts to flow back to last night's roller coaster of events, back to her conversations and interactions with John in years gone by.

The campfire crackled again. Cicadas whirred in the treetops, hissing, buzzing. Someone laughed in the background while Susannah helped John with supper cleanup. She scrubbed multi-tool camping forks in the pot of water she'd heated over the fire and set them on a nubby linen cloth to dry. The summer sun sank beneath a mountain, but it wasn't dark yet. Twilight.

"Any tortillas left for tomorrow morning?" he'd asked. She replied, no, they'd all been eaten by the hungry work crew. He stepped to her side and peered over her shoulder.

"You ever read any Louis L'Amour books?" She hadn't. "This place kind of reminds me of one—big sky, mountains, sound of running water. You ought to read one sometime."

"I bet I already know how the story went. Let me guess: at the end the guy gets the girl and the ranch."

"Yep." He smiled, and she looked up at him. "That's the beauty of it. You know the end, but the joy is in the journey, finding out how the cowboy gets from point A to point B."

She'd never thought of formula fiction as being an example of "the joy is in the journey" before. Lately, it seemed she was discovering countless things she'd never thought of before.

Other memories came flitting in: his showing her how to pound a nail into a board with one small tap followed by one swift whack; hiking to the spring as a group, when he made sure her footing was safe on the rock near the waterfall; singing with everyone around the campfire; he knew the harmony to a few hymns, and the two of them ended up in a duet; the mudslide . . .

"Look at those clouds." John pointed skyward to the south.

"Menacing." The black thunderheads had appeared out of nowhere, as they often did in this mountainous place. Today's looked more threatening than usual.

"We'd better secure the pipeline before the storm rolls in. The village leader warned me about mudslides this time of year."

The warning was no understatement. In fact, the wall of mud missed the project's campsite by less than 50 yards. Susannah felt lucky to be safe; however, the pipeline and its ditch did not fare so well.

"This storm set us back by two weeks. Maybe three." John surveyed the damage with dismay. "We're so remote here we can't bring in a backhoe; shovels are our only hope."

Before John could say another word, Susannah stalked off. A few minutes later she returned with two shovels and a sparkle in her smile. "Let's get going, Captain Wentworth," and she tossed the first shovelful of heavy mud down the mountainside. Following their lead, the rest of the project pitched in, working twice as hard and for much longer hours than they originally expected. But with combined efforts, as well as an inventive plan of a mud-break made of large stones, the waterway project eventually got back on schedule.

Unfortunately, the strain of the effort took its toll on Susannah. In her enthusiasm and fatigue, she'd mistakenly taken a long drink from the village's substandard cistern. The result was a nasty bout of waterborne bacterial infection that left her bedridden with fever and vomiting. A sweet native lady brought bowls of vegetable and root broth, which did some good, but her days were utter misery, and her nights were worse. She felt like a burden on the project and wished she could simply go home. No transportation was available until project's end, however, unless a leader's time was sacrificed to take her to the city and ship her home. Everyone assured her the illness would pass in a few days' time, but death began to look like a welcome relief.

On the third night of her misery, John Wentworth surprised her. He'd come every night before, but not with such an offering as he bore with him this night.

"Um, this may look like a poverty row meal, but I thought maybe you might appreciate it." He held out a wooden bowl filled with what looked like cylindrical gold.

"Kraft Macaroni and Cheese!" she gasped, expending what energy she possessed.

"I know, I know. It isn't a meal unless it's black beans and rice."

"No, no! Did you know it's my favorite meal? How did you know?" She wasn't lying. Macaroni and cheese represented comfort and warmth and home more than any other food on earth, more than almost any other tangible object on earth. She ate it both greedily and gingerly. It was the first thing that had tasted delicious to her palate since arriving in Central America, and her nose felt like it was going to run as her eyes welled with tears of homesickness and relief. "I love it, John. Thank you." It was the first time she'd dared to simply call him by his first name.

He smiled briefly, then looked around sheepishly for a second. "You take care, Suzie." He patted her hand, took the bowl, and bid her good night. From then on, a new feeling of friendship and trust was forged between them and they found themselves working more and more often side by side.

Memories. All alone in the Chocolate Bar lantern light.

"Susannah, are you even listening to me?" Colette snapped her with a dish towel. "I said, is he still good-looking?"

"Who?"

"Look, I know there must be a history between you and this John Wentworth yahoo. Was he named for the recipient of the Wentworth Letter, origin of the Articles of Faith, or what?"

Susannah shrugged. Her knowledge of Church history was

sketchy, limited to the film versions of *The Work and the Glory* and *Legacy*. "Yeah, still knee-wobbling, but in an off-limits, dating-someone kind of way."

"Oh, that's right. Even Sasha was in here talking about Mr. Crab Boat Baron and Camie Kimball. I hear Camie's the spokes-waif for Tahitian Noni these days. So what was the returned native doing at your place?"

"Not clear. Did I mention? He says he plans to go back and re-examine the porch sag in daylight." Susannah shrugged back when Colette mouthed, Why? "I could go back and wait around to ask, or I can try to avoid him. Or I can request a restraining order. What do you think?"

"Ask questions first, call police later."

"Good policy." But as she began considering when her opportunity would come to "ask questions," the only sure-fire location appeared to be the dratted Capitol Hills Park Ward, a place she dreaded now more than ever as it housed the membership records of both John Wentworth and Brigham Talmage, and she knew she possessed neither the poise nor the social skills to balance her feelings for both of them during a three-hour block each and every Sunday. She could turn into a human roller coaster. Blast.

Colette was still staring at her suspiciously, so Susannah realized she needed to shift back into reality. "Now. What's on the menu for Monday? Do we have enough dried blueberries? What about cherries? We need a fresh batch of Trev's Killer Hot Fudge Sauce."

Today's morning crowd included a few new sister missionaries, sans Sister Havel, who had finally transferred out for a proselytizing stint to beautiful downtown Delta. Trailing in after them by a few minutes was the quiet girl from defensive driving. She cautiously found her customary seat near the kitchen. A serious blush crept up the girl's neck and covered her face as she glanced in Trevor's direction. Clearly, Colette could stand her own ignorance no longer.

"Hi. I'm Colette. I don't think we've been formally introduced, even though you come in here so often. I totally apologize for that. You're so sweet to support our little shop. We just love seeing you in here. And Trevor loves the fact that you always order his special of the day. I think at this point he's thinking them up just for you."

Colette hit a nerve there, or an ink jet, because the redness of the girl's blush went four shades darker, into a pioneer brick color.

"I used to be a plain old housewife and do hair highlights on the side, but now Susannah's dragged me into this crazy restaurant-running lifestyle. We don't have any kids yet, so I can do pretty much whatever job I want, and Blaine, that's my husband, loves when I bring home the leftover chocolate cream pie. I'm sorry. What's your name? I'm starting to feel dumb that I don't know it."

"Jackie. Jackie Cousins."

"Pleased to meet you. I should really let you order now. Let me guess: the daily special." Colette accepted the menu from Jackie, who smiled. "Are you from Salt Lake originally?"

Over the next fifteen minutes, Colette worked her magic jaw-greasing machine on the quiet girl, extracting the information that Jackie grew up in West Jordan, went to LDS Business College, now lived with her brother—who was on the highway patrol—in a townhouse near the airport, and worked as a loan officer at one of the downtown branches of Zions Bank. Jackie liked the Utah Jazz and the Utah Symphony but hated Indian food—curry gave her hives.

Ah, it was good to see a true artist at work. Susannah periodically passed the two ladies in conversation, catching snippets here and there. She didn't need to bother to overhear the details; she knew Colette would give a full report later.

"She's totally into you, Trev." Colette hiss-whispered this toward him during one pass through the kitchen. "She mentioned you three times. Voluntarily."

"Me? No. She only mentioned me because it was common ground."

"Um, no. I know women, Trev. This one likes you."

"You should get her number, Cheffy Boy." Susannah jabbed him in the rib on her way through the kitchen with clean towels for the bar top.

"I can't do that. What would I say if I called her? 'Uh, I heard you like me. Can I make you a cake or something?' Aiyaiyai. Not likely."

"Something like that would be absolutely perfect." Susannah winked at Colette and bustled out, but then she returned almost immediately to participate in the rest of the discussion. "Yeah. Like that but not exactly that."

Colette chewed her nails, pondering. "And not in that tone of voice. I agree with Susannah. Do you want me to grease the skids for you? I could ask her to pay with a check and we could sleuth out her home phone number that way."

"Thanks, ladies, but I'll handle it—if I decide to, that is." He was quiet for a minute. "She is kind of . . . gorgeous, isn't she? No wonder I failed that defensive driving course. She had on the wildest perfume. It was like vanilla orchids."

Susannah and Colette shot each other knowing glances. It was a done deal. If only Trevor could scrape up the courage to start the deal, that was. He needed a catalyst.

"Come on guys. You're totally blowing it out of proportion. Have you seen me? I'm out of proportion. And the freckles. They're heinous. Be realistic. She's a shy but stunning girl who likes chocolate and likes to try new things. She also happens to be a very, very bad driver at the same time I am. Twice." Something in that sounded too coincidental.

"Trev, did you by any chance ask her what she was in for? At defensive driving, I mean."

"Actually, yeah. She was kind of vague about it. I figured she was embarrassed, so I didn't keep asking her. She seemed more interested in how I wrecked that motor home with my motorcycle."

"I can see why. How did the motorcycle fare, by the way?"

"As you know, I've made the crossover into motorless bikes. But going over that hill to get here from North Salt Lake practically gives me cardiac arrest."

"Too bad you don't have freakish strength like that wiry guy at your gym."

He frowned at the comment and turned back to his stove.

After a pause he called, "Look. If the moment were right, I could summon more strength than ten of your wiry guy types. I'm telling you, that was a fluke. I'll get back in contention for the top slot."

"He coulda been a contender, Susannah. You hear that?" Colette snickered.

At that, Trevor turned up the Dean Martin crooner number.

Colette hollered over it, "Are you making Chocolate Soup for the soup kitchen donation again this week? I hear they liked it a lot."

Ivy came in that afternoon and brought her five-year-old daughter, Ruth. They ordered a piece of Trevor's White Chocolate Almond Apricot Pizza and shared it. Colette reported that Ivy was giving her daughter a girls' day out. They smiled and talked as Susannah watched out of the corner of her eye from the cash register.

After a while, Ivy waved Colette over to their booth. "Ruth wants to know if she can ask you a question, Colette." Ivy gave a slight shrug and pulled a face, indicating that she hadn't a clue what Ruth's question would be.

"Who takes care of your kids while you're gone?" Ruthie asked, wide eyed. "'Cause when my mommy's gone, my nana takes care of me. She likes to see me every week. Who takes care of your kids?"

Susannah eyed Colette carefully. How would her childless friend answer this innocent girl who was six years younger than Colette's own daughter would have been by now?

"I'm still letting Heavenly Father take care of my kids. He watches them every day for me," Colette replied matter-of-factly.

"That's a good idea," Ruthie approved. "I bet He's a real good babysitter. But I bet He doesn't let them watch TV on Sunday."

"Probably not." Colette shook Ruthie's outstretched hand. Ruthie told her thanks for the chocolate. Ivy looked like she wanted to crumble like dry meringue, but Colette gave her a reassuring look that seemed to assuage things, although Ivy didn't stay much longer.

Of course, Ruthie's keen eye didn't leave Susannah unscathed. As Ivy and Ruthie walked out the door, Susannah saw the little girl point her way, "That other one isn't a mom. I can tell."

"How can you tell?"

"Because she isn't soft yet."

Susannah didn't know whether to take the critique as a compliment or a criticism. She decided to take it like it was given: at face value. No, she wasn't soft. And she wasn't a mom. But the word "yet" lingered in her ear. It sounded like Ruthie held out hope for Susannah's future mommyhood. She decided to plant that part in her mind.

"Susannah, a call." She took it in her office. It was Carly. Speaking of pregnancies!

"They put me on bed rest, Suzie." Carly's voice trembled. Susannah felt her fear. With four energetic other children to care for, Carly's plight was real, added upon the fear of a high-risk pregnancy and what might become of their baby.

"Can you come help me? Only on Sundays. Ian's mom can be here the other days, but she's got stuff on Sundays at church, and your restaurant's closed, right? If I had another option I'd take it. I hate that Mom's in Brazil. Doesn't she know we need her?" Those were the pregnancy hormones talking. Carly always went berserk when she was expecting and said stuff she wouldn't dream of uttering otherwise. Susannah knew the drill by round five.

"I'd love to. Don't worry. I can't believe you'd even hesitate to ask." It wasn't only because Susannah loved Carly's kids. The opportunity secretly overjoyed her. It was the perfect excuse to avoid going to the dreaded Capitol Hills Park Ward.

KILLER HOT FUDGE SAUCE

1 cup sugar
2 tablespoons cocoa
2 tablespoons butter
7/8 cup evaporated milk
1 teaspoon vanilla

Mix sugar and cocoa; stir dry over low heat for two minutes. Add butter and milk, turn up heat and boil 2 minutes. Remove from heat, add vanilla. Double the recipe for double the pleasure and double the fun!

❤ Black Forest Bar

This is festive food at its most beautiful and delicious. Its delectable base is a cake mix, but tell your holiday guests it's all homemade; no one will dream you're fibbing.

"Oh, I love Howard Jones," Susannah fibbed as she lobbed one into the back court. Brigham returned it easily, and she had to scramble to her own back court to make the save. "I can't believe he's still touring. I thought he dropped off the map years ago, after that song about filling the cushions but can't have a seat." Plunk. Out of bounds.

"Fifteen all. Feel the cushions. I looked it up on the CD case lyric listing," Brigham replied matter-of-factly as he served it into the net. It was his first net serve of the game. Thank goodness. Susannah was starting to think he was the invincible server. "And, yeah. He flies out to Salt Lake once a year or so. He has quite a following here, probably stronger than anywhere else in the country. I can't believe you haven't gone to see him if you're a fan."

With all her late hours at Pointman Westerford and now The Chocolate Bar, '80s synthesizer-pop flashback concerts never came to the top of Susannah's priority list. She served a perfect smash right on the back line. Thirty/fifteen. Ha! And to describe herself as a fan would stretch the truth.

"He's doing all his old stuff, plus some of his new tunes. I listened to them on the 'net, but Hojo's classics are all still fresh. The concert's at The Depot, which is in the old Union Pacific train station downtown. Hot venue. Great Asian fusion restaurant in there, as well. Can't miss." Brigham nailed a return of her lob and smiled simultaneously.

It was a chilly day for tennis, and they were the only pair on the court. The weather was unseasonably cool, but in Susannah's opinion, the chill was a mercy. The gourmet hot chocolate sales were soaring. Everyone had caught autumn fever early and wanted to taste it as well.

"I guess I should say, I loved him when I loved him. And when a song comes on the radio, I'm always shocked that I can remember all the words—oh, except that feeling/filling thing, of course. It's been a while since I listened to him on purpose."

They each ran to the net, alternately, and then backed off to their ready stance positions. The ball plunked in her front court, then his back. She was getting quite a workout for her money this time. He was the strongest competitor she'd faced in forever, maybe since college. It was refreshing. He wasn't letting her off the hook at all. It did give her a twinge of satisfaction to see the trickle of sweat running down his brow last time they met in the front court.

"Isn't it amazing, the power of music to get us to remember stuff?" He lobbed one high. "It's like they said about Primary. I don't remember a single lesson, but I do remember about a hundred songs." Little did he know, he'd jabbed his date in the most tender place in her heart, the Primary-chorister-spurned place. Even though she understood the renegade ward clerk's initiative wasn't intended to cause her pain (Brother Goaty Green had probably been reading something that used the word "proactive" in its text), it still felt like someone twisting a corkscrew into her soul.

"Match point." She served it high and wide. He scrambled for the volley; she ran to the net to return it hard to the far side of his back court. He dove to lob it back her way. She reached for it with all her might and ticked it back with the tip of her racquet, stumbling back as she did so, and then popping back on her feet again just in time to get him with a crushing back hand. He couldn't make it to the backcourt in time.

"Oh! Beaten by a girl." He pounded his heart and hung his head with a grin. "I'll never live this down at the firm." He acted like he was kidding, but she wondered. It was kind of fun to see Mr. Everything squirm a bit. Of course, maybe he just let her win.

"So. Friday night, then? Is that when the concert is?"

"Yeah. And there's a pre-concert reception thing in the Blue Goose Club—upstairs from the Depot's stage. It's sold out. I'm thinking about getting a membership, and I could get us in, if you want to go. Howard is going to be signing greatest hits CDs and chatting." Going to the concert was one thing. Hitting the total fan mania circuit was another. She didn't know if she could play the part of devotee for that long and keep up an un-bored charade.

"I would, but I ought to get a few things done on my house that afternoon—jam them in after work and before that dratted sunset. Make hay while the sun shines."

"Okay, girl. You go make that hay." He said it in a flirty voice as he tossed her a chilled water bottle. She cough-laughed at him. He didn't mind. "So just the concert, right?" She nodded, grateful that he understood. "And dinner afterward, naturally."

"Naturally." She liked a guy who naturally thought of food and included her in those thoughts. Being around Brigham Talmage was far different from her other dating experiences in recent years. Chitchat flowed like water, his charm like molasses. He always had a plan. He was courting her on purpose. No wonder girls everywhere swerved their cars at the sight of him—there was good reason to, especially when he smiled that smile. What was a girl to do?

"Anyone helping you with the remodeling? Who's your contractor?" They crossed the court and left the gate to walk through the grassy park. The soft earth felt good under her feet.

"Me."

"You? You're doing it alone?" He stopped briefly and looked at her in surprise, then they continued walking. Her racquet banged against her hip in that familiar way. She stole a glance at him out of the corner of her eye. She always liked the way men's tennis uniforms turned their wearers into these neat, preppy cleanies. Even the biggest chump looked like a champ in white tennis shorts, polo shirts, and V-neck sweaters with a stripe.

"Not totally alone. I've had a few people show up and help."

"Oh, yeah? Who?"

She debated about whether to tell him. Would he care? Why

should she hesitate? It was a non-issue, right, since John was tight with Camie Kimball anyway?

"Do you know John Wentworth?"

"It sounds familiar." He wandered toward the drinking fountain beside a picnic bench. "Oh, yeah. Crab boat guy. From the ward. Wilderness survival nut, right?"

She nodded while she gulped the sweet, cool water from the old stone fountain. The wind rustled in the drying leaves above, autumn's announcement of its impending arrival.

"I think I was his dad's lawyer way back when. Did his will and stuff. I only do a few of those here and there—did a guy's from Pointman before it went into the death spiral. Harville. You know him?" He gulped some water, and she nodded. Then they crossed the grassy field toward the parking lot. "I'd rather do wills and trusts than accidents, but I have to pay the bills."

She knew all about bills these days and hoped The Chocolate Bar would soon become solvent enough to start paying its own. They reached the parking lot, and Brigham must have changed mental gears because he suddenly checked his phone and wrapped things up quickly.

"Friday, then?"

"Friday."

"But not too late. I don't want to miss the opening act. Peter Breinholt." Peter! With that, Brigham Talmage roared away in his Porsche, while she tooled off on the Vespa. Ah, tennis. It had been too long since she'd played, and she knew she was going to pay for it tomorrow.

She thought about Brigham as she made her way back to the shop. Charming. Almost what she'd call a Prince Charming. No white horse. But in a loud place, like a helicopter or a factory, the words "white horse" and "white Porsche" would be indistinguishable to most human ears, so she decided to count it. And his energy in pursuing her was admirable. Persistent was one word that could describe him. So were undaunted, incorrigible, indefatigable, relentless. Next week's plan included a scary-gorgeous hot air balloon ride over Park City. They'd been up flying in his buddy's twin-engine plane once already. They flew over the Heber Valley, with Brigham pointing out each city, each ski resort, and each highway so she could orient herself. His pursuit of her fell somewhere between fairy tale and freaky.

She zipped to her parents' house to change back into work clothes, when it occurred to her—Brigham Talmage was the first guy to turn her head in a long time. Three years, maybe. Maybe more. It struck her that the timing was unfortunate—both Brigham and John entering (or re-entering, respectively) her life at the same time. Why did life always work like that? Feast or famine. No one interesting enough to say boo to for eons, then the two most interesting men she'd ever met show up at the same time. Dang. She wished she could honestly count John as re-entering, seeing as how he was taken, girlfriended, attached.

But if by some miraculous, happy chance his attachment freed up, why, oh why would fate make this coincidence of two roads diverging in a yellow wood for her, forcing her to make a harrowing choice between good and good? Or, in other words, why must she choose between the great, spectacular superstar Brigham Talmage, most eligible bachelor in possibly a thousand-mile radius, and John Wentworth, the love of her life?

It scared her.

A few afternoons later, Susannah was happily listening to the chatter of the café.

"Do you think my car has auto immune deficiency?"

"Oh, no. Is it in the shop again? That's the fourth time in six weeks. Your mechanic must have a daughter with a wedding coming up, and you're financing it."

"Actually, he's not married. Young, too."

"Is he cute?"

"In an overalls-and-grease kind of way, yeah."

"He totally likes you. Is he charging you?"

"Only for parts."

"Not labor? It's love for sure. Do you want him to call you?"

"I don't know. Maybe. He seems pretty nice. Kind of shy. Do you really think—"

Conversations floated up to Susannah's ears as she floated around the café, taking orders, serving chocolate concoctions like cherry-laden Black Forest Bars, clearing china. She finally understood what poets meant when they talked about lovers' feet having wings.

"Tonight's the night I challenge for third chair. I'm so nervous I can hardly lift my cello."

"Wow. Good luck. Don't drink too much of that dark cocoa. It'll give you the jitters."

"It might improve my vibrato. . . ."

"I can't date him anymore. He has this giggle. . . ."

Susannah tried to get her mind to sing the lyrics to that fill the cushions song in her head to get excited for her date. They weren't forthcoming just now.

"Adopt a highway? Please. That's so nineties! . . ."

". . . He always says he's getting his 'ducks in a row,'" the ponytailed Ingrid sighed, exhaling with her very fit lungs. "I finally quit pestering him about the ring because it wasn't helping. Did I tell you, meanwhile, he's obsessed with reptile poison?"

When the afternoon crowd drifted away, Trevor charged out of the kitchen with a grin.

"What's up Trev? You got a hot date?"

"With a contender, I do. It's fight night."

"Don't tell me you're boxing now. We can't afford to lose your hands, pal."

"No, no. I'm just ready to arm wrestle that punk again. He's a punk and he knows it, and freakish strength or not, he's going down. You want to come and watch?"

Colette shook her head. "I'm closing up. Susannah here has a hot date for Hojo tonight."

"Is that some kind of Korean food?"

"Howard Jones. Singer from the '80s. You know."

"Before my time—but wave a lighter in the air for me, eh? I'm off. Stop by Gold's Gym on your way home and see my shiny trophy if you really want to impress your date." The bells on the door jingled as he lumbered out. Colette and Susannah each raised an eyebrow at one another and shrugged. "I hope he can nail it this time."

"I know. He'll be unbearable if he loses. He'll slink away to Las Vegas and take that pastry chef job at the Ritz Carlton like he's always threatening to do. I wish they'd stop offering it to him. Las Vegas presents a tempting world for an arm wrestling fanatic of his caliber." Susannah absentmindedly pulled the strings of her apron and hung it on the hook behind the bar. "What he needs is a girl."

"No kidding. I've got my eye on a few. Jackie certainly is sweet on him. Why does he avoid asking her out?"

"Why do men do anything they do?"

"Who knows? Let's see. Male motivations: lust, greed—"

"Ah. And hunger. Just like women." Susannah grinned and took a bite of her positively last butter cookie of the day. She was still acting kind of dreamy.

"Precisely. Have fun tonight. Close your eyes in the ballads and put your head on his shoulder. That will do it every time. You haven't kissed him yet, have you?"

Susannah crashed back to reality. Kiss him? Brigham Talmage? It hadn't crossed her mind. Well, not in the last hour. She sort of didn't feel worthy. Oh, but he did sport those heavenly teeth. And the killer smile. And he was totally into her. Hm. With Peter Breinholt's mellow sounds, the mood could ostensibly strike. Would Brig be expecting anything? He'd been a "perfect gentleman" up until this point. The question of why he hadn't tried to kiss her yet had been a mild concern. Wasn't the third date the charm for people of their generation?

However, even if she didn't count lunches and tennis matches, their third-official-date bell had gone off some time ago, maybe on the plane ride, although it was impossible to hear its chime over the engines.

Maybe he wasn't totally into her after all. Maybe she was blowing it all out of proportion, getting her hopes up unnecessarily. Her mouth and throat went dry. She wished she hadn't put all the glasses into the scalding hot water of their industrial dishwasher.

"Not yet." She tried to say the "yet" as softly as she could, but it wasn't lost on Colette.

"It wouldn't hurt a thing for your lips to be reintroduced to other lips. They're somewhat out of practice, you know."

Wouldn't hurt a thing? Or would it? She wasn't sure.

Despite her best intentions of making hay while the sun shone, Susannah realized before leaving she didn't have the right hacksaw for her plumbing project, and the trip back and forth to Sugarhouse for it on the Vespa would cost all her sunshine time. She drove past the Cottage of Thrills and Chills on a surveillance sweep on her way home, anyway. To her disappointment, no Wentworth Jeep Cherokee darkened the driveway. She ignored the fact that a cottage drive-by was nothing like "on her way home." Admitting so meant owning up to the fact she was behaving like a giddy high-school-drive-by girl, hoping to catch a glimpse of her love interest at home. Never mind the fact that it was her own home and not his. Oh, mercy. Her thoughts began to garble. She decided to drop by Barbara Russell's for a quick brain-palette cleanser.

"Susannah, darling girl. What uncanny timing you have." Barbara led her back into her spacious kitchen with its Italian tile backsplashes and stainless steel appliances, where Susannah took a seat on her usual barstool and watched Barbara peel garlic cloves into her pot of Mulligan stew. "Frank just called, and the car is done!"

"He called you about my Jetta? Ugh. It's worth less than it will cost to fix it."

"No, no. That thing needs to go. You should donate it to the Lung Association for a tax write-off. No, I'm talking about the convertible—my Mercedes. Madeleine wrecked it ages ago, and I've been letting it languish. But Frank fixed it up for a song, and here." Barbara pulled a set of keys from a wooden box atop her refrigerator. "Here are the spare keys. You've got to get off that moped and back into an actual vehicle. Can you pick it up? Do you have plans for tonight?"

"Actually, yeah. Pretty good ones. You know how I love Peter Breinholt?" And Susannah filled Barbara in on the date's details.

"Brigham Talmage! Holy smoke. Where did he come from?"

Swallowing her pride, Susannah sang the song of doom, "Dun dun dun dun. The Capitol Hills Park Ward."

To her credit, Barbara resisted even registering an I-told-you-so on her face, but beamed happiness instead. "Is he as wonderful as everyone seems to think he is?"

"As a matter of fact, he actually seems like it." And Susannah described their recent dates. "We really seem to click conversationally, and he's quite a tennis player. You'd like him."

"I remember when he beat Josh Johnson, U of U's only tennis player to ever go pro." Barbara smiled and began humming to herself. An unexpected thrill went through Susannah at the thought of the happiness it would give those who loved her if she finally settled down happily. "But no pressure, Susannah. Take your time. Get to know him."

She picked up the car, arranged for the Vespa to be returned to Ian, thanked Barbara profusely by phone, and finally got home to Sugarhouse. Unfortunately, she couldn't figure out how to put up the Mercedes' rag top, so it stayed down as she crossed town on the fall evening. Surely she could worry about the top later. For now, being the driver of a convertible Mercedes made her feel like Grace Kelly in *To Catch A Thief*, motoring along the French Riviera.

At home, she unclipped her long hair from its ribboned ponytail and let it fall over her shoulders, hoping it didn't have a ponytail bend in it. With all the car stuff, her wardrobe selection time was shot. She rummaged through her closet and grabbed her only clean black pants, her best heels, and her favorite red sweater, not clean, but clean enough.

Just as she cinched her calfskin jacket, she heard the rumble of the Porsche pulling into her driveway. Thank goodness her lipstick was in her coat pocket. She put it on—sparingly and expectantly. Then she thought twice and slathered on one more coat, for safety. There are some fear boundaries even the boldest guy won't cross, and a heavy layer of blood red lipstick is definitely one of them. All those Hollywood portrayals of men kissing perfectly made-up women? Complete fiction. Real men would rather let their lips suffer eternal solitude than sully them with smeary Scarlet Shimmer.

She opened the door. What she saw made her suck in her breath. "Wow. You look—" He looked like Black Satin Raspberry Cake with Walnut Parfait to her starving soul.

"I was just going to say the same thing. You look—" Brigham Talmage took her by the arm and led her to the car. He'd set up the CD changer to create the mood for the night's entertainment. It was all Howard and Peter all the way to the old train station.

"I know we said dinner afterward, but are you sure you don't want to get a bite to eat before we go? We can hit it a bit late. I don't mind." He said it like he didn't mean it, so even though the only thing she'd eaten since noon was one of Trevor's Aprichocolate Jubilees, Susannah declined. Besides, there was something about an empty stomach that made butterflies beat their wings more intensely. They were all a-flit, and she liked it.

Once inside the Depot, Brigham took her arm and led her to their table. As yet, piped-in music still played in muted, over-bassed tones. Soon, however, a scraggly-bearded fellow came to a mic on the stage beside a lone, tall wooden stool.

"Hey, Salt Lake City. Peter Breinholt." That was all the intro needed and all anyone got. Peter took the stage. He played all her favorites, his originals, his best cover tunes, and a few from his new CD. Susannah sat spellbound, barely noticing when Brigham took her hand during "Jerusalem." It jolted her trance briefly when Peter did a cover of Dan Fogelberg's "Longer," a song fraught with memories for Susannah, but it was brief, and she recovered.

When he was finished, she cheered for Peter as enthusiastically as any high-school-drive-by-girl could.

"Glad you like the show. You seemed kind of lukewarm about it when I asked you."

"I am lukewarm about Howard; but Peter? Totally warm."

"Yes you are." He slid his arm around her waist and sat close enough to lean in and nuzzle the perfume on her neck. Paralysis set in, while the tummy butterflies performed stunts previously unknown to butterfly-kind.

Peter sang one more song, an upbeat tune with his signature

folk-pop blend sound, not unlike Dan Fogelberg's in his glory days, but at table fifteen it was all slow dancing between Susannah and Brig, at least on Brig's end. Too internally apoplectic, Susannah's body refused to sway while Brigham Talmage rested his chin on her shoulder and breathed.

Applause provided a welcome interruption when Peter left the stage. Scraggly boy reappeared. "Okay, SLC. It's going to be a minute while we roll out the piano, so you all have a barrel of fun and go buy some drinks or something while you wait." The lights came up—as much as they ever do in a concert venue.

"Can I get you a juice or something?" Brigham asked. Susannah was about to give her enthusiastic yes when a shadow loomed above her. She shaded her eyes from the stage lights to see who it was. John! Of all people.

"Brother Wentworth. How are you?" Brigham offered John his hand, but John just scowled. Rude, Susannah thought. Bizarre and rude. Finally, John consented to shake it. Brigham glanced sideways at Susannah, saying, "I'll be right back with . . . cranberry? Orange?"

Susannah nodded at orange juice and stood to talk to John. She had to remind herself to breathe. Be calm. Be cool. Be reasonable—a twist on President Hinckley's six Be's.

"John. What a surprise. I'm so glad to see you!" That was calm. Ish. She searched his eyes for his response. They were still hard from a moment before, but couldn't she soften them? "You look great. Did you see Peter? He's soooo amazing."

"Listen, Susannah." He got serious—just when she thought she was kneading him well with chitchat. "I have to warn you. Brigham Talmage, though you may think he's prince charming, is Machiavelli's Prince incarnate."

Susannah struggled to remember who Machiavelli was. Oh, yeah. Ends-justifies-the-means guy.

John's voice grew confidential as Brigham approached from the drink table. He leaned in close to her ear, the very ear where Brigham's breath brushed her neck a few minutes before.

"Trust me, please, Susannah. Wherever you've gotten yourself at this point, he's not going to take you anyplace better." John Wentworth spoke this plea quickly and stalked away into the semi-darkness after shooting a scowl in Brigham's general direction.

Susannah knit her brow in confusion. What just happened there? She absently took the juice and drank it much faster than was polite, owing to her hunger and shock.

"Thirsty? Can I get you another?"

"Oh. Thanks. No. Sorry. I was thinking and downed it. How lame. Forgive me." She shook her puzzled head in embarrassment. "I'm good." She patted her tummy for proof, and they sat down again. He leaned in close, seemingly trying to recapture the feelings of "Jerusalem."

"What did old Wentworth have to say? You know, I've wondered if he's not the original John Wentworth, New Hampshire signer of the Articles of Confederation, still kicking around. He's getting ancient enough to incite suspicion." Brigham played with her fingers. "Kidding. Kidding. I like the old codger." It bugged her to hear him demean John—for his age. As if anyone had any control over age. Brigham wasn't more than a stone's throw from 35 himself.

Howard Jones came out and sat down at his piano, and the audience cheered from the dance floor to the mezzanine above. Susannah cheered internally because it gave her a chance to be alone with her thoughts. Why would John say such a thing? Truly bizarre protectiveness. Perhaps he saw her as a little sister. Was there something about Brigham Talmage that Susannah didn't know? Not likely. She'd heard every tidbit of gossip about him for forever, and particularly more so since she started seeing him, and there was nothing in the tales about him, or in his demeanor, to give her pause.

What was John's assertion? Machiavelli. In other words, that Brig was only concerned about money. Sure, it might appear that way to someone with less money—he was freakishly rich—but Susannah had other information, behavioral evidence, to go on. At their first meeting, he explained away the Porsche as an in-kind payment for legal work. Other trappings of wealth were as easily explained away, and he hardly ever mentioned them, which was another sign to her that he definitely wasn't caught up in it. Besides, he lived in her old apartment. If that wasn't a sign of humility, what was? Other guys she'd dated in the past, with far less in the way of gadgets and cash, had talked incessantly about getting more and more things, and their materialism far outstripped anything she could even suspect in Brigham's case.

Brig swooped in again. Oh. Sweater breathing. Hmm. He scooted his chair behind hers and was leaning in very close now. It was a slow song. Howard performed unplugged tonight, the man and his piano, which left the repertoire heavy on the ballad side, for better or worse.

So was John's motivation jealousy? Couldn't he bear to see her with another man's chin resting on her shoulder, breathing her hair?

Her head felt off balance. She sneezed, and Brig sat up. Swooning, Susannah glanced around the joint. Off in the corner sat John, staring her direction and drumming his fingers on a napkin. Camie Kimball, Miniature Marvel, giggled with another teeny bopper and her older date beside them. A flash flood of her own jealousy snarled through Susannah's heart, but indignation soon replaced it.

Sheesh. What right did John Wentworth have to tell her who she should or shouldn't date, especially when his own future was locked up with The Agile One? What was he to Susannah now? Technically, nothing, nothing more than a guy she flirted with on a trip to Central America ages ago. Sure, he gave her unpaid help at the cottage, but it was also unsolicited help, and perhaps unwelcome help if he expected to use that as leverage to be able to tell her how to run her life.

Who did he think he was? Her big brother, looking over her shoulder, telling her not to date the most spellbinding millionaire who'd ever darkened her doorstep, someone who her friends and family all approved of? And where had John been himself these past years? Money grubbing in the frozen north. Machiavelli? Whatever.

More galling was the fact John offered her nothing as a replacement. He simply sat on his judgment seat and . . . judged. A growl of irritation forced its way through her trachea. She'd prove to Mr. High and Mighty she could do what she wanted, with or without his approval.

One of Hojo's lovey-est paeans, "Tears to Tell," came to a trilling end, and Susannah used the song energy to turn her head slightly (it was all that was necessary) and plant a smackeroo right on Brigham Talmage's mouth. It certainly wasn't the best kiss of her life—she was way out of practice—but it wasn't the worst either, and when it was over Brigham's face wore a satisfied look. She couldn't resist glancing toward John's table to try to gauge his reaction.

It was easy to gauge: holding Camie by her delicate wrist, he was stalking out the door.

♥ ♥ ♥

The next morning in a groggy haze of self-loathing, she staggered toward the shower of her parents' basement when she suddenly remembered she'd promised to spend the afternoon with Carly's kids. Ian needed the day to study for his CPA exam, and Susannah relished the idea of a half day away from the scary realities of her life. She pulled her clothes on and sailed in to work for the morning before heading to Carly's.

"I know you kissed him. You have to tell me what happened. This is The Chocolate Bar. We always kiss and tell here. Especially on Saturday mornings. It's like confessional."

"Colette, I don't ask you to kiss and tell about Blaine."

"Aha! I knew it. I just knew it." Colette had only been fishing for confirmation. "Besides, Blaine and I are already married. It would bore you to tears to tell our kissing stories while we watch *Magnum P.I.* reruns."

"Enough information, thanks." Trevor waved his big hand from the kitchen.

Susannah desperately needed to change the subject. "How did it go at Gold's Gym, Trev? Total smackdown?"

"The chicken didn't show up. He knows I'm going to whup up on him, like I'm doing to this here heavy whupping cream, and he's scared."

"Does he know you're a pastry chef, Trev?"

"Everyone knows I'm a pastry chef, Suze. You had it written up in the paper. My brother will never let me live it down. He keeps a laminated copy of the article in his wallet and flashes it at everyone we meet. Some pal."

"Hey, you're the best chef this side of the Great Salt Lake, so be proud."

"You think there's a better chef where? In the West Desert?"

"Oh, I don't know. I bet somewhere there's a cute little lady on the Goshute Indian Reservation in that West Desert who can whup up a mean whupped cream. You want to go Iron Chef with her? I can sleuth her out if you want."

The door chimes rang and the day began, much to Susannah's kiss and tell relief. A Grandmas-and-Girls tea party bubbled in, so, luckily, chaos allowed her to avoid one on one conversations with Colette for the rest of the morning. She wasn't ready to divulge any more of what happened last night, from the wacky, whispered warning to her anger-inspired kiss. The worst possible reason to kiss one person is that you're mad at another person.

"Oh, did you hear about Suffo-Cade?" Colette, fortunately, had other things on her mind.

"Oh, no. Is he toast again already?"

"Already? Gosh, he's been dating Naomi for four-and-a-half weeks. It's a new record."

"So, she hasn't called the cops on him yet?"

"No! Can you believe it?"

"I can't. Not after the silver-dipped rose thing. It seems impossible. Has she been out of the country or something?"

"Nope. Ivy says they're still seeing each other every day. And, get this! Naomi calls him almost as often as he calls her. It's completely weird."

Something about the Suffo-Cade update, despite its happy tidings, deflated Susannah. Of course, she realized it was only probably a matter of days now before Cade got the pink slip from Naomi, but the fact that even Suffo-Cade could land a relationship gave Susannah's heart a twinge of pain. Was she even weirder than that? Even with the hot, hot pursuit of BLT, self-doubt nagged at her. The bells jingled again. Speak—er, think—of the devil.

"Susannah in?" It was Brig. A hush fell over the female populace of the café. Almost reverential. For the first time she could hear what mind-reading Colette must be hearing all the time: the thoughts of women around her. At first, they centered on shock: Brigham Talmage! It's him! Then they pleaded silently: Notice me! Notice me! But his eyes didn't stray from his object. When he caught sight of Susannah peeking her head over the bar, his chiseled face softened into a huge, dazzling smile.

"These are for you." He pushed a gigantic, cellophane-wrapped pile of fall flowers—broad, butter-yellow roses, warm sunflowers, and fragrant eucalyptus—across the honey wood of the bar. Collective girl thoughts she'd been hearing a moment before fell silent in Susannah's head as they all heaved sighs of disappointment and retreated into whispered conversations.

Wow. If he wanted to get her attention, this was a fabulous way. Yellow roses always made her take notice. As did personal flower deliveries, in front of dozens of total strangers. It was working, the effect was immediate and strong.

"I'll call you. Let's do dinner Tuesday. Thai."

"Thai. Love it," was all she could say, and he was gone with a sleigh bell's jingle. She smelled the roses, and about ten of the braver customers flocked around the bar to get their own whiff of Talmage essence.

"Was that really Brigham Talmage? He's even better in person!"

"Somebody get me some water."

"For the flowers?"

"No. For me."

Eventually the hubbub died down, and Colette was able to find a receptacle in the kitchen large enough for the bouquet. It was about three feet in diameter. "I think he made things pretty clear, there, Suzie-Q. Have you ever seen so many of these baby straw flowers?"

Susannah hadn't seen past the sunflowers to the small, deep purple blooms.

"I can dry these for you so you can make them into a keepsake, if you want. After they've served their purpose here, naturally." Colette, whose dry but colorful hair itself resembled deep purple straw flowers today, hefted them onto the far corner of the sleek wood of the bar, careful not to potentially block Jackie's view of Trevor in the kitchen.

♥ ♥ ♥

"Aunt Zannie!" Poppy, the three year-old, ran to Susannah's arms. She scooped her up and put her on her hip, where Poppy promptly yanked Susannah's earring out of her ear and put it in her mouth. Somehow Susannah was simultaneously able to fish the choking hazard out of her niece's cheek and check her own ear for blood. None. So this was how motherhood felt.

"Show me your bike, Poppy. How does it go?" Poppy toddled away to scoot around the driveway on her tricycle. Carly appeared through the window from her post on the sofa in the front room and gave a half-hearted wave.

During her afternoon stay, Susannah accomplished a few things around the house that needed doing. It reenergized her flagging spirits and took her mind off the mistakes of the night before. She cooked a huge batch of her best chicken burritos, the ones with the fresh green peppers and onions, and put three dozen in the freezer for Ian's lunches. They were his favorite. She also helped Carly get her crib set up and the baby boxes down from the attic. They went through and discarded old, stained items from two kids ago.

"So, have you decided on a name yet?"

"We're still thinking about Pamela. Do you think it's too old-fashioned?"

"I like it. What about for a boy?"

"That's still up in the air. It makes me hope for a girl. Besides, Poppy needs a little sister." They chatted as they worked, and the kids came whizzing in and out during the cool afternoon. Susannah didn't even think three times about the café. After a lovely dinner of grilled cheese sandwiches and tomato soup, Susannah set the kids up downstairs watching a video.

"Oh, I didn't tell you about Mary Lucas, did I?" Carly reclined on the couch with a pile of magazines in a basket and a telephone beside her. "Don't leave yet. You have to hear this."

"Yeah, I remember her. She was so nice to me even though she was two grades older. We used to go to the high school sock hops together. Man, I haven't heard anything about her since I saw her husband's obituary in the paper. He was in Iraq, wasn't he?"

"Uh-huh. Oh, Suzie. It gets worse. After he was killed, she was in a bad car accident, and now she's basically confined to a bed. I mean, yeah, I'm on bed rest and it's horrid, but I only have to endure for another few months. She's stuck."

"Where is she?"

"That's just it. She's in some kind of a home. Her parents are elderly, and she spent most of her money on doctors and the rest on ambulance-chasing lawyers, so now she's basically impoverished and living in this place where a nurse comes in twice a day. It's so sad."

"Where's the place?"

"Somewhere near the hospital on the north end of Salt Lake. Not too far from your shop. Speaking of your shop, can you save me one of those candied orange peels next time your chef makes them? I crave them day and night."

Susannah assured her she would, and she promised herself she'd visit Mary Lucas as soon as possible. Widowed and confined? It made Susannah's plight of choosing between two great men look paltry. She would never, ever feel self-pity again.

As soon as possible turned out to be the next afternoon. Ian took the family for a drive after church and Sunday dinner, so Susannah happily left the Carly and Ian family to themselves. She looked up the care center's address and breezed over there in her fabulous new car. Before leaving, she glanced around her house to see if there was anything she could take to brighten Mary Lucas's room, and her eye fell on the flowers from Brigham Talmage. Perfect.

The two old friends greeted one another joyously. It had been several years since they'd met, but warm feelings emerged instantly. And despite Mary's apparent negative circumstances, her spirits remained as positive and upbeat as ever in the light-filtered sunny room. A wedding picture hung on the wall beside a wooden plaque that read, "Your Name is Safe In Our Home."

"Chrysanthemums! Did you know those are my favorite flower?"

"No, but what a lucky break." They had a brief but smile-filled reunion visit, just long enough for Mary to tire, and Susannah left her resting, with a promise to return soon. She exited the care center lighter of heart than she'd felt in many days.

The next morning dawned bright and clean. The smog held captive by the infamous temperature inversion over the city cleared out with a strong overnight wind, and the leaves on the trees blushed red and orange with fall's onset.

"Where are your flowers? I thought you'd keep them on the counter to get people to ask us about them. Then I could brag to all our customers about how you're dating that dashing Brigham Talmage. And their eyes would peel back in wonder and they'd ask, 'You mean the guy from the billboards? That one from TV? I didn't know he was—'"

"That's enough, Colette. I don't really want it spread around that Brigham Talmage brought me the world's hugest bouquet of flowers. It's too personal, too embarrassing."

"Flowers? Embarrassing? Since when? They're the symbol of a man's love!"

"I thought the minivan was the current symbol of a man's love," Trevor chimed.

"Flowers will never go out of style. But minivans? Not so sure." Colette bustled back to her work after stuffing half a Mini-Soufflé in her mouth, and Susannah fingered the note in her apron pocket. It was from Brigham, telling her he was sorry about Thai Tuesday. He'd be out of town for a few weeks, but he promised to call her when he returned.

When Monday's after-lunch crowd began to assemble at the bar, Ingrid's high ponytail bounced in accompanied by more than the usual spring in her Jazzercize step.

"Ingrid, what do you think about flowers? Are they out of style as a love declaration?" Colette set a china teacup in front of her. "You're looking quite glowing today."

"Flowers? Oh, heavenly. My fiancé brought me the massivest pile of sunflowers and roses ever. You would have had to see them to believe them. And, drum roll, please!"

Colette and a couple of other patrons obliged by drumming their fingers on the hardwood bar. "Among the flowers was . . . this!" She held out her slender, well-tanned hand. Adorning her ring finger was what had to be a five-carat princess-cut diamond solitaire on a wide platinum band. From the looks of it, Ingrid was sporting a $10,000 ring. Susannah stared in wonder. None of them ever figured Ingrid's fiancé to be so, for lack of a better word, loaded.

"Finally! We've been dating for about four years. And he's been promising this for three and a half. It was his grandma's. I told him I would wait, but I had no idea it would be this long. And so, we still haven't set the date, but he says he is ten giant steps closer to being ready, that his 'master plan' is totally underway, and it's only a matter of time now until we can finally be together. I can't believe it. Aren't you so happy for me? I'm so excited. I find I don't even care about his reptile poisoning fetish. It's a dream come true!" Ingrid's voice babbled on like a brook over rocks in the springtime, infectiously causing the whole café to smile.

"Well, I guess Ingrid's true love isn't such a louse after all. Did you see that big, square rock?" Colette asked Trevor a little later behind closed kitchen doors while she flipped through a baking gadgets catalog. Susannah passed in and out with trays of Deep Dark Chocolate Fudge Cookies, but was able to catch most of their conversation.

"I saw it. But the no-date thing is still a big, square, red flag." Trevor waved an imaginary red flag with his arm to demonstrate.

"Why? He's probably just careful and wants to be prepared to be a good provider for her."

"Maybe." Trevor brushed some flour off his nose doubtfully. "But most guys who are really in love and have their priorities straight are not willing to put off official engagements years and years at a time. Guys are not like that. Real guys want to get married." Trev retied his apron strings tightly at his back for emphasis.

"The flowers and the ring were a big step in the right direction, anyway."

"But, no date? Smells like fish. Fishy. Fishy-fishy." Trev held his nose, and Susannah's mind conjured up odors of bracing salt air and crab nets brimming with squirming, displaced shellfish. "Hey, Suze. Your old buddy Sasha Perrier was in here."

"Yeah, what did she want?"

"To argue with me about, get this, frosting-covered doggie bones with the word 'Utes' on it. I said no way."

"You're heartless, Trev. Heartless."

"Hey, check these out. I'm definitely buying these." He pointed to a picture in Colette's catalogue. "Kevlar gloves."

"Kevlar? Like they use to make body armor?"

"Exact-a-mundo. Ha! No matter how sharp my knives are, they won't cut through those. No more Band-Aids, baby." Trevor chuckled as he dog-eared the page of the invention and stirred a pot of Mexican chocolate sauce, the kind with a pinch of cinnamon, to be served over his famous homemade ice cream.

Several days later, while Colette tended to a minimal crowd in the late afternoon's fading autumn sun, Susannah hunkered down in her office to catch up on mail and bookkeeping. She needed to drop off yet another bouquet of flowers from Brigham—this time perhaps at the women's shelter—besides doing a hundred other tasks. However, her mind kept trailing off on Hojo tangents. Memories of the ill-motivated kiss played on a sickening loop through her wandering mind, making her cringe. John's words echoed behind them. Confusion still dominated her perception of the event, and she tried to sort it out as she sorted the mail, a frown tugging at her recently kissed lips.

Suddenly, a legal-size envelope captured her attention. "Office of City Development, Renewal, and Vehicle Management." Oh, mercy. Evidence that government bureaucracy ballooned at every level. What could they want, another business license fee? No.

Far worse.

"Colette, look at this!" Susannah stomped out to the front where the final afternoon customers' jingle signaled their exit. "Can you believe it? Of all things!" Susannah's staccato, angry voice punctuated the air of the empty café.

Colette slid the papers from Susannah's hand and began to read. Trevor joined them from the kitchen after hearing the commotion.

"What? No!" Colette stomped her foot. "They can't just take away people's businesses and livelihoods!" She stomped it again.

Trevor stomped his own foot. "Girls. What are we foot-stomping for?"

"This says we're being targeted by a large conglomerate as being situated in the so-called perfect spot for additional parking for Temple Square patrons," Susannah explained, seething. "A major construction company submitted a proposal to city planners to purchase and plow down my shop and thirteen surrounding homes and businesses to build a six story parking garage." She planted her hands firmly on her hips. "Now isn't that something to stomp about?"

"It certainly is!" Trevor's huge foot responded appropriately.

Colette sighed, "Oh, it's precisely like that 'oooh-bop!' song where they pave paradise and put up a parking lot."

With less than a full year's financial figures, Susannah flailed unarmed when it came to presenting a firm case of "economic boon to the city" on behalf of her establishment.

"Hey, you ought to get a lawyer." Colette raised a knowing eyebrow. "Where's a dashing young member of the Utah Bar Association when you need one?"

"Hopelessly out of town," Susannah mourned. "Out of cell phone range, too. Even for emergencies." And this was an emergency. The daily dozen roses being sent to her were no substitute for his legal expertise now. The hearing on the matter was slated for six weeks from today, hardly a nanosecond when it came to financial and legal presentations, as Susannah well knew. So many details would need to be compiled! She wanted to cry, but the doorbells jingled, and in came a familiar sight.

"Sister Hapsburg!" The sweet voice giggled. "I mean, Susannah. I can't seem to stop thinking of you as my Beehive teacher." Camie Kimball. Miniature Marvel. She always did have perfect timing, as the Olympic judges often commented. The jeans-clad perky one sat herself energetically on a barstool beside a bouncy young friend and pulled out a menu. "I love this place. Can I get a water?"

Susannah obligingly smiled and listened as Camie trilled on about her post-Beehive years, her college classes, her 'roomies,' and her trip last year to Mazatlan. "I love cruise ships, don't you? It's like a never-ending floating food feast. Oh! Can I get one of these fruit thingies—but without the cream? Mmm." Her friend took one, too.

Colette sidled up. "I'm done with everything in back, Suze. Oh, hi. You must be Camie Kimball. I recognize you from the vitamin drink commercial. Wow. That's so cool, right?"

"Thanks. My mom and dad wanted me to do it. They wanted me to do all this gymnastics stuff. I can't wait to be done with college so I can get on with life. Susannah taught me that—way back in Young Women. I remember the lesson was on finishing things we start and being true to our commitments. I wanted to quit gymnastics clear back then, but—integrity! It really struck me at the time, and now, here I am talking to her again." She giggled and a look of enlightenment crossed her cute visage. "Wow. It's been, like, most of my life since then."

It surprised Susannah that Camie remembered anything from such a long time ago, especially anything from Young Women lessons. Those Beehives constantly buzzed amongst themselves, as far as she as their teacher could recall.

"It's neat to run into you again, Camie. I'm so proud of you and how you've turned out. What's up next for you?" Susannah knew it was a dangerous question, and she also knew it was an underhanded, selfish question; but her heart compelled her to ask.

"Oh, I don't know. After graduation in the spring I want to travel more."

Her sidekick finally spoke. "Honeymoon?" and elbowed the elf-child.

"Wouldn't you like to know?" Camie sipped her water through a straw. "Candidly, I'd have to say a big, 'Not sure.' I mean, I'm dating this guy—we see each other all the time and stuff. And he's totally cute and rich and smart and wise—and he's an amazing hiker. He knows absolutely everything about everything. That's why I like him." Camie paused to take another bite of her creamless tart.

Susannah thought, *That's why I like him*. Except the hiking part. It seemed superfluous.

"But I don't know. I have to wait and see. I mean, hey. He's not young. In fact, he's kinda old. If he were serious, I think he'd have asked me by now. It's like part of him is living in the past, and sometimes he gets all cloudy. Whatever. Anyway, he's leaving next week."

"Oh, really?" Susannah kicked herself for letting the eagerness in her voice show, but Camie didn't seem to notice, obviously having no clue the reason for Susannah's intense interest.

"Yeah, he's heading back to Alaska to check on his crab boats for the season. October is the first big month up there. You know why I like October, though? The end of Capri season. Yesss! And I have to say, I am so done with Capri pants. They make my legs look even shorter than they are! Now I can officially go back to jeans and keep praying those horrid cropped pants'll be out of style by the time the hot months roll around again."

Camie's friend pulled a napkin from the dispenser for herself and one for Camie. "Something bugs me about the crab boats."

"You, too? I know it's his job and all, but don't you secretly feel sorry for the little animals?" Little Olympian twittered on about the welfare of crustaceans, and Susannah, weary from the pendulum reaction of alternately loving and hating her former student, retreated behind closed kitchen doors, the burden of the past few weeks' information and experiences weighing heavily on her shoulders. Her muddled mind couldn't determine whether

Camie's words gave cause for hope or despair. And her feelings for Brigham L. Talmage were conspicuously absent from her emotional equation.

BLACK FOREST BAR

1 package fudge cake mix
1 teaspoon almond extract
2 eggs
1 can cherry pie filling

Combine and bake in a greased loaf pan at 350 degrees for 30 minutes or until done. Frost with the following:

1½ cups sugar

5 tablespoon butter
⅓ cup milk
1 cup chocolate chips

Boil sugar, butter and milk one minute. Add chocolate. Stir until melted. Pour over hot cake. Eat while it's still warm. It will melt your mouth like a good kiss.

♡
Chocolate Chili

*At the next chili cook-off, bring this winner. You'll
laugh when a large group of friends circles
around you asking what your secret ingredient
is, and you'll commence a classic romance
between many families and this recipe.*

One Tuesday evening, Felicia Patterson brought in a large group of friends for the screening of *Shop Around the Corner*, a black-and-white classic romance. Susannah wondered if they would have all enjoyed it more if Felicia had piped down during even five minutes of the show; she was so full of silver screen trivia that she simply couldn't contain herself. The friends, however, didn't seem to mind, and—besides their other selections—they ordered three quarts of Trevor's Aztec Super-Dark Chocolate Ice Cream to share.

"This movie was the basis of *You've Got Mail*. Did you know that?"

"That's one of my favorite movies!" Fortunately, there were only a few other customers that night, as the Jazz had a home game, so her facts were welcome. Even the genealogy ladies seemed to enjoy them. It sparked a conversation among a couple of the older women.

"I remember corresponding by mail with my husband while he was away in Europe with the military after the war. Conversations took forever then, but they were more satisfying."

Felicia's same crowd made another appearance the next evening for fondue, and Susannah and Colette nodded triumphantly at one another at the sight of more regular customers. It looked like the café could really be a go.

Susannah felt manically busy. With work and Carly's family and hopeless efforts at her cottage, she only spent enough time in Sugarhouse to sleep and occasionally do her laundry. In the wee hours of the early morning, she researched everything she could find on the Internet about eminent domain, a.k.a. land grabs by cities for the public good. If the city council decided to take her café, there was basically nothing she could do about it, short of a hairy lawsuit. However, cases of it were rare because of bad publicity for the city council members. The fact that four of them were up for reelection this cycle gave her hope. But, darn it, the parking-plow-down simply cut one more facet in her already sparkling gem of stressful drama. Susannah decided not to ask Brigham Talmage for free legal advice (even if he was blowing a huge sum on flowers for her). Besides, she didn't dare ask his going rate.

Susannah trudged through the sludge of the parking-lot war alone. To make matters worse, her mind wouldn't stop swirling back to the ten minutes of cringing torment at the concert. She longed for an opportunity to see John Wentworth face to face and somehow apologize or explain away her foolish actions and to ask him to clarify his comment. The trouble was, every time she concocted an excuse-conversation it fizzled, and her mind's eye watched his face turn from stony to scornful just before he turned on his heel and walked away from her. Again.

One evening, right before closing time, a couple of vaguely familiar faces appeared in the far booth. When Colette went to take their orders, they specifically requested Susannah, so she excused herself from a conversation at the bar and went to serve them.

"Hi, ladies. May I help you?"

"Susannah! Suze! It's us. Remember?"

Susannah squinted her eyes briefly. "Lori? Wendy? Wow. I haven't see you guys for years. How are you?"

"Doing great." Lori and Wendy were Susannah's roommates her first year of college, but Wendy got married to her high school boyfriend after their freshman year, and Lori after her sophomore year to an RM she had met in a French class. It felt like a million years ago.

"It seems like just yesterday we were roomies, Suze," Wendy sighed. "Can you believe it's been thirteen years? Remember those guys who lived upstairs from us—Zach and Tony? Tony had such a crush on you, and you drove his car into that canal—"

"Oh, yeah," Lori interjected. "And when Zach wore that trench coat to class with shorts and we were all afraid he was a flasher?"

"And when Bartley Matthews sang that serenade under our balcony to ask Melanie to homecoming?" They proceeded to drag Susannah along through distant cloudy memories of days that seemed like they were from another life, they were so long ago. By the time she'd pulled up the file for the face to match the name from her deep storage memory banks, the women had shot off four more names and totally backlogged her brain. She couldn't help but look bewildered.

"Gee, look at you, Suze. You look like a zillion bucks. How do you keep thin working here? Look at us. We've gotten so fat. You know I've got six kids, don't you? And Lori's got three. I should be twice as fat, by rights." Wendy giggled and Lori began pulling out photos of the children. Susannah looked and made appropriate coos over the kids. They were, in fact, quite cute. She took their order for Chocolate Chili and let them visit while she did some other things, but as they sucked down their Black Cows, Lori waved Susannah over once again.

"Oh, and I just remembered! Halloween? Jan's huge boat of a car and going through that narrow drive-through for French fries and getting wedged on one side?" Lori started her signature snort-laugh, and Susannah gave a courtesy chuckle. That freshman incident must have been deleted from her files during a reboot on her mission or any of the intervening ten years. She shook her head in non-recognition. To her surprise, Lori took it personally.

"Sheemanee, Suze. What's with you? It's like you don't remember any of the fun times." Her voice was accusatory, and then Wendy frowned, too. "Every time we bring up all these cool people it's like you forgot everyone, and, like, everything. Well. Oh, well." Lori pulled some bills from her huge Cookie Monster diaper bag purse and laid them on the table. She gave Susannah a perfunctory hug,

Wendy gave one, too, and they left, allowing an icy gust of wind to whip through the dining area.

Their visit deflated Susannah to a surprising degree. She didn't usually let blasts from the past get to her. Luckily it was closing time. She flipped the sign over to show "Closed" and locked the door. After a quick clean up, she gathered her day's bouquet in her arms and made for the convertible. The same frigid gust threatened to mar her latest flowers' delicate petals, and she attempted to cover them with one flap of her wool pea coat. Her spirits were alternating between agitated and plain old down, and she knew nothing would help unless she worked off some of her frustration, so she headed for Capitol Hill, Doom Habitat Central.

She pulled onto the two-cement-strip driveway in a huff and jammed the gearshift into park, exhaling in annoyance. As she rattled tools in the steel box on the back seat, she muttered loudly to herself. Suddenly, to her mild shock, she felt a warm presence at her side.

"Are you talking to someone?"

She looked up. "Oh! John! I'm so . . . I don't know. Annoyed!" John Wentworth. Here. That she didn't pull back in embarrassment when he shielded her from the wind was evidence of how deeply the day's events frustrated her. A visible, angry huff steamed the chilly air as she rattled off a stream of complaints while he listened.

"Why is it that people who are married take it so personally when you can't remember all the details of your own life that coincided with theirs when they were single? All those stories are still fresh in their minds, and they expect them to be the same for you, like who was dating who in 1994, and who wore what to which dance, and all this garbage, but what they don't realize is that you have another fifteen years of the single, dating drama details to keep track of, in addition to what happened when they were single for their, like, nanosecond, and it's still like it only barely recently happened for them because all their intrigues stopped at that point and it's all they have to look back on, and then they get all huffy about it if you can't recall every little specific point about when you were a freshman in college and try to make you feel stupid or like you didn't care about them when you happen to play such a big role in their own memory of being young, and they get all offended and act like you're this big loser who can't remember things that have intrinsic significance, when all that really happened was that in your own mind it was a long time ago and you're still lonely and alone and they have these husbands and lives and nine kids and two minivans between them?" She hiccupped. A tear slipped from her eye.

"Ho, there. Slow down. Take a breath." He put his calm-inducing, warm arm over her shoulders. "What happened? Did you see someone today?"

She did take a breath and started slowly, while he guided her across the yard.

"Two of my college roommates. Lori and Wendy."

"And they wanted to take a trip down memory lane. Only it was their memories, and not necessarily yours."

"Right!" He got her.

"And . . . when you didn't remember some of their cherished tales, they were—?"

"Offended."

"—offended. But you couldn't do anything about that."

"Right. But it annoys me that they were bugged by that."

"I can see that."

Oh. Did it show so much? Suddenly she clued in to her surroundings: sunset, dream cottage, sitting on a step, with John Wentworth at her side, sympathizing with her, his arm still resting on her shoulders, a salve for her pain.

Pain. What was pain? That she'd kissed Brig Talmage right before John's eyes with the express purpose of causing this healer pain the last time she'd seen him. Oh! How could she have been so stupid? New waves of pain washed up on her soul's shore as he calmly responded.

"Last year I ran into a couple of guys I knew right after my mission. They were golfing, and we played a round together, but by the time we hit the sixteenth hole, I think they were ready to slice me into the rough. They wanted to talk about drives we took four-wheeling up the canyon in a truck I'd forgotten I owned. When I gave them the golfing equivalent of a blank stare, they got mad and wanted to leave me in my sandtrap. They ended up finishing with the group ahead of me. It was weird."

"You golf?"

"Not well. Do you still play tennis?"

"Sometimes. Not like I used to."

"You were on the U's team." He remembered? "You'd have to play hours a day to keep at that level. I doubt you have time for that now."

"Not really, with the business and all."

"How's your business going, anyway?" He asked timidly, glancing at her car. Susannah laughed inwardly, knowing Barbara's convertible Mercedes looked exactly like the trappings of success, and simultaneously knowing the truth of her vehicular situation. "Did your boyfriend get you that car?"

"My boyfriend?" Uh. No. What boyfriend? "No, this is Barbara Russell's car. You remember her." She didn't want to dwell on the Barbara Russell topic too long, for his sake. "My wheels are still my beeeeautiful 1992 Volkswagen Jetta, which as we speak, languishes on the back lot of Frank's Garage in Sugarhouse. The Flux Capacitor konked out, and it's going to cost a jillion dollars to ever be able to drive it again. Barbara lent me this because she thought I looked undignified on my brother-in-law's Vespa and wanted me to have something safer for the winter months."

John's face softened, and a smile tugged at the corner of his mouth. Susannah felt like someone had unhinged her jaw, and now it wouldn't stop.

"Um, the only problem with this car and winter is I can't put up the rag top. Mechanically disinclined. " She shrugged helplessly, and he took her hint without hesitation. Walking over to the car and reaching under the dash, he located the lever and began the process of covering the car. "To tell the truth, I hate convertibles. The wind makes my skin go numb."

"You should try the wind on the deck of a crab fishing boat."

"No, thanks. Hey—aren't you supposed to be up there in

Alaska? I mean—" She didn't want to reveal her snooping weakness, so she backtracked. "I mean, isn't the season starting up?"

"I'm leaving in the morning. I thought I'd stop by before I left again." He did? Her heart slammed momentarily. He thought of her? Wasn't he angry—about the past or the kiss? She searched his face in the pause until he spoke again. "I haven't seen you at church in a while."

"I've been taking care of my nieces and nephews while my sister is on bed rest. They let me be Primary chorister in their ward temporarily, so I'm back in my element. Did I ever tell you how they released me from my calling during sacrament meeting without giving me a heads-up? Worst. The worst."

"When was that?" John asked hesitantly.

"At the beginning of the summer. I kept going to the ward for a while until the clerk told me my records were gone. I was wondering why they didn't give me a different calling. Records gone, I was suddenly anathema to them. You membership clerks are a predatory species, I say."

He didn't answer, looking lost in thought. Finally he snapped back to attention.

"Well, we've missed you. I mean, I've missed you."

Now, Susannah had never been to Alaska, but she had watched her fair share of *Northern Exposure* episodes back in the day (and had sighed appropriately over John Corbett in his pre-*Greek Wedding* youth), so she knew about the loud crrrrack which accompanies the breaking of the ice at the onset of the annual spring thaw. Tonight, north of Salt Lake's Capitol Hill, a sonic boom sounded from Hill Air Force Base in Ogden. Both John and Susannah looked up instinctively, but Susannah convinced herself the thunder signaled the first thaw of John's long-icy heart. I've missed you. Crrrrack!

"I, uh, just came by to bring you this letter. It's about the safe. Remember? From the closet?" Closet of Amontillado—how could she forget? "They're shipping it to Minnesota to a specialist. I didn't know where else to find you. This place is the only address I have."

"Oh, well, you should have come by my work. I'm there day and night. Except when I'm at my sister Carly's. Here." She scrawled The Chocolate Bar's address on a scrap of paper from her purse.

Susannah's watch beeped to announce the hour. "Oh, dear. I'm late for that blasted City Development, Renewal, and Vehicle Management planning and zoning meeting."

"Why are you going to a zoning meeting?"

"Oh, some rich twit-fest company thinks they can plow down my chocolate café and put up additional city parking. A six-story cement monstrosity to house cars instead of a Tudor-style brick home that serves wholesome desserts to the women of this fair city? How on earth will that improve downtown? Tell me."

John glanced down at the paper she'd handed him. "The Chocolate Bar?" he asked aloud, then sat silent a moment. Susannah couldn't tell if his quiet denoted apathy or shock or deep contemplation. Eventually, he spoke. "I guess you'd better get going."

Apathy. Undoubtedly apathy. Visions of herself cruelly kissing Brigham Talmage in front of John and Camie and Howard Jones and everyone spattered in her head like sledge-hammered plaster. She roared away in the now-covered convertible to face her enemies—the ones other than herself.

CHOCOLATE CHILI

1 lb ground beef, browned
2 Tbsp dried onion
½ teaspoon garlic salt
½ teaspoon cumin
3-15 oz cans chili-style diced tomatoes, undrained
2 cans (15-oz each) black beans, drained, rinsed
1 can (15-oz) kidney beans, drained, rinsed
1 square unsweetened chocolate

Combine all ingredients; bring to a boil. Reduce heat and simmer 10 minutes, stirring occasionally. Garnish with shredded cheddar cheese, of course.

Devilishly Hot Hot Chocolate

With cayenne-spiced whipping cream and a real cinnamon stick for a swizzle, this hot cocoa is diabolically delicious.

"I can't believe their diabolical plan. They are so cruel! It was precisely as awful as I imagined it would be." Susannah frowned as she looked out the care center's window across the frosty Sunday afternoon. Practically all of Salt Lake's tree-lined streets were being guarded by the skeletons of the once-lush deciduous trees. This year's autumn had been less than splendid and cut tragically short by huge winds from the canyons and gusts whipping in from the lake. The view from Mary Lucas's care center room window afforded little cheer to an already gloomy situation; however, Mary's eye glowed bright and a smile intermittently rippled across her concerned face as she listened to Susannah's report of the zoning meeting. The bedridden girl was too happy to receive a friend not to show moments of gladness.

"Oh, Susannah. I'm sure you'll figure out the best thing to do. I wish I could recommend a fair lawyer to help you out, but I've only had the most atrocious luck with that breed myself."

"Please, if it's not too painful to talk about, can you tell me how this whole awful thing happened to you?" In her several visits, Susannah had never been able to get more than a few sketchy details about the events that led to Mary's current situation. Either the unfortunate woman had been too weak or tired, or she'd been reluctant to dredge up the past. However, today, chatty and chipper, she willingly glossed over the main points of the tragic circumstances, giving Susannah a fair understanding of how it all came about.

"I bet you miss your husband so much."

"I do. It's strange, though. We were married such a short time before he went to Kuwait for the war. I actually didn't know him very well."

"And then, that whole thing with the bad lawyers! What an outrage!"

"Lawyer. Just one. I forked over the cash to pay for one, and then he totally took advantage of me. By the time I realized fully what was happening, I was too weak and too broke to fight back. And, besides, he covered his tracks very, very well. There was nothing we could prove; he did the whole thing legally, if not ethically." Mary frowned. "Oh, well. I'm trying not to dwell on the negative, and I honestly believe that's what is healing my heart, as well as my body. You may not believe this, but I think I've finally, totally forgiven him."

"Completely?"

"Almost. The only remaining shard of pain is concern that he might strike again—dupe some unsuspecting helpless soul out of his life. I don't want to sully anyone, so I've resolved not to mention his name again, but I really wish there were something I could do to stop him."

Susannah couldn't help wondering, so she ventured to ask. "How do you do it? How do you keep such a smiling, warm attitude under the circumstances?"

"Oh, Susannah, you're right. The circumstances are not ideal." That put it mildly. Mary Lucas had nothing: no home, no husband, no health, no church calling, no money, no children, no job, no personal mobility, nothing. All the things from which Susannah derived her self-worth and personal satisfaction were missing in Mary's life. It looked empty, and yet her friend smiled.

"Naturally, at first I felt horrible. I cried. A lot. Especially when my parents' health failed and I had no help, even from them. Plus, I couldn't come to their aid, either. I missed my husband terribly.

I'd be lying if I said there were no down times. Most of all I missed being able to be of some use to someone, anyone. Before all this happened, I was a list-maker. Crossing stuff off it every day gave me a sense of power and usefulness. I'd done something!

"And then I couldn't. I couldn't even make a list anymore.

"Eventually, through prayer some thoughts came to me. I came to understand my value didn't depend on what I could do, what I could accomplish. My worth came in being loved by my Father. It's kind of like a newborn baby. We don't love them because they're so useful, or even for their potential usefulness. We love them because they're ours. When I came to realize the Lord loved me because I was His, it calmed me. He loves us all that way, Susannah, and it's priceless." Mary smiled, tired now. Susannah hugged her sweet friend, and walked (on her two working legs) out to her (working) car, pondering on how useful Mary's words felt today.

Three or four weeks went by, when the world's largest poinsettia arrived at The Chocolate Bar in a red foil-covered pot, tied with a sparkling green satin bow and accompanied by a card that read, "Susannah. You and me. Solitude. Night skiing. Saturday. Dress snowrific. Your Brig."

"Snowrific? He used the word 'snowrific.' In print?"

"How spastastic of him." Trevor guffawed from his perch on the counter. Even granite sagged a little under his enormous weight.

"Hey. Maybe he didn't get the Sponge Bob memo," Colette defended him. "Remember: he also signed it 'Your Brig.' Isn't that just—" She ahhhed. Susannah looked at her in surprise, then in fear. Not an article of clothing in Susannah's closet could be considered ski-worthy. And 'Her Brig' was coming back to town. It all came pounding down.

"Colette, what am I going to do?"

"You, my dear, are going to take Barbara Russell and head over to Gart Sports. But not until I wake up from a little nap. This headache requires me to lie down for a spell. Can you handle the front without me?"

Susannah could—right after she phoned Barbara, who agreed to be the ski-fashion consultant that evening when the shop closed.

Later, Ivy came in pulling a bewildered but darling curly-haired blonde of about 22.

"Hi, Susannah. Where's Colette? I want everyone to meet my future sister-in-law, Naomi!" A massive grin covered Ivy's entire face, and a matching one covered Naomi's. The two of them sat down at the bar, and Naomi began poring over the menu.

"Oh, this Chocolate Velvet Cake looks like heaven. Two pieces—both for me! Celebration day. Mm. And a cup of that Devilishly Hot Hot Chocolate. Love the cayenne idea! What are you having, Ivy? My treat."

Ah, a girl after all their own hearts. Susannah retrieved Colette from her nap in the back room, and she came out to embrace the future bride with open arms. It was impossible to tell which of the future sisters looked more elated.

Soon after, Jackie came in with a smile and left with three gold foil-lined boxes of today's specials: two for friends at work, and one for her brother the policeman. The Chocolate Cranberry Sponge, with its sharp contrast between sour and sweet, was worth passing on.

"When are you going to ask her out, Trev? How much more of her patience are you going to try?" Colette couldn't hide her exasperation as they worked in the kitchen a few minutes later.

"What do you mean, when? It's more a question of if." He set down his whisk and lit the flame on the gas stovetop, then turned it to its lowest setting and added a cup of milk to his sugar and cocoa mix. "I once heard a saying: 'Nothing is so difficult to marry as a large nose.'"

"But, Trev, your nose isn't that large," Susannah said.

"Everything about me is large, girls. Face it."

"Wait. I know. You're just avoiding it to keep her guessing."

"Exactly. And you should be afraid, be very afraid of my asking her out, Susannah."

"Why's that?"

"Because if I do, and she hates me, and there's a better than 75 percent chance she will, you'll lose your best customer. She'll never come back in here again."

"You overestimate the power of your anti-charm to push her away."

"And you underestimate the power of my chocolate to draw her in here."

"Come on, Trev. Suffo-Cade did it."

"Cade." The huge Hawaiian got quiet. "Suffo-Cade did do it, didn't he." It wasn't a question. Susannah and Colette knew they'd made an important advancement in their battle.

Late that afternoon, Susannah returned from her sporting goods outing. "So, guys, how do I look?" She spun to model the parka and ski pants Barbara helped her select.

"All you need now is the headband with the pink ears, snow bunny babe."

"Thanks a lot. I'll go change back into my work-rific clothes now."

She hadn't seen Brigham Talmage yet since he'd been home. In fact, she'd only spoken to him on the phone briefly to confirm details of their date. He sounded swamped, and she sympathized. She herself was drowning in a sea of details.

No progress could be made on her utilities-free cottage in the icy cold weather, so Susannah immersed herself in scratching together a presentation to persuade the city zoners not to shut her down. Unfortunately, no overpoweringly strong arguments materialized. She began to wonder if a parking garage might actually be the right thing for "the greater good" of the area.

It distressed her.

A first-year capital loss normally wouldn't prove tragic for a business, but with the city breathing down her neck, this year's numbers must shake out in the black. Besides, her own financial solvency was at stake: for her to make the cottage's mortgage and scrape together year-end business taxes, the money had to be there. Potentially she could go belly-up on both house and café, and together they were the embodiment of all her dreams.

Well, almost all of them.

Now thoughts of Brigham Talmage and John Wentworth entered her mind and sent it spinning. She couldn't deal with that right now. She returned to the cash register to gather the day's receipts and overheard two customers discussing the merits of dark versus milk chocolate. One of the ladies concluded by saying, "Both are so delicious. How can I possibly choose?"

The statement reverberated in Susannah's mind. Both Brigham and John were so . . . well, delicious seemed like a silly word, but good—both men were such good men. How could she possibly choose?

"Ouch!" She banged her shin against a shelf in the kitchen. It banged her mind right back into reality. Ha. As if choosing John Wentworth were even an option. As if. Ha.

"So, Susannah. Brig seems pretty serious about you," Trev called as she trundled past him. "Flowers. Night skiing. He's getting ready to propose."

"Propose! No!" Susannah recoiled at the words. It hadn't occurred to her—today.

"Of course he is. He's playing his gentleman cards one by one. Talmage has calculated the whole thing. He's a serious go-getter in the courtroom, I hear. My brother's friend got him as his lawyer for a slip-and-fall case, and bam! The deal was done. He doesn't mess around when he goes for what he wants." Trevor came out into the bar area, which was mercifully empty during this discussion of Susannah's private life, to add his manly opinion.

"The details all add up, Suze. He's methodically leading the witness to the clincher question. Romantic evening on the slopes is about two steps away from proposal for a regular guy. For him, it could be more like one step away."

She knit her brows in disbelief and fear. Naw, she concluded. She liked Brigham, yes. Immensely. He had an unquenchable fire for whatever his deed was. It attracted her—like some kind of . . . moth? But the fire, even if it warmed her, made her nervous. She really didn't want to get burned. Nope. Trevor was wrong. What did he know about men and women, anyway? She overruled his objection and went back into her office to change.

"Hello?" She picked up the ringing phone in her office.

"Susannah?" It was a man's voice. "It's me. John. Wentworth.

I know it's the end of the month and you probably didn't expect to hear from me yet, but I wondered if I could get together with you sometime before tomorrow. It's kind of urgent."

John? He wanted to get together with her? Part of her soul began to reply helplessly, "Yes, John. Anytime, anyplace you say," but prudence restrained her. As did her schedule, which began frantically beeping on her PDA at that moment, signaling she had only five remaining minutes to become snow bunny babe before Brigham Talmage arrived to pick her up.

"John. You're back. Wow. Hey, I'm really sorry. It's going to be impossible tonight. Will tomorrow be too late?" She almost felt herself pleading with him.

"I guess not." They signed off. She wished for even two seconds to ruminate on the strange exchange, but it was a luxury she couldn't afford. The call of the slopes beckoned.

DEVILISHLY HOT HOT CHOCOLATE

4 cups whole milk
4 cinnamon sticks
6 whole cloves
dash cayenne pepper
½ cup sugar
1 tablespoon vanilla
6 oz dark chocolate, finely chopped and melted

Combine milk and spices in pot on stove and bring to a boil. Boil 5 minutes. Remove cinnamon sticks. Wisk in chocolate and sugar until dissolves. Remove from heat and add vanilla. Serve with cayenne-spiced whipped cream and a cinnamon swizzle stick to heat up any cold winter evening.

Chocolate Avalanche

The ground beneath you will begin to slip away as you immerse your taste buds in this avalanche of chocolate.

"Wow. You look like hot buttered toast, Susannah. You'll melt the slope. Avalanche!" Brigham took her by the arm as he balanced both their skis on his other shoulder, and they clunked out of the lodge in their big fiberglass boots. Once outside, she bent her knee forward and latched the boots shut. Ah, the old familiar pain in the shin of wearing ski gear. Even if she felt like a clunky, gawky dweeb who would potentially yard sale it so badly on the bunny slope that the helicopter would have to airlift her to University Hospital, she didn't care because she knew she looked absolutely snowrific in her new ski jacket and pants.

Brigham was right. The night sky, clear and starry, and only barely affected by the light pollution of the Salt Lake Valley below, was enchanting. With each slice of their skis down the mountain, tiny snow crystals sparkled in the moonlight before landing on her hot cheeks, melting there, cool and fresh. A recent snowfall still weighed heavily on the boughs of the evergreens lining the runs, and she and Brig were two of only a few dozen people to take advantage of the night's beauty. The sky, the mountain, the trees, the brisk air—all theirs.

They skied side by side part of the time, and then Brig would crouch into speed-skier stance and call, "I'll meet you at the bottom, gorgeous," and leave her in his frosty wake. She didn't bother keeping up but took her time in leisurely runs down the hill. True to his word, he met her at the base of the slope and rode beside her on the bouncy, cabled ski lift that took them clear above the tops of the firs, giving her a view of the world she'd never before seen: dark and white, bluish-black treetops contrasting with the fields of snow. Breathtaking.

What with the burden of the impending loss of her livelihood on her mind, it was nice to take an energizing break, but she still longed to talk to Brigham about her concerns. Eventually she gathered the nerve to broach the topic in the most tactful manner she could.

"So, as a lawyer," she asked as they drew near the top of the hill on the lift, "how do you handle it when friends approach you for free legal advice?" The lift chair dumped them off, and they hurried to slide quickly out of its way.

"A real friend would never ask." Hm. Perhaps it was his pat answer. Surely if he knew the magnitude of the trouble she was in, this knight would come immediately to her rescue. But how could she tell him now?

Brigham took her hand. "One last run. They'll shut down the lift at nine," he told her. She actually regretted it, losing the beauty of the night, and he noticed. "Hey, my love, don't fear. The lodge serves dinner and cocoa until midnight. We've still got time together."

A few minutes later, with her skis thrust into a drift behind the lodge and her boots parked at the back door, Susannah stood in her stocking feet and wet ski bunny clothes beside a roaring fire to warm the blood in her veins.

"How about some cocoa? I need to make some phone calls. I'll be back." She assented through chattering teeth, and Brig left her leaning near the screen to see how close she could get her fingers to the flame without detrimentally singeing them.

"I never notice how cold I am until I start warming up." A familiar voice sounded behind her. "Are you to the painful part yet, when the feeling comes back to your extremities?"

She turned around to see John. John! What was he doing here?

"I'm glad I ran into you."

What a surprise to see him—wind-burnt and a little thinner,

but none the worse for wear. In fact, he might look a bit better for wear, with his haircut grown out and curling up at his brow. What was he doing here?

"What are you doing here?"

"I had a meeting with Ty Sparks, from the county's planning commission." Oh, that's right. John still did some emergency management consulting. "This was the only time of day he could meet with me."

Ugh. Don't remind her. So many planning commissions, so little joy! Her woes followed her to high altitudes now. "Why? I mean, what kind of meeting?"

"Several things. Mostly earthquake stuff. Fault lines and that. A little bit on avalanche prevention. I had some stuff to talk over with him, so he agreed to meet me up here tonight during his ski vacation. Nice guy."

"So, was I in a near-avalanche out there tonight?"

"I don't know. Were you on any non-machine-packed hillsides?"

"The bunny slope." She cocked her head to the side, smirking.

"Ah, no. No avalanche danger for you."

"How can you tell where it's dangerous?" She'd always wondered about that.

"Come outside. Maybe we can see a couple of spots. It's a bright night."

She slipped into her regular boots, the ones with the fluffy warm sheepskin lining, and followed him out behind the lodge to where her skis sat jabbed into the drift. Brigham had acted like his calls might take a while when he left her by the fire, and she counted on that as she relaxed comfortably under the instructive arm of John Wentworth, while his other arm pointed off toward a nearby mountainside.

"Can you see that snowpack over there? See how there's that thick layer of snow near the overhang? It's just at the next ridge." She squinted her eyes and searched a minute, then discovered where he meant.

"I see it. Are they worried about it?"

"There are approximately ten avalanches a year, small ones mostly, at this ski resort, and even more at Alta and Brighton. It's always a concern. Every heavy snowfall increases the risk, although they need the snowfall for their livelihood. It's a necessary evil."

"So what turns a pack like that into an avalanche?" The word gave her an idea for a new recipe for the shop. She could call them Chocolate Avalanches.

"Oh, a minor quake can set it off, or any loud sound with the right frequency. A gunshot, an engine. That, or additional snow, a sudden melting, or even simply someone snowshoeing or riding a snowmobile across it."

"How far away is that slope? Could I yodel and bring it all down?" She began humming "Lonely Goatherd" from *The Sound of Music*, her favorite Austrian-set Broadway musical. He laughed. She started singing, turning to face him jokingly but keeping her eyes on the faraway avalancheable slope. It didn't budge, so she continued. Soon he hummed along, and eventually joined her with his voice on the "Yodelayeeodelayeeodeloo" part, by which point they were both giving it great gusto. Suddenly, she heard a faint snap and the whooshing swish of sliding snow. It wasn't the thundering she'd expected, and no foamy clouds of snow appeared on the far mountain. The sound was coming from much nearer, from close behind and above them, in fact. She stopped yodeling and turned barely in time to see a huge mass of accumulated snow sliding off the lodge's A-frame roof directly toward where they stood under its eaves.

"Look out!" John shouted and pushed her aside. But they were too late. A crush of frozen moisture landed on their heads and shoulders, knocking them on their backsides and covering their laps and shoulders and the tops of their heads.

"Like I said," John eked out between laughter bursts, "any loud noise can set one off."

"Gotcha. Noted." She leaned back in the pile and found her own gasps of breath. Soon he was helping her up and brushing the snow from her shoulders and legs.

"Excuse me. What are you doing to my date?"

Susannah looked up in horror to see Brigham Talmage standing beside them with a perplexed look on his face and his hands on his parkaed hips. "Wentworth. Is that you? You're everywhere. Susannah, honey. Would you like me to take care of this? Legally? Is he bothering you?" Before she could answer emphatically in the negative, Brig's cell phone gave a ringtone to the tune of coins clinking. He glanced at the caller ID screen. "So sorry, Suze. I have to take this. Client. Urgent business. I'll be right back to help you out of this . . . pile of snow. Wentworth, I suggest you clear off." He turned and stalked around the corner of the lodge for privacy, with a brief glance over his shoulder at the two of them.

"John, I—"

"Oh. Susannah, I didn't know you were here on a date. I mean," he glanced around, "I mean, I guess I should have figured." He shot a withering look in the now-departed Brigham's general direction. "Anyway. At least I can count our conversation."

"Count it?"

"For h-home teaching," he stuttered. "Even if it's not at your home it still counts, doesn't it?"

Wait a minute. Home teaching?

"Oh. So was that why it was urgent that you talk to me tonight—before the end of the month? You're my home teacher?" Was that why he acted so interested in whether she showed up at church, why he appeared at her house willing to help her with fix-it-type chores, why he erased all malice from his face when he talked to her? She heard from far away another faint snapping sound, but this time it wasn't a sonic boom, and it wasn't the thawing of the ice in Alaska or around John Wentworth's frozen heart; it was the breaking of her own. Bitterness bled forth from it. "So, you're my assigned friend."

"Uh, no. I mean, yes. I mean, how should I answer that?" His jaw twitched, and it was impossible to tell if his aloof manner denoted apathy or emotional self-preservation. "Listen, Susannah. You and I have known one another too long to—look. I told the elders quorum president I couldn't be assigned to you. He said, 'Yeah, Wentworth, two-thirds of the people in this here singles ward have a history,' and he didn't let me off the hook. I didn't want this any more than you did."

He sounded almost mad, which caught Susannah off guard, and she had to think about whether she would have wanted him in her life back at the beginning of the summer. There was no question. Susannah had wanted him in her life every minute of every day since she saw him for the very first time. And the way John had treated her—and looked at her—lately, even tonight, made her suddenly realize she believed he had reasons beyond simple duty.

John stared at her intently as she worked this through in her mind. "Look." His voice softened. "The reason I finally took the calling was when I saw you hadn't been to church in the whole three months since your records showed up, I hoped maybe an old acquaintance might be a good influence on you. And when the sister missionaries told me you were running a bar—and that first night I stopped by, when I heard you calling off your live-in guy Guido guard dog, well, I worried you were lost." He looked up at the stars. "It killed me," he whispered. He swallowed visibly and paused while he sniffed back emotion. Finally he continued, more composedly. "I figured I'd have to simply be a friend, do some service as a friend, not a home teacher. I didn't want to scare you off."

"You thought I was inactive? A bar owner? With a live-in boyfriend?" Susannah's head was spinning. If what John was saying was true, how wacked out his opinion of her must be! Everything he'd said made her want to cry. "I thought you knew me better than that. Knew my character, my faith, better than that."

He kicked a hole in the snow with his boot. "I thought I did, too. Can't you imagine how it made me feel, to see you, to see you so—" John's voice was strained, aching. The longing in it was undeniable.

And then she remembered he saw her making an indiscreet public display of affection at The Depot with BLT. Her shame overrode her dismay at his mistaken idea of her, although a bubble of annoyance rose within her at his lack of trust in her, his unwillingness to come to her directly to discover the truth.

"Don't you know, John, who I really am?"

"I might." He whispered. "I might." A sharp gust of wind sprayed fine snow crystals on Susannah's cheek where they melted instantly. On John's they shone in the night moonglow. He looked at her searchingly. Then the door of the lodge banged, and Brigham Talmage came boot-clunking their direction. Her mind felt like it was being torn in two.

"Um," he backed away both physically and emotionally. "Susannah? I have some papers I want to give you. I'll drop them off at your house. Look for them." As his eyes fell on Brigham, a look of disappointment washed over and remained on John's face, which he then directed at Susannah. He turned and walked away toward the lodge as Brigham approached. An icy blast rushed by, and it froze the snowdrops on her skin and in her hair. She was starting to feel dangerously cold now.

"What was that old codger doing around here?"

"Oh, he's my home teacher. Last day of the month, you know." The words felt like sandpaper in her throat.

Brigham led Susannah by the hand toward the warm, dry lodge. "Let's get you out of those wet things and into something dry and more comfortable." His voice carried loud, and the night air turned the tear on Susannah's cheek to ice.

"Oh, you're shivering!" Brigham peeled the sopping parka from her shoulders. Her sweater underneath was damp, too, but a few minutes near the fire were enough to turn that moisture to steam and give it a dry feeling again. Her jeans beneath the parka were a bad choice, Brigham said. Cotton soaks up moisture like a sponge, and heavy denim takes a long time to dry. Eventually the fire dried the jeans. Nevertheless, she remained chilled to the core. He looked at her with an eye of concern.

"You're cold. Really cold. Your head was unprotected out there. Promise me you'll take better care of yourself. If not for you, for me." He took her in his arms. "Let's warm you up. I don't think even cocoa or hot cider will work. We've got to arrange a heat transfer."

It sounded like one of those hideous teen-love-survival-movie plot machinations, but she was too cold to care. Standing beside her at the roaring bonfire, he held her close to try to return her to a state of steady and even breathing, and to quell the random quakes that cramped in her abdomen and arms and thighs. She attempted to wrinkle her nose. It went up fine but came down slowly. She stayed pressed in his arms a few moments longer, then tried again. A little quicker coming down.

She was thawing out, thawing out in the fiery warmth of a kind, attentive, good-looking and charming Plan B. It appeared Plan A had just morphed into Disappointment Part 2, The Decade Later, and she realized she should now swallow her pride, cut her losses, and begin to fully accept Brig's warm attentions. What she'd interpreted as John's love, was love, but brotherly. It explained the warning at Howard Jones, the frequent helps, the attention. Her home teacher. If she'd known sooner, she might not have made such a fool of herself, dripping emotion all over him. Wait. She didn't. She'd never given him encouragement. John didn't even know she still held him in the highest esteem.

So, here she stood, in the warmth of the handsomest man of her acquaintance. A good man, with heavenly teeth and who sacrificed his heat for hers. For so many months she had withheld emotion toward him, and at last, it began now to flow. Even though she had initially regarded him with skepticism, took her time trusting him, deeming him sincere in his attentions, she believed their friendship was growing in the right direction. A friendship based on kindness and mutual respect and understanding could certainly evolve. No one was naïve enough to believe that a relationship, an eternal one, wouldn't develop as the partners grew. What did President Kimball say? Any righteous man and any righteous woman can have a good marriage.

Susannah, calmer now in body and mind, pulled back to look up at Brigham and felt his dark eyes look through hers. She imagined they looked down into her heart and saw the affectionate spot she'd finally created for him. Satisfaction tugged the left side of his smile back, as if he'd found a long-awaited chance. He took her by both shoulders, guiding her to sit beside him on the deep leather sofa beside the blaze. She instinctively drew a nearby fleecy blanket over her shoulders and legs. But then to her great surprise, Brigham dropped to the floor beside her and rested his folded arms across her lap and looked up into her face.

"Susannah. This may seem fast. Please, don't panic. This is how I am. You'll get used to it soon enough—that is, if— What I'm trying to say is, Susannah Hapsburg, will you marry me?" He pulled from his pocket a velvet box and creaked it open. There on a black satin background sat a diamond that made Sasha Perrier's full carat trillion look like a blue light special. This diamond sparkled, not only with the flickers of the nearby blaze, but from a fire of its own in the round-cut solitaire set on a glistening gold band. It was so huge it almost looked like an industrial-use stone, but the brilliant fire refuted that.

"Cubic Z! My favorite!" Her nervous habit of humor under stress kicked in, an innate defense mechanism under pressure.

"Oh, you're so witty. That's one of the many things I love about you."

"No, I was going to say—how did you get your hands on the Hope Diamond? I thought it was in the Smithsonian."

"The Hope Diamond is blue. This F color is as clear as you are pure." Oh, his persuasive words. And what a monstrous, gorgeous rock! It took her breath away. "So? What do you say? What do you say to becoming Mrs. Brigham Talmage? It's never been done before. I want you to be the first." That was a weird thing to say. Of course, everyone says weird things from time to time, and he was probably a nervous wreck, proposing and all. She let it slide.

"Brigham. Oh, look at it, this—" He placed it on her finger. It even felt heavy. "It's amazing. I love it! It's so—"

"Like you, so beautiful. I've been wanting you since before I met you. That's why I found you. When you appeared in my world that Sunday, I knew. I knew I couldn't waste a moment. I know it's fast, but I've seen enough to know what I want. Some guys wait around. They want something, but they don't know how to get it, or they're scared and hesitate." That sounded like someone she thought she knew. Like John, perhaps. But she'd been wrong about his intentions after all, hadn't she? Never again. Oh! Should she be thinking about another man at this moment? No! Focus! "Not me. He who hesitates falters. I've always been one to decide and then seize the day, or the case, or the girl—meaning you, fair Susannah. Your deep brown eyes, they really see me. You're everything I've ever wanted in a woman, a wife. So, so beautiful, my beautiful Susannah."

Nine-tenths of the speech's power was in the delivery. She saw why he could sway a jury. It stirred her heart even more than her own softening thoughts toward him, even more than the five carat feat of nature resting on her ring finger. But, despite all this, she couldn't answer immediately. It was so sudden.

"Brig. Brigham. My friend. My goodness!" She stuttered, slurred her words alternately. "This is— Forgive me for being taken off guard a bit. I feel like I've been offered a deal of a lifetime here. Wow. That's what it is, isn't it?" Or longer, as Mormon marriages go. Every word sounded lame, she knew. But she couldn't stop herself. A "yes" wouldn't come out, and she didn't have time or the presence of mind to concoct a perfectly tactful "not sure yet." "But I'm a businesswoman. It's just like me to need a bit of time to review the paperwork. Can I, could I, I mean, could you please allow me a few days to think this over? It's just I hadn't dreamed today would be the day—"

A twinkle formed in his eye that said she'd revealed that she had been expecting this proposal. He took his chance and sealed the moment with a good kiss. A good, good kiss.

"Yes, Susannah Hapsburg. Take all the time you need. But remember, I'm in agony every moment you make me wait. Keep the ring on, please. For me. It's yours. Besides, it will remind you of me while you decide." He pressed her hand and gave her one more light kiss. "Now, let's get something warm inside you. Dinner is ready for us in the restaurant."

CHOCOLATE AVALANCHE

4 square semi-sweet chocolate
1 cup butter
1¾ cup sugar
1 cup flour
4 large eggs
1 teaspoon vanilla
1½ cup pecans

Melt chocolate and butter together in a saucepan. Stir in nuts until well coated. Combine sugar, flour, eggs, and vanilla. Mix only until blended. Add chocolate-nut mixture, again mixing carefully. Turn into paper cups and bake at 325 degrees for 35 minutes. Do not frost if you value your life. Store in an airtight container, unless you eat them all in one great avalanche of gluttony.

Chocolate Mousse Filling For Crêpes

Go ahead. Eat a few crêpes filled with this creamy delight after dinner, but it's a sure thing you'll find yourself sneaking to the refrigerator for a spoonful in the wee hours of the morning.

In the wee hours of early Wednesday morning, the fire of the diamond sparkled a bit differently than it had beside the roaring flame at the Solitude lodge, and the ring weighed heavily on her finger as she rested her clasped hands across her stomach while lying in her bedroom before the dawn's early light.

The room's ceiling had the same familiar patterns she saw in the shadows of its spackle as when she was a little girl. She could still pick out the pictures which her mind had interpreted in the texture so long ago—the train, the dog with the fluffy tail, the shooting star. All she felt like doing this morning was staring.

Her thoughts all jumbled together. Nothing emerged clearly as an answer. She'd prayed at length, though vaguely in her swirling-thoughts state, but the heavens weren't exactly forthcoming with answers. It seemed like she needed to reason this out on her own.

Remembering last night's events irked her. How had she let things go so far off course? At the beginning of the night she was secretly contemplating giving Brig the heave-ho, and now she was wearing a massive diamond ring that showed she planned to let him possess her from now until forever. She slipped it off her hand momentarily and then slid it back on. It came off pretty easily. How much would it cost to get it sized?

If she tried, she could briefly recapture that feeling, if only for a wink of an instant, with John. Every time she spoke to him she felt her entire inside turn into a big maybe. Maybe, maybe. It seemed like every encounter she'd ever had with John left her in a lurch of maybes.

Boy, if ever there were a time she could use her patriarchal blessing, it was now. How long ago had it disappeared? It seemed like a year. She felt lost without it.

Turning onto her side, she slid the diamond off and set it in the drawer of the nightstand beside her bed. It didn't feel right to wear the ring when she wasn't sure. It made her feel like an engage-o-path, those girls who leave in their wakes the jetsam of wasted hopes.

Something whispered in her mind. She didn't catch it. What was it? She listened again. It whispered for her to open the nightstand drawer. No—not the ring again. But could that be the answer? That she should put the ring back on? Oh, dear. Could it be? If so, it was an answer she wasn't ready for. She kept reasoning things out in her mind. She put the pros and cons of her decision into two mental columns—assets and liabilities.

Brig had obvious assets. Number one, that he loved her, loved her with enough fire to want to make her his own—forever. A big asset, for sure. Then there was the security he offered her for her future life. Making sure her hobby business came out in the black accounting-wise might never worry her little head again. Women crave security. Brigham Talmage's wife would have it in spades. She adored his confidence, his keenness to achieve his goals—whatever they might be. He didn't hold back. And when she considered her own risk-averse personality, she recognized a complement: his strengths in that area compensated for her lack.

Then, of course, there were his sharp mind and wit, his incomparable good looks, and the charm. All definite assets. He went to church, as far as she knew, every Sunday, and his knowledge of the gospel never gave her cause to question.

On the other hand, she couldn't ignore the liabilities. Naturally she believed everyone's character is much deeper than a few months' acquaintance can reveal; however, she often felt like she'd barely scratched the surface of Brigham's character, even though last night he declared her deep brown eyes really saw him. She longed to know him better, especially before she made such a solemn, binding commitment. In fact, it made her wish she'd lived in the days of arranged marriages. Those women seldom knew their spouses before the wedding, but they didn't have to take any personal responsibility for that fact. They simply went into it expecting to make the best of whatever hand they were dealt. If an unhappy union resulted, at least the bride could blame the matchmaker.

Besides that, John's warning about him still clinked around in her mind.

However, all these concerns rested firmly in the "not enough information" zone. The pressure bothered her—but she talked herself out of that. Brigham wasn't pressuring her. He simply had a seize-the-moment personality; he knew they were right for one another first. Nothing was inherently wrong with that. In fact, perhaps his certainty served as evidence of his stewardship over their relationship already taking hold, and she ought to heed his counsel. Could that be?

The whisper to open the nightstand drawer came again. Yikes. The ring was calling to her—like that creepy gold band from J.R.R. Tolkien. Double yikes.

Now, for John's assets and liabilities. While she was dissecting, she might as well throw him onto the cutting board, even though Home Teacher Guy with Gymnast Girlfriend pretty much yanked himself off the surgical table. Nevertheless, this was her own personal early morning daydream, and she allowed herself to indulge it.

John's assets came easily. Years of observation taught her he, too, possessed self-assurance at his own rock-solid value system, which included serving others and serving God. From the jungles of Guatemala to the home teaching assignment at the Cottage of Broken Bank Accounts, to a boring computer desk in the ward clerk's office, John Wentworth upheld his priorities of loving the Lord and his fellow man. The other things about John—his strong work ethic, his broad knowledge of things of the earth, his constancy in personality—they fell secondary to his faithfulness in matters of values.

Her mind sloshed on. John spoke gently, made her feel calm. He made her laugh, taught her interesting (albeit trivial) facts. He was brave in the face of Poe-esque danger. He had courage to taste a substance from a jar labeled 1953. Could she in good conscience list that as an asset? She wasn't sure, but it wasn't a liability, so she fudged it. Okay, okay. She could go on all morning and miss work if she kept listing things she liked about John.

Oh, and must she mention his ruggedly handsome face? Or the fact that with his freaky-rich Alaskan crab business, security wouldn't be a concern for his future wife either?

Future wife. Ah, that pinpointed John's number one, overriding liability. She had rejected his hand, and he had moved on, selected another to take to his heart. All the faithfulness she could ever receive from him again would come in the form of a monthly stewardship visit.

The drawer whispered again.

"Gaa! Fine!" She succumbed to the nudging with a gasp of exasperation. "If I have to, I will. But I won't like it." She jerked the drawer all the way open, and a piece of paper at the back caught her eye. Sliding her fingernail under its edge to pry it up, she extracted it, ignoring the ring as it tumbled into the front corner of the nightstand drawer. She unfolded the document.

"Patriarchal Blessing, given to Susannah Marie Hapsburg, 2 February 1989." It was here all along? She never would have brought it here. She took a closer look. In the top right hand corner were the typed words "Copy #2." It was done with an old daisy-wheel typewriter, and Susannah ran her finger across the indentations of each punctuation mark and letter. The paper was getting slightly brittle at its creases.

Copy #2—a vague memory of misplacing her original wisped through her mind. That was right: she'd written to the Church to ask them for a duplicate. It took two long weeks and two hard-earned dollars (of her dad's) for it to arrive. But that was shortly after she'd received it in high school. Naturally, she'd located the original two days after the mail brought the duplicate. She, or her mom, must have placed this one here, where it had lain for the ensuing years.

Her eyes scanned the document. It was all there. Susannah sank back onto the pillows propped against the headboard and began to reread the familiar paragraphs carefully.

On the first read, nothing jumped out at her as being the perfect answer to all her questions. It disappointed her a bit. She'd been banking on the likelihood that some important phrase would somehow be neon-lit, or at least underlined with pink highlighter, to direct her mind in the matter. But no, it still didn't come right out and say who she should marry, only that she would marry (whew), "in the due time of the Lord" (drat that phrase), and advised her to counsel with her father in times of decision and indecision.

Odd. This copy perpetuated a typo from her original blessing. She'd cringed every time her eyes slid across the word "father." Didn't the typist here or there or anywhere see the glaringly plain need for a capital letter when referring to Deity?

She comforted herself with the knowledge that she'd been faithfully seeking the counsel of her Father in Heaven as she groped her way through this blind spot. In recent weeks her prayers had been more sincere, her scripture study more in-depth than ever before. She'd cross-referenced herself into places like Obadiah and Lamentations, seldom-trodden ground. But the messages remained encrypted, and she couldn't seem to break the code with fasting or prayer.

Now, a third reading of her blessing proved similarly unprofitable, and she told herself she only had time for one last stare before she absolutely had to get up and get ready for work or her hair would never dry and would freeze upon contact with the outside world.

However, this time through, her eyes stopped once again on the phrase "counsel with your father." Bammo! It was like something whacked her upside the head. It wasn't a typo, after all. The word "father" referred specifically to her earthly father, Glenn Hapsburg! Suddenly it made perfect sense, and she wanted to shake herself violently by the shoulders for not seeing it before. If only it had said daddy instead . . . No. There were no excuses for her blindness. Unless, of course, it was simply understanding that had been enlightened to her in due time.

Dad. How she longed to sit beside him at their kitchen table ask him his opinion in this weighty matter. His words soothed her, even as she imagined their resonance falling from his smiling, usually-chapped lips. Dad. But how could she counsel with him? He was not merely Dad or Glenn Hapsburg at this point. He was President Hapsburg of the Brazil Porto Valencia Mission, a hemisphere away in his shirt sleeves in some steaming jungle—a whole summer away from her blastingly icy winter. She exhaled dejectedly. "Finally, after all this searching, I decode the map to understanding, and I can't follow it." Crusher.

💔 💔 💔

"So, I'm sick of you guys' scheming. You can quit it because I'm going to ask her out."

"Jackie? Jackie Cousins?"

"Yeah. Now lay off, okay?" Trevor asserted himself like the macho huge man he was, but Susannah didn't miss the lilt in his voice or the spark in his eye. She and Colette gave each other an excited-shiver look. They didn't say anything, so as not to jinx it, but Trevor muttered, "I think I'm going to offer to bake Cade's wedding cake. Pro bono. That bloke deserves it."

Fortunately Sasha Perrier made her grand, purse-dog-accompanied entrance after Trevor's magnanimous wedding cake pronouncement. Her ring, which she'd managed to fit on the outside of her leather driving gloves, flashed like a Christmas light as she sashayed through the jingle-belled door.

"Seasonal greetings, all. Colette, dear, what can you get Trevor to whip up for me? I need impressive refreshments for a top qual' bridal shower I'm helping with. My own little bridal shower, which won't be little, mind you, isn't planned until springtime when the local tulips are in bloom. They're far too expensive to import from Holland." Sasha rolled her eyes for effect. "So, what do you suggest,

Colette? I need something fancy that tastes good, too. Ooh! I like this!" and she pointed to a line on the menu: Chocolate Nutmeg Soufflé with Crème Anglaise. "Can I get enough of this to feed fifty for under a hundred dollars?"

"Uh, probably not." She guided Sasha to a section of the menu more suited to her budget.

"Oh, well. When I become Mrs. Barclay Barnes I won't have to worry about the cost. We'll fly them in from Paris, won't we Yo-yo, sweetie?" Yo-yo stuck his trembling head out of the poinsettia-decorated purse momentarily, then retreated like a prairie dog spotting a coyote.

Fortunately, all the hubbub surrounding the love lives of others in the café mercifully distracted Colette and Trevor from asking about Susannah's ski date last night. That is, until a messenger shivered in with a large turquoise envelope for Susannah. The return address label read 'Talmage and Associates, Attorneys at Law.'

She retreated to the privacy of her office before she tore it open. When she did, out fell a long, wide folder with a blue and red graphic of a jet on the side. Delta. "Come Fly With Me" was scrawled across the page in black ink. It looked like Brigham's handwriting.

As she opened the Delta folder, a tinny version of the Bobby Darin song met her ears. The envelope was rigged to play it. "Come fly with me, let's float down to Peru. In lemon land there's a one-man band and he'll toot his flute for you. Come fly with me, we'll take off in the blue." She loved that song's swinging style—it was a staple on the play-list for their restaurant.

She slid the envelope's contents into her hand: an itinerary. Depart any day the week of January 1 from Salt Lake City, change planes at LAX, and from there to Quito, Ecuador. Next a puddle jumper to Galapagos. Hen-scratched in the margin were the words, "Beach Cabana, seven days, six nights." Return via LAX any day the week of January 8. Her name and Brigham's were on the tickets for which she held a photocopy.

"Girl, that has honeymoon written all over it." Colette had come up behind her silently. To Susannah it had "pressure" written all over it. "Did he propose last night? I'm your Colette, here. You have to tell me."

"He did." Susannah shushed her as Colette practically jumped up and down. "But no shrieks of delight yet, dear."

"Why? Didn't you accept? Was he too chintzy to fork over a ring? Where is the ring?"

"It's at my parents' house. In a little wooden drawer."

"Why?"

"Partly because I don't feel right wearing it until I know for sure I want to advertise what it suggests."

"What about the other partly part?"

"Oh, that. Partly because this morning I suspected it had some evil whispering power, and I thought it would be safer out of reach."

"Precioussss," Colette hissed. "But why didn't you accept? Isn't he good enough for you?" She was teasing, Susannah knew, but it hit a nerve.

"Oh, Colette. I wish I knew. There's so much pressure, and I feel like I'm wandering in mists of darkness. I wish I could talk to my dad, but he's in far-off Brazil. I don't even have the phone number of the mission office—if I could remember in my current deranged mental state how to make an international call anyway."

The look on Colette's face softened. It wasn't very often as a business partner that she saw the vulnerable side of her colleague. The very good friend side of her took charge.

"Give me five minutes." She left Susannah pondering, trying not to weep. The words "seven days and six nights" blinked before her eyes. A week alone with Brigham—it would give her what she needed, the chance to peel back the suave layers of his exterior and really look inside. Another voice reassured her, buoying her self-esteem incalculably, "He picked you. He picked you!"

Exactly four minutes and forty-three seconds later, Colette reappeared.

"There's a guy out there eating Chocolate Mousse-filled Crêpes who has a sister in China, and he calls her all the time with a great international rate he got online. Like two cents a minute. Here's the site." She handed Susannah a scribble on the back of a napkin. "It has rates to Brazil, too." Susannah looked it over and stuffed the paper in her purse. She might check it out. "And, I'm not done yet." Colette demanded more attention. "Sister Blackwelder reminded me to tell you you're on Temple Square. Someone here knows the phone number of every mission office on the face of the planet. She said she'll walk over and ask her president for it before her shift starts in an hour. In fact, she already left—at a dead shuffle-run—trying not to slip on the ice. And, I'm not done yet—Trev wanted to remind you that even though they have a different season there, it's probably fairly close to the same time of day. Think of the earth's spinning on its axis and the sun coming up in the east and all, he advised."

It was funny to hear this reminder. Of course as a former PW investment team member, one acutely aware of international business practices, Susannah should know about South American time zones, but with the swirling perplexity of her brain cloud, it seemed like her parents must be in a different time warp, not a different time zone. Letters took so long to travel, months really, and the seasons being different, it seemed like they were much farther away by time than they actually were. She thanked Colette.

"You didn't tell anyone about my situation, I hope." Susannah cringed at the thought.

"Of course not. But give me something to share soon, okay? Are those wedding bells I hear?" Colette cupped her hand to her ear. Her eyes got a faraway look.

"Ignore them for now. Remember: ask not for whom the bell tolls."

"It tolls for thee."

"I'm saying it doesn't. For now." Susannah tried to be emphatic.

"Whatever. Ga-la-pa-gos, chicky baby. Galapagos! It's so unusual. So romantic. A man with a plan who's not afraid to execute it. Shazam. At least tell me how he proposed."

Susannah did her best to relay the bare bones of the events, in all their weirdness, without wasting too much time or being disloyal to the private feelings of Brigham or herself or John.

"You mean, Brig told John to take a hike? After you started a mini avalanche with a yodel? John saved you, only to leave you to be proposed to by another man? Bonkers. Why didn't he stick up for himself? For you? If he was your home teacher all this time why didn't he say so?" Colette paused a moment and tapped shave-and-a-haircut on the doorframe with her fake nails, then pointed at her friend. "Bizarro world, Suze. You've got to do some air clearing with John before you answer Brig. You'll never rest easy until you do."

Maybe she was right. But then again, she didn't know. All Susannah knew was that she wanted to, needed to, talk to her dad. "All I know is I need to talk to my dad."

"You need to talk to your dad?" Trevor poked his head in her office door. "What's that plane ticket? Hey, Colette. There are about ten people waiting out front." Colette left in a bustle. "Suze. Go home and call your dad. Sister Blackwelder just came back and dropped off his phone number—got it from her mission pres. Here." He tossed her another slip of napkin, and it fluttered onto her desk. "We've got things handled here. Come back when you're done, if you want." He had an unusually jaunty air, and despite her own woes, Susannah had to ask.

"Was Jackie in here already today?"

"Just left."

"Oh really? Anything I should know?"

"What do you mean? If you mean are we going to dinner tomorrow night, yeah. You should know because I won't be able to stay late and make the gelato. We'll have to strike it from the menu for a few days. It's cold enough only penguins want it now, anyway." Trev leaned to go, still holding the door frame and looking like he was about to kick up his heels. "She's a nice girl. Quiet, but real nice."

"Sure is. Good choice, Trev. We all like her." Susannah watched him go, and a happy feeling filled her momentarily. She loved love, especially in people she loved. She felt homesick for love, herself. Susannah crossed her fingers that no disasters would befall Trevor's date tomorrow night. Then she shoved the musical plane ticket in the top center drawer of her desk, snatched up her napkin notes, and made for Sugarhouse across the slick streets of the wintry day descending to its close.

A short time later, the ringer on the other end made a strange beeping sound. She couldn't tell if it was ringing or if it was a busy signal. As she was about to hang up and wait a bit to try again, there was a click and a slight delay, and then a young man's voice answered on the other end. He said something she couldn't make out, probably in Portuguese. The only familiar syllables were Jesus Cristo, but they were enough to tell her she had the right number. Brief concern flashed through her mind—what if the missionary was a native Brazilian? He wouldn't be able to understand her. Then she remembered her days in Austria, where many of the natives spoke better English than the Americans, and she forged ahead.

"Hello. Is President Hapsburg there?"

"Sí, just a moment, okay? Can I tell him who's calling?" An American.

She waited forever, hoping he wasn't in an important meeting with the prophet or anything. It would be exactly her luck.

"Hello! Susannah? Is that you?" Even with the delay, she could detect the audible swallowing of food. One of her inborn talents was the uncanny ability to call people during mealtime. "Is everything all right?" It hadn't occurred to her that her phone call might alarm him. After a few moments of calming his nerves, and a short, chit-chatty update to gloss over the major aspects of her life, she launched into her purpose in phoning him, giving him at least 89.9 cents worth of details. As she did so, she felt more like a little child than she had in years. She had to restrain herself from calling him daddy, like she had as a little girl racing to embrace him when he came home from work at night.

"Well, Susannah. It looks like you are in a situation. A ring, huh? Do you like it?"

"It's nice. Gorgeous. Huger than huge."

"Hmm. That's good, but am I right that you seem more interested in this John Wentworth? I remember his name."

"The Articles of Faith, Dad. It's the same name as from the Wentworth Letter."

"No, sweetheart. I remember him from when you came back from Guatemala, before your mission. Same fellow, right?"

"Yes. You remember?"

"I'm your father. I remember." Something about that statement made Susannah's breath catch in her throat and stinging tears well up in her eyes.

"Oh, Dad. I wish I could just turn it off—the switch that makes me want to be in love. It's unnatural. It's inconvenient. It's—it's bugging me and wrecking my peace of mind."

"Of course it is, Susannah." He let her sob a moment. "But, sweetheart, you've got something backwards. It's not unnatural at all. In fact, its intrinsic to us." He cleared his throat, and his soothing voice gathered strength. Susannah's limbs went limp, and she began to soak in her father's certain wisdom.

"You know, we had a visiting general authority—Elder Groberg—here not too long ago, and he taught us something really interesting about love. It was this: that we're all children of God, who is the source of all love. Nothing new there, I know, but he also said one of the strongest connections we have with our pre-mortal life is how much our Father and Christ loved us—and how much we loved them. Every time we sense true love here, it awakens a longing in us we can't deny."

For months, years now, Susannah had been trying desperately to deny the longing. In fact, she'd prayed intently three nights in a row that the yearning could somehow be assuaged for a time, so she could focus and get a little peace.

"As His children, children of love, we all respond to it," her dad continued. "In fact, we all have a powerful desire to reconnect here with the love we felt there."

The tears had begun to flow freely down her cheeks, but Susannah didn't bother to wipe them away. She knew how powerful that wish for love and connection felt. It distracted her from her duties, making her miserable and empty. It dictated many if not most of her actions—trying to fill the need for love by whiling away hours with Carly's children, by visiting Mary Lucas with flowers whenever she could, by pouring cup after cup of steaming cocoa for strangers also in need of love and caring. She gave and she gave, but oh, how she longed to receive.

Her father waited for a response, and hearing none, he went on, "Susannah, you are no exception to Elder Groberg's explanation. You are a child of God and therefore have a great desire and capacity to love and be loved." Could he read her thoughts? It felt like it. The word capacity—what faith he showed in her to say she had a great capacity to love—and to be loved. Her father was always so wise, and her soul pleaded that he might be wise in this also.

"You think so, Dad?"

"I do."

"What, specifically, do you think I should do? In this matter?"

"Suzie, I think you need to take time—and use the Spirit—to help you discern when that love is true."

She would try. Their phone time had run long. "Thanks, Dad. Really."

"Good. Now, do you think there's any way the postal services could transport me a piece of your best chocolate cake? Your mom would love me forever, although I hope she's planning to anyway."

CHOCOLATE MOUSSE FILLING FOR CRÊPES

1 cup milk
1 cup heavy whipping cream
1 small package instant chocolate pudding

Combine all ingredients and whip with hand mixer until soft peaks form. Delicious in crêpes, and as filling for cream puffs, or elegant as its own sinful dessert. (Other flavors of pudding, such as French Vanilla or Cheesecake, can, of course, be substituted, but why?)

Bleeding Heart Chocolate Cupcakes

Not too sweet and loaded with chocolate, these cupcakes may appear sunken and underdone when they emerge from the oven, but don't let their appearance fool you. Their moussey middles ooze with every bite. Your heart will bleed with desire for another, and the only bandage will be to give in to your craving.

"Trevor—what are those bandages on your arm? You can't very well cook here if you're bleeding, you know."

"Oh, they're not for blood. They're for muscle strain."

Colette caught Susannah's gaze and then rolled her own eyes. "Muscle strain? Exactly what kind of a date did you and Jackie have?"

"It was just dinner. We were heading up to Bountiful to take in a movie at that old theater where they bring root beer and pizza to your table, but we caught sight of her brother just off the road. She made me wheel around and check it out."

"What was her brother doing off the road? Was he okay?" Susannah set down her morning market acquisitions, including some serendipitous, fresh Bing cherries from Chile.

"He's the policeman, isn't he?" Colette chirped up as she sampled some of the tart-sweet Bings and pulled a pan of Trevor's Bleeding Heart Cupcakes from the oven.

"That's the one. He was fine, just at the scene of a gruesome accident. Not gruesome, I guess. But it could have been. Potentially gruesome, I should say."

"What are you saying, Trevor?" Susannah loved it when Trevor got discombobulated, bogged down in the details of the story. He was so cute that way. The jingle bells on the front door shook, and in walked the girl Jackie herself. Susannah noted the light that came into her chef's round, freckled face. "Hello there, Jackie. Colette and I were just quizzing Trevor about your date. It would be fun to get your more intelligible side of the tale."

"Oh, I bet he's too modest to give you the full extent of it. You should have seen him. He was like the Incredible Hulk!"

"What are you talking about?"

Trevor stood back, nearly blushing, as much as a jolly brown Hawaiian giant can, while Jackie related the strange events of the evening.

"My brother was radioing an ambulance, when another accident occurred a few blocks down, and he got sent over there. Trevor and I stayed on the first scene. I know CPR, and I wanted to help. You should have seen this car, Colette. It looked like—"

"—like a soda can that someone stepped on the side of," Trevor interjected.

"Exactly. A Red Cream Soda can," Jackie continued. "The driver's side door was indented pretty bad, and the driver got pinned under the steering wheel, so there was no way to get her out through the windshield or the side window. She was losing some blood, but we couldn't tell how much. The ambulance still wasn't there, and none of the other police on the scene could un-jam the door."

During the retelling, Jackie slid toward Trevor and was now talking to them while nestled beneath his chin. "Trevor—he was so awesome—got irritated with how long everything was taking. He could tell the poor girl was going into shock in the car. Boy Scout! And so he finally took matters into his own hands. He marched right up to that car, pushed a bunch of these helpless oafs aside, and with a burst of power yanked the door back, and then—get this!—he twisted the door off its hinge and threw it into the barrow pit! Everyone who was standing there about went crackers, but he slid the poor girl's seat back just as the ambulance pulled up, and the paramedics were able to extract her."

"Without the jaws of life, I must add here," Trevor gave his little input, arms folded across his chest. Jackie leaned up against those arms now.

"So from there, we followed the ambulance to the hospital. Trevor wanted to see if she was all right. By the time we got there, she was completely stabilized, and the EMTs told us that police on the scene of the accident had radioed. They needed to talk to Trevor to get some details for their report, so we went back to where the accident happened."

"I get to tell this part. This is the funny part."

"You go ahead, Trev." Jackie was calling him Trev! Colette crinkled her eyes slyly.

"So we got back over there, and this shorty officer was telling his buddy, 'Yeah man, you should have seen it. That big Samoan guy twisted that door right off its hinges. He looked like the Incredible Hulk, only not as green.'"

"Not as green. That's good." Colette chuckled.

"I know. So I felt bad for the guy, who must have been feeling like some kind of wimpy weakling at that point, and I wanted to show him that the car was made out of cheap tinfoil. I patted his shoulder. 'Hey, buddy. It's no big deal. Anyone could do it.' And I went around to the other side—the only-sorta-smashed side. 'Look,' I said, and I opened the door and twisted it as hard as I could. It wouldn't budge. Not an inch. I tried again. I even grunted. But it was solid. No give. The cops laughed it up a bit and gave me the thumbs up. I didn't really care because that's when Jackie here came over and said those magic words. Say them again for me, Jack."

"Okay, but I have no idea why they strike you so." She smiled and obliged him. "I said, 'Don't worry about it, Trev. We all saw you earlier. You totally had freakish strength from that adrenaline rush. You saved that girl.' It was weird because all of the sudden, when I said that, Trev took those big arms of his and gave me this huge hug." And the way she and Trevor looked at each other, it was as if they recognized one another as long-lost loves who didn't even need any reacquaintance time.

"Wow. And to think, if Trev hadn't needed that defensive driving school, you two never would have met." Colette patted Jackie's hand. "You never told us what you were in there for." The four sauntered from the kitchen toward the café's seating area.

"Oh, that? The first time I had a few speeding tickets, and I wanted to get them off my insurance." Jackie and Trevor sat down in Jackie's assigned booth.

"Weren't you in there twice with him? That was odd timing, or providential, wasn't it?"

"It wasn't either," Trevor jumped in. "She fixed it. That second time she got her brother to pull me over, and then she showed up at my session of driving school. She was stalking me!"

Jackie laughed, Trevor laughed louder, and Colette and Susannah left the lovebirds to their nest in the front booth. Colette pulled the Cardamom Cream Horns out of the refrigerator. They were much better the third day, as the spicy cream softened the chocolate cookie to perfection and the flavors seeped into each other.

"Have you come to a decision on your own problem yet, Susannah? I still don't see that fabled ring on your finger. Is it such a little tiny thing it embarrasses you?"

"Trust me. The only rival for my colossus is Ingrid's princess-cut beaut." Susannah looked away as Colette's jaw dropped. Ingrid's ring was legendary. "And, the answer to your question is yes, and no. But I have a few things to work out before I can tell anybody anything."

"Oh, I forgot. This package was in the door for you when I got here. Sorry! I can't believe I forgot to give it to you first thing."

It was another large envelope, official-looking, with a logo on the return address label that read Grant, Woodruff, Goldberg, and Osmond. Who were they? CPAs? She'd never heard of them in the accounting world. Probably more lawyers. She was surrounded by lawyers these days—they couldn't seem to get enough of her. She tore open the back flap.

Dear Ms. Hapsburg:

As executors for the estate of Mr. Joseph Harville, it is our duty to inform you that you have been named in his will. You are requested to be in attendance, either personally or by legal proxy, at the below listed time and location for the reading of of the estate's division.

Sincerely,

Jerry L. Woodruff, Attorney at Law

"Look at this, Colette. Mr. Harville died. The partner from Pointman. I didn't even know! Missed the funeral and everything. How sad."

"Sorry to hear it. You liked him." Colette was right. Susannah did like him. "So, what's that for?"

"It says I'm named in Mr. Harville's will. Strangely thoughtful."

"What did you inherit?"

"I don't know. I didn't think he had anything left after the firm went under. I always figured all his wealth was tied up in PW. I have to go to some reading of the will on Monday. Can you cover for me here?" Colette nodded. "Wow. This is really sad. He was an odd one, but so nice. I'll miss him."

"Maybe you could send flowers to his widow."

"He never married. No kids. Plus he was an only child. Pointman Westerford kind of became his life. I bet when it went down it broke his heart."

"Oh, that is sad! Do you think that's how he died?"

"Of a broken heart? I don't know. But now it's making me really sad. Shoot! I wish I could have done something." Susannah retreated to her office to reflect for a while on the loss of her friend. Not a close friend, but a friend nonetheless. She found his obituary online and read it through. "I never knew he taught at Princeton and Brown and Texas A&M before joining Pointman." There were a dozen other "I never knew" statements. She was always too busy for people in those days. How grateful she was for this new leaf she'd turned over in her life by opening The Chocolate Bar, which provided her time to be interested in and enjoy the minutiae of the lives of people around her. To mourn with those that mourn, as well as to rejoice with those who rejoice.

"What time is the will reading?" Colette leaned into the office to ask. Susannah told her five o'clock. "Oh, good. I can do that. I have something else at 2:30 that afternoon, but I can be back before five, no prob." Colette chewed her nails while Susannah looked through the rest of her mail. Oh, fabulous. Another envelope from another attorney's office appeared. What was with all these lawyers?

She found a letter from some bloke named Pete Pannabaker at Pannabaker, Jensen and Siegfried, Attorneys at Law, summoning her to a closed meeting regarding the development of the land parcel 14932§34A. She guessed her café sat directly atop that scarily numbered lot. Dang it. She didn't want her dream business to become a parking garage! There had to be something she could do.

"Did you have a chance to ask your 'attorney' about the situation?" Colette prodded later while they poured cocoa and served the last of the steaming crêpes. Tonight the crêpes themselves were chocolate with sautéed bananas and butter pecan ice cream for the filling.

"It didn't come up."

"Couldn't we sign a petition or something?" asked a regular patron through a full mouth. Everyone who came in found out about the looming disaster sooner or later. Patrons talked, even if owners seldom did.

"We have to have somewhere to eat dessert in this part of town."

"What about light rail? I thought that was going to solve all the downtown parking problems."

Susannah's dilemma was the hot topic for about twenty minutes among her customers until they settled back in to the regular banter of their own concerns.

"When will the Boy Scouts of America enter the 21st century and discover Velcro? Enough with the sew-on patches. I think we should file a class-action suit against them."

"Have you tried Wunder Under? It totally works. For a while, at least."

Susannah retreated into her own mental world to fight her own legal battles.

♡ ♡ ♡

Arms laden with plywood, and toting a book entitled *How to Make Emergency Repairs to Your Roof to Prevent Further Damage to Your House*, Susannah trudged through the murky yard of the blight she once believed to be her dream home. It was getting dark, but the TV weatherman predicted a deluge tonight, possibly turning into a blizzard. She had to minimize the leakage if she could. She'd barely extracted her longest ladder from the tool shed when a bright yellow paper taped to her front door—inside the swinging screen door—caught her eye.

"Attention: Condemned Property." There was more, along with technical jargon, but her tear-bleared eyes prevented her from reading it.

Condemned? Her cottage of joy! She would have sat down hard on the porch and bawled, but she was afraid it might collapse. Shoving the ill-hung door ajar, she pushed her way into the front room. Her shadow hadn't darkened the indoor portion of the eyesore for weeks. Scattered across the wood slats were envelopes, all addressed to her. John had promised he would leave her some papers, hadn't he? In a haze of sadness and discouragement, she stuffed the envelopes into her briefcase and only plucked the smallest, pinkest one from the mess and tore it open.

"You are cordially invited to attend a bridal shower for Camie Kimball . . ."

It was more than Susannah could take. Casting the omen of eternal loneliness into the depths of her briefcase, she made a break for her car, not even bothering to shut the gaping door, turning her back on her dreams, probably forever.

BLEEDING HEART CHOCOLATE CUPCAKES

1 cup butter
8 oz semi-sweet chocolate; chopped
¾ cup sugar
½ teaspoon vanilla extract
7 eggs
pinch salt
7 tablespoons flour

In a large heavy saucepan over medium heat, begin melting the butter, stirring occasionally. When it's half melted, add the chocolate and continue cooking until the chocolate is half melted. Remove from the heat and continue stirring until mixture is smooth. Mix in the sugar, vanilla, eggs, and salt until smooth. Mix in the flour, just until blended. Ladle the batter into the muffin tin, filling each cup about three-quarters full. Bake for 15 minutes at 325 degrees in a greased 12-cup muffin tin until the edges are set but the centers are still wet and sunken. Cool on a rack for 5 minutes. Run a knife around the edge of each cupcake and carefully remove to a cooling rack. Cool for 10 minutes more. The centers will be liquid. Serve warm.

Chocolate
Zucchini Cake

Keep telling yourself it's a vegetable,
that it's part of a healthy diet. Then
bid a fond farewell to your will.

"And now for the reading of the will." The man in the dark suit with the oil spill comb-over cleared his throat, again, and resumed his phlegm-punctuated droning. Susannah had already been bored into oblivion for ninety-four straight minutes by legal technicalities regarding the deceased. At least one potential heir had slyly left the room after a loud whisper to a spouse to "Call me when he gets to a point." Once again, Susannah found herself wishing she had a husband to lean on, this time for ultra-selfish reasons.

The sheer tedium of the will-reading gave her a moment to think, a rare luxury lately, what with working six days a week and minding Carly's kids on Sundays. For a few, very long minutes, the dull meeting was a blessing in disguise.

She was powerless against the tendrils of defeat pulling her thoughts down. Her business was about to be demolished in favor of a pile of cars. Her dream home had officially been condemned, a title it deserved long ago, but which sent her hopes into the abyss. And after so many hours of labor, so many dollars, so much loving effort, it was defeat at its most poignant.

Well, almost its most poignant.

Clearly her most poignant defeat lay in that square pink envelope announcing the bridal shower of her darling former Beehive Camie. After all these years of wondering, John Wentworth reentered her life, only to make a square pink exit—and Susannah had utterly failed to put up a fight for him.

A bell in her mind sounded the death knell of her dreams. Gongggg!

And so, defeat pulled Susannah downward, downward. No matter what her tacky little inheritance from Harville might be, it certainly wouldn't be enough to remedy her current ills of unemployment, homelessness, and eternal solitude. In her haze of self-pity she conveniently ignored the fact she'd been proposed to by Captain Courtroom, and her reply remained to be made.

Eventually, Droning Phlegm, Esq., from the law firm of Grant, Woodruff, Goldberg, and Osmond got to the interesting stuff. Mr. Harville had no natural heirs, and although most of his wealth (retirement, etc.) had been tied up in Pointman Westerford and had gone down with the ship, he retained a few personal possessions of interest: Sly Exit and his patient wife were the happy recipients of Harville's low-mileage Jaguar and a set of copper cookware; a woman with a lap dog got an antique four-poster bed and all Harville's clothing. Susannah saw her wince slightly at the mention of the clothes and in her mind's eye could see it all going in a single load to the thrift store. Too bad, because Mr. Harville was always a snappy dresser.

Other items that were disposed of included baseball cards from the 1950s; another, less interesting vehicle; six giant wooden masks from some Polynesian island (Susannah harbored no regret at not being named for those); a painting by an artist Susannah had never heard of, but the man who got it teared up when his name was read as its recipient.

The clock kept ticking. Dusk fell. Susannah still didn't know why she was there. Nothing so far had been left to her, and she couldn't imagine feeling anything but uncomfortable accepting any of Mr. Harville's personal effects.

Monotonous Oil Slick cleared his throat. "Harumph. Those of you already named may now leave if you wish. The remaining items in Mr. Harville's will require technical explanation and will be of little interest to the rest of you." Practically everyone else in the room rose immediately and gathered their things. Heirs, pleased and not so pleased, cleared out in a flash. Soon only Susannah and two or three lawyers remained. She looked around nervously and shifted in her seat. Technical explanation? Oh, dear.

"Miss Susannah Hapsburg?"

"Yes."

"Mr. Harville's will specifies that you are to be the recipient of and future guardian of his most valued possession. He requested that you be informed you were selected due to your kindness, your gentle care, your youth and vigor, and your excellent sense of responsibility. According to a detailed statement of the deceased, no other person in Mr. Harville's acquaintance existed on whom he could rely for such a high duty as that of caring for an item of such import as this heritage pet."

"Heritage pet?" What was a heritage pet? A sense of foreboding swept through her.

"Yes. Heritage pet, in the form of Mr. Harville's prized tortoise, Beagle." Beagle! Beagle the tortoise. "During some time in the past two years, Miss Hapsburg, Mr. Harville left Beagle in your care for a time. He was so impressed with your gentleness toward the aged creature that he felt impressed you would be the best person among everyone he knew to inherit this animal."

Grrrreat. It took all the willpower of her entire being not to roll her eyes and sigh heavily. "You may or may not know, harumph, that Beagle is not any ordinary Galapagos tortoise. He is, in fact, the very tortoise that the famed Charles Darwin retrieved and brought home with him from his momentous voyage, the voyage in which he charted the natural life of the Galapagos Islands. You may recall that the ship aboard which Darwin traveled was christened *The Beagle*. It is that ship for which this tortoise is named."

But how? When was Darwin's voyage? Forever ago, like the 1850s. Maybe earlier.

"How can that be, Mr., uh—"

"Udall. It is highly unusual for a tortoise to live this long. Beagle, as you may have noted, is a unique animal, very special. Along with the animal himself, you will also be given official paperwork documenting his past care, all the way back to Darwin himself."

Right. She still didn't believe it. And she certainly didn't have anywhere to keep a tortoise. Continual nightmare. Her life was one continual nightmare. She pinched herself. This couldn't really be happening. A tortoise with patents of nobility?

Mr. Udall handed her a large enveloped marked "Beagle Documentation." She resisted the urge to look inside immediately because Mr. Udall persisted in droning.

"As you must realize, a great deal of responsibility, accountability, comes with an animal of Beagle's importance. Mr. Harville could have easily left Beagle to a museum or to a zoological society. He is, as you must see, a creature of international significance. I'm sure you're wondering how Mr. Harville acquired Beagle in the first place."

The question hadn't yet occurred to Susannah.

"Mr. Harville's great-grandfather was the gardener for Charles Darwin's nephew. The nephew had taken charge of Beagle upon Darwin's demise and gave it all proper care and attention, with the valued assistance of his gardener. Darwin's nephew, in turn, went the way of all the earth, leaving no heir and, therefore, assigned care of the tortoise to his trusted gardener, Beagle's caretaker during the nephew's declining years. Along with Beagle went a monetary sum, generating an annuity, to provide for its every need. This was converted into a trust fund when Beagle crossed the great Atlantic once again, this time aboard the Queen Mary as an adult rather than aboard its namesake as a baby. By now, the fund had accrued substantially, although Mr. Harville himself depleted it by constructing what he thought best for Beagle's comfort, a tortoise playground of sorts known as Beagle Gate." Beagle Gate? Perrrfect.

Udall was on a roll, so she didn't interrupt with her opinion on the idiocy of the entire situation. Put it out to sea, for heaven's sake! Use the cash to send the poor, plodding thing back to the island. Her own weekend with it a couple of years ago was enough to convince her that Salt Lake City was no environment for that thing. She had no doubt that her mother's no-indoor-pets-in-my-house edict included giant tortoises. Oh, mercy. Mercy, mercy, mercy.

"You will, as Mr. Harville's heir, take possession of Beagle immediately, as well as all his effects." A turtle had effects? Oh, brother. "Here are the keys to Beagle Gate, his home." He handed her a small manila key envelope. It clinked from within. "You also take possession of the Beagle Gate property, address included." She didn't check its location. Where could it be? Rose Park? Murray? Ooh! Maybe it was in Magna—out in the country. Beagle would like the country, surely.

There were other "effects." A recommended diet. The number for a veterinarian on retainer. On retainer! A few papers she didn't understand immediately.

"And now, Miss Hapsburg, we come to the heart of the matter. Beagle's age is quite advanced. Exact years are unknown. However, it is stated explicitly in Mr. Harville's will that the person who inherits Beagle will also be the executor of the trust fund and, in the unfortunate event of Beagle's death, will inherit the balance of the fund. There is a condition for this." Of course there was a condition.

Susannah wished she could vanish out of her life right now. There was no way. Absolutely no way. She said an almost involuntary silent prayer that she might not have to own a priceless heritage pet tortoise also owned by Charles Darwin. She didn't even like Charles Darwin! Now she liked him even less.

"The stipulation is that the trustee will only inherit the fund if it can be determined that Beagle died of natural causes." There went that plan. One she hadn't even thought of yet, and the rug was pulled right out from under her. Oh, no. She knew she couldn't seriously consider torticide. Or whatever. "In the event of Beagle's death, here are the numbers you will contact."

She thanked Mr. Udall for all his time, shoved the molehill of paperwork into her handbag and clicked her way out of the room. A giant Galapagos tortoise might be the loser gift for a zoo-themed TV game show, but it certainly didn't qualify in Susannah's opinion as a consolation prize for the utter desolation of her social life and house and business dreams.

"Wait, Miss Hapsburg. Don't forget Beagle."

She turned to see the tortoise looking blankly at her with his elderly eyes. He'd been plodding around chewing lettuce in the corner of the room all this time. Mustering her every whit of courage she stepped up to her responsibility. Darn it. The closest thing she had to a vegetable in her parents' fridge was some leftover Chocolate Zucchini cake. Her mind lingered briefly on wording for a possible want ad: Tortoise for sale. Pet only. No soup.

♡ ♡ ♡

"Susannah." It was a crackling, cell-to-cell call. "It's me. I need to see you. I can't wait."

"I need to see you too, Brigham." Talmage. She forced herself not to add the last name aloud. She thought she'd have more time, a few more days or hours to consider things before she came face to face with him again. She wasn't ready. In fact, she was a bit emotionally shattered, what with the awful reptile in her parents' front room. Facing the marriage decision right now overwhelmed her. Susannah drooped. Then again, perhaps Brigham could soothe her, give her some lovely food, a kind word and a comforting pat on the shoulder, then tell her to take her time, that he'd wait for her as long as she needed him to, until the moon fell. Hmm.

Beagle looked at her with his old, old eyes, and she tossed him an extra serving of lettuce, wishing he could impart his wisdom to her.

Within ninety seconds the doorbell rang. That couldn't be Brigham so soon, could it? She felt her hair, jumped up and smoothed her skirt and sweater, then, touching her finger, raced downstairs to grab that massive chunk of pressurized carbon from the nightstand drawer. She hoped her shoes didn't clunk too audibly as she ran back up the wood floor steps.

"Hi, beautiful. Come ride with me. Do you have your coat?" He pulled her black calfskin jacket from a hook in the entryway and took her by the hand. She followed, unconsciously grabbing her briefcase, her mind and resolve swinging like a pendulum.

Was a "no" to a marriage proposal an appropriate thing to drop on a guy while in a moving vehicle? It seemed more like a stopped activity. She let him fill the air with idle chatter as they sped westward along I-80 and then met the freeway exchange onto I-15 southbound toward Las Vegas. She always wondered why the road here was marked with that particular city as an endpoint. Why not I-15 South Los Angeles? That was a more logical endpoint, near the ocean. Why not I-15 South Cedar City? Why not I-15 South Lehi? Or Beaver? Any of those seemed like valid points along the line or endpoints for more Utah drivers than Las Vegas. She considered writing to UDOT with her opinion.

The lights of Salt Lake, Sandy, Draper, blurred past. They were cresting Point of the Mountain now. The golden lights of the state prison glowed in the night sky. She wondered if her attorney friend knew anyone in the state prison. She wondered where Brigham Talmage was taking her. It was too late at night to be off to meet the family at a holiday gathering. It was getting too late for dinner. Or dessert.

With cloud cover and snowflakes, it was not the night for romantic stargazing. Susannah gazed over at Brig's profile, and he took her hand naturally. He did have a handsome face. It was a perfect Hollywood profile. She had to admit she approved of his neatly trimmed sideburns and his strong chin. He fingered the diamond on her ring finger. She'd put it on for safe-keeping. You never know when there's going to be a hole in your coat pocket, she reasoned.

"It suits you."

"What?"

"My grandmother's ring." Oh, what now? Now she was the recipient of a family heirloom? No wonder Suffo-Cade's one gal made a run for it. High anxiety! Now that the cat was out of the bag about the family gem, she couldn't trust any pocket. This thing welded itself onto her finger.

He squeezed her hand. Replies died in her throat. If only he would stop the car so she could take both his hands in hers, look into his eyes and tell him kindly. His deep, torrid eyes. His warm,

warm hands. She'd have to kiss him first, of course. It might be her last chance . . .

Oh, curses! Her will was failing her. Here in his Porsche with his kabillion dollar ring on her finger and his burning hand locked over hers, with his perfect profile and love professions sprinkling over her like tiny fires from a sparkler, her best-laid plans looked naïve. They began to evaporate like snow in the sun. How could she give him up? How could she hurt him? Especially considering the alternative: nothing. Considering the fact of Camie Kimball's bridal shower.

His CD changer shifted and a Breinholt ballad washed over her and into her heart. She closed her eyes. Surely she would awaken when Brigham stopped the car where he wanted to take her. Wherever he wanted to take her . . .

Her eyes popped open as she felt a warm hand on her cheek and neck. To her surprise, fingers of dawn's faint rays reflected in the side view mirror. Where were they? Cookie-cutter houses and then stretches of desert, then more houses bleared past her eyes.

"We're almost there, Susannah. I thought you'd want to be awake for this." Her briefcase flopped against her shin, and she slid it to the door side of her legs so the hot air could come out of the heater vent and warm up her toes.

Awake for what? Then, as she saw the sign, she swallowed her gum in horror. "Las Vegas?"

"It's like I told you. I couldn't wait."

"Couldn't wait? I thought you meant to see me—"

"I did. And I meant to be with you. I told it all to you on the way here. Everything. Didn't it sink into your soul as you slept?" He pulled into a parking lot of a small building. "I know I saw a smile pull at your soft mouth when I told you how much I care for you, about all my plans for you and me and our future. Don't tell me you didn't hear it all. I know you did. You can't fool an experienced lie detector like Brigham Talmage, Esquire." He flipped down his visor, straightened his only stray strand of dark hair and turned to her with a glistening smile. "You know I meant I couldn't wait to be with you—to really be together. To marry you."

Marry? She looked around herself in panic. Las Vegas. Early morning. Swept away in the night. Her eyes suddenly came into focus on the name of the small grey building: "Chapel of Dreams." Dreams was wrong. Nightmare was more like it.

"Brig. Oh. Oh, I'm so—"

"You don't have to say it, my darling, my love. I know this is tacky. We'll do things right—as soon as your parents get back from Brazil. They wouldn't want to miss the real wedding, later." He was out his door and opening hers before she knew what was happening. The air, even in Vegas, blew bitingly cold at this time of a winter morning. "Come on. It's warm inside. Mr. Martino is waiting for us. I phoned ahead from Mesquite. We can still honeymoon in Galapagos in a couple of weeks. You got the tickets I sent, didn't you?"

It was no use being indecisive out here in the frostbitten wind. She followed him helplessly, a despair welling in her heart. What should she do? All her resolve seemed distant—a thousand miles gone. All self-confidence so remote. Really, under what circumstances could marrying Brigham Talmage be so bad? Here he was, so anxious for her to be his wife that he eloped with her without question or hesitation. Who was she to think he might be wrong? But simply because she was right for him, did that mean he was right for her? It might.

Presence of mind restored itself as she defrosted in the foyer while Brigham consulted with a sleepy-eyed Mr. Martino. Reality flashed briefly into her mind, pointing out that she stood shivering in a Las Vegas wedding chapel. To be married. By some stranger called Mr. Martino. Yuck! To marry a man she had no intention of marrying 12 hours ago. Moreover, she was wearing her work clothes from yesterday, and she hadn't brushed her teeth.

Brigham made his way back to her with a big, happy grin on his face. It was now or never: she had to break it to him now.

"Brigham. I wish I'd known this was your plan before you blew all that gasoline on carting me down here."

"It was no problem. I tried to get plane tickets, but you know how that is these days. It was much quicker to drive. And, Susannah, my dearest, dearest Susannah, tomorrow wouldn't do. It had to be today. Now." He was looking into her eyes again, darn him, kissing her hands, pulling her close. No! She squared her shoulders with all the strength she possessed.

"Brigham. This is so hard for me to say."

"Then don't say it. Save it until later. After we're man and wife. Then I'll have to listen to you because I'll be your dear and loving husband." He was making this hard for her. Those were words she'd waited 31 years to hear someone to say to her. 'Dear and loving husband.' How could he have known? Wait. This was all wrong. Well, maybe not all wrong. It was too confusing for that. But she did know it wasn't all right. She needed more time to think.

"I thought I told you I needed a few days to think about it."

"It's been a few days. This is Friday. Do you want to slip into one of the bridal gowns I had brought over for you from Saks? There are four or five to choose from. I think I know your style, or at least what I thought would look best on you. My tux is here, too."

Gowns from Saks 5th Avenue. Hmm. Susannah ought to at least see what they looked like before she totally dumped him. He did go to all the trouble, after all. Oh, what if there was a heavy silk one? She'd always wanted to be married in silk. And he was right about her parents' wanting to be there for the sealing, later. Frankly, Sister Hapsburg would be so overjoyed their daughter finally made a commitment and got married, she probably wouldn't care about an elopement to Las Vegas. Right? Brigham was now sitting beside her, close at her hip, and he pulled her long, fair hair back to whisper in her ear.

"I know this is sudden, Susannah. It's sudden for me too. I've been waiting all my life for someone like you. For you. The last few years of waiting have been torture. And when I finally discovered you, I knew exactly what I wanted and decided I'd stop at nothing." He rested his head on her shoulder but looked up into her face. "Please, hear the cry of a desperate man. Marry me. Here. Now." He rested his lips on her cheek. She felt his warm breathing and closed her eyes. A tear surprised her as it rolled down. Was there a silk dress in that lot? He pulled back, and she looked at him once again. Then light caught the ring and Susannah noticed again how utterly vast the table on the top of the stone was, how brilliantly it sparkled on her hand in the candlelight of the foyer; it cast a spell on her. Without speaking, she stood and left his side and went through the doorway labeled "Brides' Room."

When she entered, her eyes landed immediately on the dress. Her briefcase dropped to the ground as her hand clutched her neck. It was as if every other object on earth disappeared into the black, and all that remained was this single, white object: the silk dress. It hung on a brass hook on the wall in absolute splendor, knobby, raw silk, yards and yards and yards of it—and a long white train, with silk rosettes. The bodice, plain and elegant, may have been made especially for her frame. Yes, this was the dress she knew from the preexistence. She checked to see if her hands were clean and then touched it lightly. The room and its objects came back into focus, and there on the table sat a bridal bouquet of lilies and orchids. There was a card attached: "To My Lovely Wife." Brig thought of everything!

But despite all the trappings of perfection, and the enchantment of the moment, still Susannah hesitated. Marriage! Today. Today? Such a leap into the unknown. Unexpectedly, the lyrics of a hymn sang in her mind.

Lead, kindly Light . . . the night is dark
and I am far from home.

Boy, was she ever. About a thousand miles from home.

Keep thou my feet, I do not ask to see
The distant scene, One step enough for me.

Faith had guided her footsteps many times in her life, and Susannah had taken risks—steps from the light into the dark, and then it was as if a lamp lit her path. But she had to make that initial step. Every time she'd done so, however, she'd felt as if she'd been following a good, sure prompting.

This time, though, confusion reigned. One moment resolve was firm, another it was gone. She'd never been so wishy-washy in her life, at least not for a very long time. Wow—and with eternal happiness hanging in the balance. Her heart caught the line, One step enough for me. It became a prayer. Her mind and heart begged for guidance, for just one step's worth of light.

I'm here. I'm about to put on this gorgeous dress. I'm about to marry a wonderful man. If this is wrong for me, please, turn me aside from this path—and soon!

The prayer left her heart and ascended toward the heavens. She paused a moment, staring up at a small window at the top of the bridal dressing room. A ray of sun caught a glinting object. Susannah wasn't sure, but it might be—it just might be the gold leafed statue of Moroni, blowing his trump atop the Las Vegas Temple. She tried pushing a plush armchair over beneath the window, but the dragging sounded so loud that she simply plopped down into the chair instead, overcome. However, the image of the angel fixed in her mind. She closed her eyes. Beneath the image, a white marble building grew, sparkling and clean. A happy, beautiful bride and groom emerged, and the groom waved to his family and did a Toyota oh-what-a-feeling jump of joy. The unbidden mental picture made Susannah laugh, and her eyes flew open. The dingy surroundings of this lame so-called chapel of dreams accosted her. Gross! The contrast was unbearably stark!

She shuddered, and her mind's muddle, all the confusion, cleared in an instant. With a miraculously lightened heart, she gathered herself and her courage and her wits to give Brigham Talmage the final word. Yes, one step ahead glinted as bright as gold leaf and shining white marble in the morning sun.

Just then, her cell phone rang in her purse. Irritation! Why did cell phones always ring at contemplative moments, at critical junctures? Chuh! She pulled it from her briefcase in annoyance and snapped it open without even looking at the caller ID. "Hello."

"Susannah?" Mary Lucas's voice sounded far away. It was a naturally weak voice, but via cell phone, it sounded more distant than ever. "I only have a couple of minutes left on the phone card you gave me, but I needed to call you."

"You're so nice, Mary. Is something wrong? Can I help you in some way?"

"I don't think so. You've done so much. It's just—I had this overwhelming, strange idea I should call and tell you about my lawyer." Nice, thoughtful, but it seemed unnecessary for Mary to be doing this, especially considering Mary had hired such a bad lawyer, never mind the fact that Susannah's legal problems required a real estate law specialist, not some hang-out-a-shingler. Besides, she wanted to hurry up and attack her situation here while her newfound resolve shone bright.

"I don't mean I want you to hire him. In fact, you should totally cross mine off your list. I know I promised myself I wouldn't speak ill of him or anyone else, but I feel compelled to pass this on, even though it's gossip, which I hate." Time ticked away, and much as she loved Mary, Susannah hoped she'd get to her point.

"Listen closely, Susannah. I'm going to give you a lot of information. First you must know, he's not a good man. He mishandled my insurance settlement, charged unconscionable fees, which I later learned he invested in a casino scheme on the Goshute Indian Reservation in the West Desert. But there's more. My money wasn't enough. He left a file in my hospital room once when he left to take a phone call. It was tucked into a pile of documents for me to read and sign, and I read quite a bit before I realized it wasn't meant for my eyes."

"What did it say?" Susannah's heart pleaded with Mary to let this conversation happen some other time, but no.

"I shouldn't retell this, but maybe, just maybe you can stop him somehow." Mary cleared her timid throat. "The document outlined a money grabbing scheme in which he marries an heiress, gets joint use of her money, invests it all in his casino. Then he uses the casino revenues to fund a nuclear waste storage facility. Nukes! In our back yard! Do you know how dangerous that is?" Dangerous, yes. Lucrative, extremely. Bad for Utah's back yard, incalculably.

Susannah's head had been spinning for the entire conversation, and now it kicked into high gear. This blackguard should be stopped, by all means. She determined to research this out and help Mary if she could. Later.

"And here's where his black heart gets completely inky,

Susannah." Mary took a deep breath. The retelling seemed to sap her energy. "As soon as his plan is funded, he divorces the poor, unsuspecting heiress and marries some bimbo—pardon the term— he's had on the side. I saw the expense accounting. He even bought two huge, five-carat diamond rings a couple of years back to set the plan in motion." Susannah's hand felt suddenly heavy.

"What was your lawyer's name again?" she squeaked out, but Susannah already knew.

"Brigham Talmage. Oh, and I'd promised myself I wouldn't say an unkind word about anyone. But I just had to. You understand? I'm so sorry."

"Me, too." Now she could see not one but two steps in front of her—in front of her bimbo self. "I'll do what I can to help, Mary. I promise."

The silk dress hanging before her lost all its appeal. She picked up her briefcase and wandered out into the lobby. Brigham was still haggling with Mr. Martino in his charming, oily way. He held up a finger to ask her to wait a moment, then kissed it and blew it in her direction. She set her briefcase on her lap and opened it to glance through and try to focus her mind.

A large envelope inside the leather clutch caught her eye—one from the pile of bad envelopes at the Cottage of Condemnation. The return address label had John's name on it. She pulled it out and tore it open. It was a topographical map with red pen drawn through it. She'd never been much with cartography; it would take her a long time to decipher. Why was John giving her a map? As a parting gift before his wedding to the Tiny Tumbler? Oh, horrible day.

Suddenly a thick pile of papers appeared on Susannah's lap between the map and her eyes.

"Didn't any of the dresses work? I can have another set brought over post haste. Mr. Martino," he called. "Have set B brought over from the boutiques immediately. Meanwhile, my gorgeous wife, can I call you that yet? Here's the marriage license for you to sign, and a couple of other things." A couple? Here sat an entire ream of paper. "And don't ask if you need your lawyer to look them over, sweetie, because you're going to have your very own, live-in attorney starting today, and for close family I don't charge."

I'm sure you don't, babe. Susannah thumbed through the papers. She felt her mind racing. First, she was furious—furious with herself for being deceived in his character. Furious with him for hurting poor Mary. Instinct and logic taught her Mary Lucas could not have lied. Plus, she was furious with him for having such egregious faults and masking them. Why her? And who was the heiress? The poor girl must be heartbroken. Susannah boiled at the thought of being forced into the position of the "other woman." For a long moment she couldn't look at him. Part of her debated whether to confront him about it, but the precariousness of her situation, hundreds of miles from home in the hands of a man of now-unknown character, led her to choose evasive action instead.

"Brigham. It's not going to happen."

"The prenup? Oh, baby. It's natural. Everybody signs them these days." Susannah glanced down and thumbed through the stack of papers nonchalantly, knowing her pen would never touch the dotted line. She thought her eye fell briefly on the word reptile, and it made a giggle rise in her throat. If anyone here was reptilian, it was this snake BLT. Her mind was so tired it was starting to pull her leg. She wondered how that sad old reptile in her living room was faring. Did she leave him enough water?

"If you want to look them over, please do. In my business—I'm only doing it to protect you, Susannah." Protect her? But what about his sad, sobbing ex he gypped out of her fortune?

"It's not that, Brigham. I'm not worried about your devotion. What I can't sign is the marriage license. I won't be marrying you today, here. I can't do it."

"Sure you can. It's simple as 'I do' at this point. Susannah." His eyes and voice plead with her. "Susannah, I need you."

She felt for him, much more than she'd expected to feel. Into her mind flashed a hundred memories of tennis and hot air balloons and dinners and kisses. It wrenched her to know she had come this close to marriage, at last, but that she'd come so close to marrying someone who had so much to hide.

"Susannah, come on. We're here. You've got the dress, the flowers, the ring. And I'm offering you everything here. Putting it all on the line for you. Do you know how often I've done that? Without you, I'm—I'm nothing."

A few minutes ago she might have seen his pleading eyes, his wide, persuasive smile and crumbled. But with the image of the trumpeting Angel Moroni fixed in her mind, and the knowledge of his true character, she knew her own mind, at last, and would not be moved.

"Brig, I wish I could. I can't." Simple. Simply put. She squeezed his hand, kissed his cheek and rose to go. Simultaneously, a bit of anger rose in that cheek of his.

"Don't do this, Susannah. Don't."

Her cell phone rang. Oh! Those cursed things! Her eye could see the caller ID light glowing down inside her briefcase. It was Ian's cell number. Something had to be wrong. Carly's husband never called.

"Susannah. Thank goodness! Where are you? You're not at work, you're not at home. Carly's having the baby. She needs you. The kids do. How quickly can you get here?"

"Taxi! Airport, please." She hustled out the door and climbed into a cold yellow Buick. "Good-bye, Brigham." She tossed him his 'grandmother's' ring. "I won't ever forget you." As she rolled down the desert highway, a shaft of light shot out of the cloudy morning sky and illuminated the road before her.

CHOCOLATE ZUCCHINI CAKE

2½ cups flour
½ cup cocoa
2½ teaspoons baking powder
1½ teaspoons soda
1 teaspoon salt
1 teaspoon cinnamon
¾ cup butter
2 cups sugar
2 teaspoons vanilla
2 teaspoons grated orange peel
2 cups grated zucchini
½ cup milk
1 cup chopped pecans

Combine dry ingredients. Set aside. Cream butter and sugar; add eggs one at a time and beat well. Stir in vanilla, orange peel, and zucchini. Alternate adding dry ingredients and milk. Bake at 350 degrees for 1 hour or until firm in center. Count it as a vegetable when you strive for five.

Chocolate-Caramel Turtles

Far superior to the stale nut concoctions available at the Christmastime drugstore, you can even snitch the creamy caramel while you drizzle chocolate over these giant pecan, classic turtle delights at home.

"Okay, kids. You can feed him a piece of lettuce, but no more riding on his back. He's a grandpa. A great-great-great grandpa."

Carly's kids were fascinated with Beagle and stared at him for the entire afternoon. "Let's name mommy's baby Turtle!"

"But she's a girl, Poppy," Perry reminded his littlest sister—correction, his second littlest sister. "Mom said she's calling her Pepper Susannah, and I like that better."

Between phone calls from Ian and Colette during her plane ride, she didn't have a moment's peace to decipher the map from John, and it had only barely registered on her emotional Richter scale with all the events of the previous night and morning. A pang of guilt and sadness at lost love, even lost bad love, spun through her mind between rings.

The café depended on three workers running it on Saturdays—this was the first time since it opened that one of them had flaked out on their busiest morning. Colette was having a conniption fit about it. She'd been so emotional about stuff lately—it was strange.

Now as Susannah sat in her living room, surrounded by little cuties and watching her giant heritage pet chew yet another stalk of celery, she relaxed and let herself breathe freely. Her mind was even beginning to clear a bit as she thumbed through the mess she called a briefcase, looking for Beagle's paperwork, when her eye fell on the map from John. She pulled it out and peered more closely at it. North East Quadrant, Salt Lake City, Utah. After a good, hard stare, Susannah finally made out the location of the topography. Yes, there was the State Capitol. There were the hills nearby, and the Avenues, the downtown area. Red pen traced a crooked path down the foothills and through Temple Square. She could just make out the street where her cottage sat, slightly off to the left of the line, and the location of The Chocolate Bar—directly bisected by red. And the line meant . . . her eyes scanned the page heading. Major Fault Line Depiction, Downtown Salt Lake City Area, North.

Fault lines—her café sat atop a major fault line! Her eyes now found the scrawled subheading, *Prediction of catastrophic destruction within one block radius of line in the event of a 5.1 or higher magnitude quake. Moderate to major damage to areas beyond.*

She tried to digest the various implications of it, and instinct told her there were both good and bad. However, her attention was suddenly diverted once again, this time by the bridal shower announcement for Camie Kimball. Lucky girl, she thought. Lucky Little Olympian. Her former Beehive had no idea what a gold medal she was earning for herself in John Wentworth. In a flash of empowering forgiveness, she pulled the square, pink envelope forth and ripped it open.

"You are cordially invited to a bridal shower for Camie Kimball, the future Mrs. Blake Townsend, at 6:00 p.m., Friday, 29 December, at Camie's mother's home."

Blake Townsend! Camie was marrying Blake Townsend! Whoever he was, Susannah loved him, loved him, loved him! She went outside to whoop for joy (so as not to disturb the sleeping Beagle and Poppy) while the snow fell thick on Peter's newly cleared sidewalk. Camie Kimball Townsend, congratulations to you!

Monday morning she returned the children to their parents' house, and she dragged herself back into the café. It felt like she'd been gone a hundred years, Rip Van Winkeling it, and everything on Earth had changed. Trevor and Colette's eyes bulged upon hearing about Beagle.

"You mean you have a giant turtle living at your parents' home?"

"Tortoise. Galapagos tortoise."

'So that's where you've been for the past three days? I never figured you for a pet girl."

"Or a reptile girl."

"Definitely not a reptile girl. I should make a batch of Chocolate Caramel Turtles in your honor."

"Yes, that's where I've been. Force-feeding him lettuce leaves, trying to get him to walk around for his daily exercise. You'd be surprised how hard it is to get a tortoise to take a walk." Susannah shook her weary head. Babysitting both tortoise and Carly's kids was turning her into a total wreck.

"It's in your parents' house. Is that a familiar environment? Maybe he's stressed."

"Well, it can't move into my frozen haunted mansion on A Street, and I'm not moving myself out to Magna, or wherever, in order to live with Beagle at Beagle Gate."

"What's that?"

"I don't know yet. But it's where the blasted thing has been living with Mr. Harville. Smacks of Ligertown. I need to go check it out sometime, figure out what exactly a tortoise playground entails and where it all is, but I don't dare leave old wrinkle-fest alone. He's too . . . valuable. And then there are the vet bills."

"For what? And how are you paying for all this?"

"Toenail care. And there's a trust fund. As Beagle's caretaker, I'm the main trustee. And that's another thing, I have no idea whether the pot of cash is a bottomless pit, or if we're nearing the end of the funding. So many things to do. No wonder I've never kept pets! I should have hired a babysitter for him today, but I couldn't find one. I think he'll be okay. I put a grandkid gate up in front of the basement stairs."

"We have to know. Have you had to clean up after him?"

"Look, don't make this worse than it is. Wait. It can't get worse. I am now the caretaker of a priceless, zillion-ton hunk of wrinkly, warty skin. And he smells. Aged reptiles—they need to be outside. It's too awful. Let's not talk about it anymore. Did anyone call me?"

"John Wentworth. He said something about your safe being open and ready to pick up. And the lady from the City Office of Development, Parking Garages and Eating Establishment Destruction called as a 'courtesy' to remind you about Thursday night's meeting."

Oh, mercy. Merciful heavens. Was the meeting this week already? Her presentation! She had absolutely no ammo. The place might as well be toppled by an earthquake today if a parking garage was going to squish it next summer anyway.

Wait. An earthquake?

"Forgive me, gang. I'll be right back. I have to check something." She ran to her office and dug through her briefcase, then returned, map in hand. "Okay, folks. I think this is it, our silver bullet." Susannah waved the topographical map in the air. Colette and the mid-day customers dropped their present conversations to listen. "See this?" She pointed out the squiggly lines and the big, bad fault, as well as its excellent implications. "This means, no parking garage!" Salt Lake citizens would surely deem it unconscionable to build a giant, six-story parking facility on a major fault line.

"Oh, hurrah! It looks like you didn't need a lawyer after all," chirped a relieved dessert eater, who unwittingly hit the nail on the head.

Susannah clutched the paper to her chest in relief, joy, not even caring that her own restaurant sat atop a fault. In bliss, she thumbed through the attached documents. The first paper summarized a study on earthquake damage estimates. The second was a CC of a letter to someone called Ty Sparks.

Dear Mr. Sparks:
Thank you again for meeting with me at Solitude Ski Resort last November 30th. Here are the earthquake-related documents you

*requested. I hope they make your job, and the whole board's job, easier
in this decision. I think the information speaks for itself. Best wishes.*
    John Wentworth
    CC: Susannah Hapsburg

Solitude. Susannah and Brig and John were all at Solitude that
night. John, John Wentworth, the wonderful John Wentworth of her
past, present, and (maybe) her future, with his earthquake expertise
had personally met with Ty Sparks of the planning board, armed
with geological facts and engineered her restaurant's miraculous
save! John had done all the work. The silver bullet had been fired
nearly a month ago into the heart of the whole dastardly, dessert-
bar-crushing scheme. She didn't even need to present information
tonight. Wa-hoo! Oh, how she loved this man, this man who was
not engaged to Camie Kimball. A vision of his face formed in her
mind, surrounded by flitting butterflies and sugar plum fairies and
rose petals.

She dialed to return the call to the woman at the city office, who
reported that the issue had been stricken from the agenda. A tear of
relief welled in Susannah's eye. Then a disturbing thought entered
her tortured mind. In spite of the unengaged state of her dragon-
slaying man, nothing in what she'd heard from him in person ought
to lead her to believe his lack of proposal to Camie implied an
impending offer to herself. There was no reason to assume a wacky
inverse of 'he loves me he loves me not,' in the form of 'he loves her
not, he loves me.' All this rescue work, in truth, may be nothing
more than any faithful home teacher might do for his charge. Last
time he saw her, on that fateful, snowy Solitude night, she'd faded
out of his life again into the wicked Brigham Talmage's arms. The
thought made her shudder, and a vision of her own face appeared
in her head surrounded by flitting bats with long fangs. Her entire
existence felt like Halloween sometimes.

Colette knocked on the office door. "Ooh. Why do you look
like that? Yipes. Hey, I'm off to my appointment. It's mandatory,
so if you have to leave for some reason, don't think twice. Just flip
the 'Closed' sign over and go. You know Trev can't handle this place

alone. He'd freak out. Oh, look, Suze. There's a note on the back of those papers. Did you see it?"

Susannah flipped it over to see the scrawl of John's red pen.

Susannah,
If you need a friend at the meeting, I have a few charts and some posters I can show the board. A six-story parking garage is clearly too big a risk to the liability insurance of the city. They'll see that, no doubt. What time is the meeting? Call me.
Love, John (your faithful home teacher)

Love . . . John. Does he really mean he loves me?

With Colette gone, Susannah gained a huge appreciation for her friend's industrious care of the shop. People demanded attention every single second, particularly with the Christmas season upon them. Wrapping truffles in foil boxes took more dexterity than Susannah had conjured up in years. Everyone wanted three times as many orders, and in five times as many varieties. One woman alone ordered eleven cheesecakes for next week: pumpkin, peppermint, orange, Oreo, raspberry truffle, turtle (ironically), sour cream, and four plain with chocolate crumb crust. Trevor would be up all night solely for her.

The regular Monday ladies came in, and Susannah tried to follow their chatty stories between pouring cocoa and passing out more peppermint swizzle sticks, but in truth, her own thoughts continually raced off to John, the man who saved the café, who loved her. Maybe.

Jackie came in at her usual time, but made a stop in the kitchen to give Trevor a huge hug before coming out to pick up her daily special.

"Susannah, you look positively glowing! Did you get a nice Christmas gift? Did someone die and leave you a million dollars?"

"A Galapagos tortoise instead."

"Oh. And thus you glow? You're an odd one, Susannah." Jackie took a big, blissful bite of Almond Chocolate Mousse. "Come on. Tell. You're in love. We missed you Friday. News? Please."

Susannah realized she possessed no solid information to share, only a hunch, so instead she gave the good news about the café's rescue to the afternoon crowd.

"Oh, that's wonderful. Your lawyer didn't pull that off for you, did he?"

"No, indeed. My disaster management consultant did."

"I'd like to pull off my lawyer." Ingrid bustled in, arms loaded with Christmas packages, and elbowed in to a spot at the bar. No ponytail on this frosty day, she wore her blonde locks down, covering her ears. A huge frown covered her taut face.

"What's the matter?" Susannah asked after she attended to some truffle-case droolers. It made her recall a story in the newspaper that said simply looking at chocolate triggered the same centers in the brain as drug addiction. "Where's your ring, Ingrid?"

"Done. Gone. Over. I'd rather kill him than wear it."

It took some doing, but Susannah used a few Colette techniques to ease it out of her.

"I've had the worst weekend. I had to dump my fiancé. I found out he was stranger than a simple reptile poison freak." That was a tall order. "When I told him to hit the road with his big fat ring he got mad and started debating with me. Do you know how hard it is to win a debate with a lawyer?"

"I do. They can be very persuasive." She never knew Ingrid's fiancé was a lawyer, too.

"Well, when I found out just how weird he was, that he claimed he was going to marry a poor unsuspecting girl and then kill her turtle just to get its money, I realized enough was enough. Sayonara, buddy. Don't forget to take your medication." And then she made a cuckoo, cuckoo noise and drew an air circle near her temple. "I don't care if Brigham Talmage is the top lawyer in the state, I've wasted way too much time on that louse. He can keep his aerobics club. I'll keep working out at good old LA Fitness. So, can you see why I need three Absolutely Deep Dark Chocolate Fudge Cookies today?"

"I can." Susannah really could see! In fact, Susannah took one for herself. If she'd had time to think for even a second between demands—but they don't call it the Christmas rush for nothing. Susannah's heart rate rushed mercilessly, as did her short-term memory banks for orders and prices and gift wrapping. Her mind cried out for mercy. No wonder Colette had been cell phone maniac the other morning.

A while later, things suddenly slowed down, and Colette returned, looking much brighter-faced than she had in some time. The afternoon off did her a world of good.

"You look great, Colette. Nice day off? You and Blaine hit the Market Street Grill for their Christmas snow crab?"

"Better. We hit the OB clinic." A gargantuan smile spread across her happy face. Susannah's eyes grew large as cocoa saucers. "Yes! It's true! We heard the heartbeat today."

Susannah erupted in a fit of joy and the two embraced until they dissolved in happy tears.

"Oh, Colette! This is the best news ever! Better than The Chocolate Bar being saved, better than my dumping Brigham Talmage, better than Ingrid dumping him, better than John not being engaged to Camie Kimball, better than everything ever!"

Then Susannah had a lot of explaining to do, but only briefly before customers demanded their attention. After a bit, they were able to get a word in sideways.

"I guess he forgot about the 'natural causes' clause in the trustee provisions."

"Who knows. Wicked people forget all kinds of things," Susannah replied carelessly. "He qualifies as one of the most schemingly wicked, dastardly devils I've come across."

"Do you realize? This makes you the heiress."

Hmm. But if she was the heiress, Beagle was the legacy; Mr. Udall said the animal's trust fund had been depleted when Mr. Harville built Turtle Land, or whatever. Why on earth would her so-called inheritance be of interest to the villainous Brigham Talmage? It wasn't like Beagle could be sold off for cash. Who would buy it? Her financial instincts told her the "Tortoise-Collecting Wealthy Eccentric" niche was impossibly small.

Susannah scrubbed plates and platters, spoons and serving

trays, and wished once again for a remedy for dishpan hands. Skin flaked up in little pointy shards on her palms. The "Closed" sign mercifully flipped around and she, Colette, and Trevor could finally breathe again, and visit.

"Susannah! You missed it!" Colette giggled as they gathered in the kitchen. "Sasha breezed in here all pinch-faced and superior to announce she'd washed that man Barclay Barnes right out of her hair last week, and, she hoped you wouldn't mind, but since you didn't need him anymore, she thought Brigham Talmage appeared to be fair game. They have a date tonight." Colette couldn't suppress her guffaws and snorts.

"I don't know which one to feel sorrier for!" Susannah joined her. "Enough about them. So! Tell me. How far along are you?"

"We won't know for sure until they do a sonogram, but the doctor thought fourteen weeks. I'm almost past the sick stage, almost out of the woods for miscarriage, he says."

"Did he want you to take it easy? If you have to quit, I totally understand. Believe me, I know your baby is waaaay more important than dessert." Susannah dried a spatula and set it in the drawer beside its hundred brothers.

"She said no. In fact, it surprised me, but she said I should keep going so I stay active, that the exercise would do me good. If things get iffy, she'll tell me to slow down. She did, however, suggest an afternoon nap. I hope that's okay. My baby needs me."

"It's marvelous. Absolutely wonderful. You nap away, dollface." Susannah loved love, and she loved seeing her dear friend begin to love a baby of her own at last.

"So! Wow! John Wentworth isn't engaged to Camie Kimball. That's fabulous, utterly fabulous. Did he call you again about the safe? Oh. You didn't call him back, did you?"

Susannah's heart dropped into the pit of her stomach. If ever a person deserved a return phone call, a call of sheer, gushing gratitude, it was John Wentworth.

"Did he leave a number when he phoned about the safe?" Susannah called over her shoulder as she whisked toward her office, where her telephone was already ringing. John?

"Susannah?" Not John. Ian, her brother-in-law. "I'm at your folks' house—I came to bring the kids some lunch and Poppy's favorite blankie that she forgot. Uh, what's this big dead thing in the living room?"

It took roughly twenty minutes to get from the closed Chocolate Bar to Sugarhouse in light traffic. Today, Susannah made it in nine flat. Screaming the entire way.

I haven't even had that thing for two weeks! And it's dead! Dead! Her screams re-echoed in her chasm of a head. She hadn't gone through all the paperwork related to owning a giant tortoise. She didn't even know where it rightfully lived. Oh! Beagle knew he was unloved and unwanted, and he gave up the ghost. Her heart wrenched at the thought.

She tore into the living room to where she'd created Beagle's makeshift pen with squared-up couch cushions. Perry, Piper, Polly, and Poppy all sat in a somber circle around the animal, 12-year-old Piper sniffling. Susannah had let them come over and pet sit Beagle today to get them out of Carly's hair, since they were all home on Christmas break.

"We'd just finished letting Beagle give little Poppy a ride," Perry reported, jaw steeled. "She loved it, and he looked like he was happy, too."

"Yeah," ten-year-old Polly chimed, "he looked real happy. Poppy fed him a piece of lettuce. He liked it." She hiccuped and pulled Poppy, who was hugging the blankie, onto her lap.

"I'm so glad you let us watch him today. So he wasn't alone when—" Piper stroked the animal's head. Beagle's eyes were closed, his head resting lightly to one side, a half-eaten leaf of lettuce near his front hoof, or foot, or whatever. It was a sad but peaceful sight. He looked like he was at rest. It comforted Susannah somewhat.

"I only knew him for a few days, Aunt Zannie," Polly sniffed. "But I loved him. A lot. He was a good old grandpa."

"I think he loved us back." Perry showed he was trying to be the strong, sensible one. Susannah agreed. Beagle did look happy when he'd been with her nieces and nephews.

"What were you doing with a big turtle, anyway?" Ian was there. She almost forgot.

"Tortoise. He was a Galapagos tortoise, Dad." Polly's voice caught. "Beagle."

"Beagle? I thought a beagle was a dog. Like Snoopy." Ian coughed.

"So did I." Susannah folded her arms reverently. At those words, Piper began crying her 12-year-old eyes out again. Poor kids. They really loved the old codger.

"That's a major pet store error, sis." Ian gave each of the children a big dad-hug and began shepherding them out to the car. "But with him dead and all, I don't see how you can get your money back now."

Money back? Money? Oh, dear. The money. This made her feel shameful all over again. What would the attorneys and veterinarians think at this sudden turn of events? Where was that number Udall gave her "in the event of Beagle's death?" She fumbled in her purse and dialed.

"Hapsburg? But Beagle, our favorite patient here at the clinic, belongs to a Mr. Harville. Are you sure we're talking about the same animal?"

"I'm sure." She finally convinced them she was Beagle's humble owner, and they agreed to begin . . . proceedings.

"Proceedings? What kind of proceedings?"

"Well, we'll have to call in a certified herpetologist, of course, for the veterinary autopsy." Veterinary autopsy! "And the closest one I'm aware of is on the Oregon coast. We'll have to fly him in. I'll contact him immediately. The animal, as you surely know, must remain in place until it can be seen by the pet coroner as well as, let's see, Dr. Vosco. Will that be convenient?"

"He's in my living room."

"Well, Miss Hapsburg, don't plan any dinner parties."

The next two days passed in a swirling mass of confusion and lawyers. She never would have believed so many lawyers could care that a reptile was dead. As she sat in her parents' kitchen with her head in her hands, the phone rang yet again. Drat! The word was out! Reporters would be calling about the dead tortoise scandal. In trepidation she lifted the receiver.

"Susannah?" It was a very crackly connection. "It's John. I wondered if I could come by. Are you free?"

In a barrage of unintelligible blurts, she attempted to explain the situation.

"Look, Suzie. We're adults. If you don't want to see me, just say so. There's no need to invent wild stories."

"Really, John. There's a dead Galapagos tortoise that once belonged to Charles Darwin in my living room, and a lawyer and a veterinary coroner are on their way here now to remove it. A certified tortologist is currently on a flight here from Oregon to perform the autopsy." Panic crept into her voice, but John didn't seem fazed.

"Don't you mean herpetologist?" He said this as though her mislabeling of the scientist was evidence of her being caught in her own web of lies.

"Oh, probably, but hey. Don't confuse me with the facts. Besides, I can't stand to say the real word. It makes me think of an icky disease."

"Susannah, things are never simple with you, are they?"

"No, John, they aren't."

He softened at the contrite tone of her voice. "I guess I ought to give you the benefit of the doubt, eh? Could you use some help? Or some company?"

"Really? Oh, yeah." Her sigh was heavy with relief. "I could."

John arrived at her door shortly, and after paying brief respects to the deceased, helped her on with her warmest coat. "Can we go for a drive? To see the lights?"

Christmas lights on the house across the street flashed gold and green, and Susannah wished she had time to decorate for the season. Maybe John could help her choose a little Christmas tree for her big, lonely, unfestive house, which he now led her away from in the snow.

"Oh, before we go, do you want to see what's in your safe? I have it right here." John opened the back door of his Jeep Cherokee where the rusty old safe sat on the back seat in, hilariously, a seat belt. "Can't be too cautious in case of a rear-end collision, eh?" This ought to be good, she thought as she climbed in beside it and cracked the safe's rusty door open.

"Just so you know, I didn't peek."

"Of course you didn't." She smiled up at him. His eye twinkled. Snowflakes fell, and one stayed on his eyelashes. He double-blinked to shake it off. Susannah had to shake herself to stay on task. His cool, clear, confident eyes sought deeper into her own than they had since the jungle. Perhaps more deeply.

The handle had been cleaned by whomever John found to crack the lock, but the hinges were so rusted it took great force to pry the door far enough open to reach her hand in. When it began to look hopeless, John stepped in and gave it a hard yank. Dust came out, but no spiders, thank goodness. Susannah reached her hand in, bravely, and pulled out a small stack of cash.

"Look! We're rich! Confederate $50 bills."

"You're kidding." Maybe this was the community property Brigham was trying to get his hands on by marrying her so quickly. If she'd come into it before their marriage, he could have had no control over it, could never have converted it into nuclear waste. Relief filled her again.

"Yes. Kidding. They're only a stack of twenties from, let's see, 1956." She flipped through and counted them, estimating their value. "Maybe $1000 here. Not bad."

"That ought to cover the cost of the locksmith and the shipping. Barely. What else is in there, Suzie?"

She liked that he called her Suzie. It made her feel young and sweet. "Some papers."

"Let me see." He took them and held them under his keychain flashlight for examination. "You won't believe it." He handed them to her.

"Stock certificates! Wow!" She'd heard of ancient stock certificates being worth a ton of money. Maybe she could sell them and finally fix her poor condemned house!

"Look closer."

"Pointman Westerford? Aw!" Worthless. Worth a fortune 15 months ago. Now not worth the paper they were printed on. Possibly less. She shook her head in dismay. "Big, bad old PW strikes again."

He laughed with her at the irony and sat down in the driver's seat, and she paused briefly before climbing in, tempted to take the center of the bench and nestle in next to him, but she didn't quite dare. She wanted to believe he felt for her what she felt for him, but everything was old and new at once. Taking liberties with his feelings looked like a risk.

"Oh, that passenger seat is wet from the snow falling on it. I should have closed the door. Do you mind sitting in the middle?"

Not at all. And they tooled off lazily through the snow to see the lights. The Capitol served as their beacon, illuminated white marble high on Capitol Hill. Any northbound street could eventually take them there. John didn't bother with the freeway, the main arteries, or the stress of finding the shortest route. Susannah relaxed in his comfortable company.

Susannah looked at his hand as it rested on the gearshift. A rough hand. A hand that had accomplished much good. A hand that knew how to build things, how to fix things. John glanced over, saw her staring at his hand, and took the hint. It felt right as it closed around her fingers, scratchy and cracked against her own dishpan hand, a good fit. She hoped he would meander for hours.

"Are you hungry? I can make you a home-cooked meal," John offered. She nodded. That sounded wonderful.

John continued making his way north, past the stunning glory of the Christmas lights on Temple Square, the beauty of which never ceased to astound her. Up Capitol Hill, but not to her Avenues house. Instead they made a left and circled over and down to the Marmalade District to John's, a cozy 1930s-era Craftsman style home with a large front porch and a narrow one-car garage. They pulled into the narrow drive. It had a similar feel to Susannah's fixer-upper, but without the apparent dangerous flaws. Inside, the remodeling process appeared to still be underway, but the finished living room and kitchen were bright and airy, the furniture vintage, sparse and comfortable. She loved the one bold rust-orange wall in the sitting room. Susannah found herself relaxing almost immediately.

From the kitchen he carried on a conversation with her—about crab fishing and his ship and crustaceans and home renovation and the power of ice. She told him her sad news about the condemned property she owned. He expressed condolences and said he felt a connection to that place, too, having spent a few dozen hours in its behalf himself. She broke the very good news about the café's rescue; internally she debated hard about whether to go give him a giant hug of gratitude. Half an hour later, she sat curled up on an easy chair with a steaming bowl of home-cooked Kraft Macaroni and Cheese. "Nostalgic, John. Very."

"Mac 'n' cheese? You still like it?" He carried his own bowl and sat down on a sofa near her easy chair and began eating with a large spoon. Their bowls and silverware were mismatched, and she found it charming.

"You remembered?"

"Suzie. There have been days when I wished I could forget a single word you ever said to me, but I can't." He shrugged helplessly and kept his eyes fixed on her face until she felt warm.

"You don't know how many times I've thought the same thing about you." She dipped her eyes so he couldn't see the emotion filling them. He took her twice-emptied bowl away and pulled her by the hand over onto the couch beside him.

"So, do you want to see my pictures of CHOICE? I was on an amateur photographer kick that year and took dozens of rolls of film. Some of them turned out quite good," he said as he lifted the lid of his storage chest coffee table and pulled out a bulging photo album.

She nestled easily under his arm, smelled his weather-beaten skin and strolled down memory lane. Good memories—the purple mountains, the villagers, a few of the other volunteers, but mostly the waterfall. The waterfall. Where John sang to her in his resonant baritone voice, "Longer." *Stronger than any mountain cathedral, Truer than any tree ever grew, Deeper than any mountain cathedral, I am in love with you.* Susannah had reciprocated the confession.

At the recollection, at its distance in the deep past, at the loss, at the possibility of regaining it, Susannah found her breath catching in her throat and tears welling up in her eyes. Could it still work for them? Had it been too long? Was there any way to beg for another chance? Here, in his cozy home, under his strong, weathered arm, with his even breath beside her, and then his lips on hers, nothing could feel more like a second chance.

♡ ♡ ♡

The next day, the day of the tortoise inquest, Susannah left the Christmas rush of work early to make it in time for the meeting with the doctors and dreaded lawyers. Traffic was light, so she took a detour via Barbara Russell's house. The lights were all ablaze, so Susannah went in. The house smelled of wassail and fudge and caramel. Christmas.

The winter sun's light glinted off the snow and slanted in through the slats of the vertical blinds in Barbara's walk-out basement.

"Do you remember," Susannah asked as she sipped her iced lemon water, "when I came back from Guatemala, and we were walking Brutus, and I talked to you about that guy I met and liked down there."

"John Wentworth? Sure. I heard he's back in town again. I saw his mother with him at the temple one morning." Barbara set down her bowl of the Deep Cocoa Ginger Trifle Susannah brought on her lap with interest. "Didn't you rule him out? I thought he wasn't your type."

"Turns out he was."

"All along?" Barbara's eyes grew wide in surprise as Susannah shrugged, chewing her own bite of the warm, spicy dessert. Barbara took another thoughtful bite and continued, "Susannah. Please don't tell me anything I said during that conversation influenced you against him, especially if he was your type all along."

"Oh, no, Barbara. No. In fact, I think I probably only shared my worries, and not my joys. I remember telling you I didn't know him very well."

"Susannah, every woman marries a stranger. There is no possible way for a woman to understand a man well enough prior to marriage to say she knows him—at all. Then she spends the rest of her life being either pleasantly or unpleasantly surprised. I lucked out. Walter was a very pleasant surprise. I look forward to getting to know him better on the other side."

Susannah thought she had an inkling of understanding of Barbara's long separation from her true love, and hope of a reunion. She hoped it would be as sweet as her own with John was proving to be.

"So, no. Don't worry that you influenced me against him. I made up my own mind to let him go. In retrospect, I think I needed Austria, I needed PW, I needed the chocolate shop experiences to prepare me to fully appreciate this man. And maybe for him to appreciate me—I've grown a lot since he first met me, in the last year, actually. Perhaps it's better for both of us. He had his own adventure in the Great White North," and she related to Barbara a few vignettes.

As Susannah meandered toward Sugarhouse, it occurred to her how far off her impression of Barbara's advice regarding John had been—for years; and how glad she was of Barbara's approval of her decision now. Perhaps Susannah didn't actually need it, but she liked to have it just the same.

At home, she changed into one of her Pointman Westerford business suits for the meeting with the lawyers and doctors. A short time later, John arrived to accompany her. At the door he gave her a long, approving look. She still couldn't read his clear eyes. Maybe with time . . . She invited him in for a home cooked meal of a peanut butter sandwich and a glass of milk. They shared it at the kitchen table, sitting beside each other, close. Everything felt cool and comfortable and natural, despite the fact that her heart beat wildly. Nevertheless, a few things needed to be cleared up. She trembled to speak them, but her conscience insisted, so after clearing the paper towels and loading the cups in the dishwasher, she ventured to speak.

"John. Look. I know I've been awful to you."

"By? By dating that heathen Talmage?"

"Oh, that guy's as ancient history as my turtle. I meant for being so unkind to you. For wasting years of my life and yours—when we could have been happy together."

"Susannah, please—" He lifted her up and sat her on the kitchen counter to look directly into her face. "You probably know that I came back from Alaska planning to find a girl and get married. To be honest, I promised myself I'd be content to get hitched to pretty much any faithful young lady—except you. I knew you were still single. My mom would have reported if you'd married. But I'd been mad for a long time, and I wasn't ready to let go of it."

"I'm so sor—"

He placed a finger on her lip to shush her and moved a little closer.

"But, after basically getting Shanghaied into being your home teacher, I gave myself an ultimatum. I knew I couldn't ever truly love you or anybody else if I couldn't fully forgive. I had to forgive you in order to move on. I knew it." His confessional was stinging Susannah's soul, but his hands rested softly on her hips, and her heart hungered to hear the truth, painful or not.

"When I got to know you in Guatemala, I determined you were far and away the finest girl I'd ever laid eyes on, the first and only I'd ever opened my soul to. It pained me to come back from Alaska and see what I thought was such a ruin come over you. Remember my confusion about Guido and the bar and all? There I was, your home teacher. At first I felt really bad for you. Strange, but the pity opened the door a crack. Then I talked to you. That night at the closet door. You were so real, and so much the same amazing girl I'd fallen for, with the same goodness and courage that never left my soul in all my years up north. I found myself re-fascinated with your energy, your wit, your outlook on life. It killed me to watch my resolve not to fall for you, well, fall apart. I felt myself not caring if you owned a bar and wished I could spend every minute with you. And when I was with you it felt like I'd never left you behind." He pulled in closer to her and searched her whole face with his eyes. "I was helpless when it came to you.

Couldn't you see it?"

"I wish. It would have made things a lot less complicated."

"Then I heard—and saw—you were dating that money-grubbing lout Brigham Talmage. Did I ever tell you how badly he screwed up my father's will? Now, there's someone I'll be a long time learning to forgive! I went berserk. I didn't allow myself to think I could have you, but I was darn sure he couldn't. No way. That's when I acted like such a jerk at the concert."

"No, I was the jerk."

"No, I was. My poor date. She had never heard of the performer, anyway, so I guess it didn't matter."

"Before her time."

"Yeah." He held her hand briefly to his cool lip and then to his rough, whiskered cheek.

"That night was horrid. I'm afraid I'll never be able to listen to Peter Brienholt again. I'm mad at that jerk Talmage for quite a few things, but most of all for spoiling Peter for me." The one bright memory was when Peter covered "Longer," the song John had sung by the waterfall.

"Oh, not forever, Susannah. Peter's all right. I mean, seeing you kiss Talmage accomplished a few things—like, I knew I wasn't over you because it made me so jealous I couldn't stay in the same room with the two of you. And," he smiled, "something told me the reason you did it was because you were angry."

"And that was a good thing?" Susannah wasn't ready to admit he'd pinpointed her motivation, even though it amused her to know he'd seen right through her.

"Well, if you were angry, it meant there was some feeling in your heart for me—you hadn't shut me out completely. The opposite of love isn't hate, it's apathy. And if you felt something toward me at all, I had reason to hope." He leaned in close. "Susannah, what I'm trying to say is this—you are still the most accomplished, beautiful, vivacious woman I know. I've grown and changed some in the eleven years since I first loved you. You have, too, no question. I'm not sure it wasn't for the best that we each had time to grow alone before we came back together."

She rested her head on his shoulder in relief. "Thanks for being with me tonight."

"Of course." He pulled back and grinned. "Naturally, I did intend to get my home teaching visits done before the holidays. People leave town, you know."

"Not me. I've got a tortoise inquest to attend." She patted him on the shoulders and jumped down. "Let's get going." She followed him out to his jeep lighter of step than she'd felt in a decade. More.

"We were beginning to think you were uninterested in the results of the autopsy." Holiday traffic, as well as the starry-eyed irresponsibility of being in love, prevented John and Susannah's timely arrival, but they spared Udall the details of an excuse.

"If the results had come back in any kind of murky fashion, I might have taken your lateness as an indication of guilt." Udall eyed Susannah skeptically. "However, I am pleased to report that Beagle, may he rest in peace,"—at that Susannah couldn't prevent her mind from wishing Beagle the blissful option of resting in peas—"died of natural causes due to advanced age."

"How advanced?" John, always practical, inquired.

"To the best of our knowledge, the herpetologist and the veterinary coroner were able to ascertain that Beagle had reached the ripe old age of 186."

"One hundred eighty-six! You've got to be kidding," Susannah gasped in surprise as her pen clattered to the ground.

"Not at all. This tends to confirm the authenticity of the paperwork accompanying the heritage pet, that he, indeed, may have once been the property of Charles Darwin." Udall shot them a satisfied look, one of hopes realized.

"Exactly how do you go about determining the age of a dead turtle? Count its rings?" She had to know.

"Tortoise," Udall corrected. "And it is something along those lines. Each year, each knob on the shell gains another stripe around it. The older the animal, the tinier the lines, which made age determination nearly impossible until recent advances in microscopy."

"I see." John nodded. "I'm glad there was no foul play involved in Beagle's death."

"So is your girl." The title fell on her like dappling shade on a hot summer's day.

"Why do you say that?"

"Because, as Beagle's final caretaker, Susannah Hapsburg becomes the sole inheritor of the remainder of Beagle's trust fund. It was, of course, depleted somewhat by the construction of Beagle Gate by Mr. Harville, but as heir of that property as well, I'm sure you won't mind too much."

Visions of trailer parks danced in Susannah's head, but she shoved them aside.

"If it doesn't suit you, Miss Hapsburg, you can always dispose of it through sale or donation."

"Thank you very much, Mr. Udall. Can you give us a ballpark of what the amount remaining in trust is?" she asked.

"It's in the paperwork I gave you at the will reading, but perhaps you've been engrossed in caring for the animal and, then, in mourning his loss." That didn't exactly fit her activities or state of mind, but she didn't bother to correct him. "Let's see." Udall pulled out a leather-bound folder and ran his finger down a column. "It appears, before funeral expenses and the accompanying medical and professional bills," it looked like he was doing some math in his head, "that the remainder is in the ballpark of $374 million."

The sound of the sum's enormity reverberated in the air. Susannah's straight, professional posture collapsed, and she swallowed hard. John, too, sat in stunned silence for a long moment. Eventually he cleared his throat and offered the observation, "Wow. Beagle could have lived very well for another 186 years on that."

"Dined on the finest butter lettuce money could buy." Udall's voice was droll. "That's of course in addition to the structures and grounds at Beagle Gate. Those must still be appraised."

"And you say Susannah now controls those funds?" It was a good thing John was there to speak for her, because Susannah was rendered utterly mute.

"Yes. And, lucky for her, inheritance taxes don't even go into effect due to Beagle's being, as you know, an animal. It was very smart of Mr. Harville to set things up in that fashion. Wise financier, Mr. Harville. At least in his younger days. Got tripped up by the DNA skin care Internet market, I hear."

Susannah nodded dully. She was the tax-free heiress of a third of a billion dollars and a dead tortoise. It couldn't be real. In her days at Pointman Westerford, she'd crunched numbers that big for international mergers, so she knew what $374 million could buy.

"The only thing that remains is to decide where to bury the old boy. May I make a suggestion or two?" Certainly Udall may. "Beagle lived a quiet and unassuming life, far from the prying eyes of tourists or looky-loos. He could have occupied a place of fame at any animal park, but he was protected from such indignity by his caretakers. There are several good taxidermists in town, should you desire to follow that publicity-ridden route, and one or two respectable pet cemeteries exist." Udall cleared his perpetually froggy throat.

"Beagle began his life in the tropical land of Galapagos, but Beagle Gate was his last and most favorite home, and I'd like to strongly suggest he rest in the green grasses there." Udall looked wistful, like he had a soft spot for the old reptile. Susannah, still aghast at the revelation, would have suggested letting Udall bury him in his own backyard could she have made any utterance. Instead, she simply nodded as John took her arm and led her from the laboratory.

Out in John's Cherokee, Susannah's shock finally dissipated. "Yes!" she shouted and began to laugh. Upon this, John's staid countenance cracked into a smile and a then a full-blown jolly grin. It was several minutes before either of them could breathe regularly enough to even think of moving the Jeep into the nighttime traffic. At last, skin still tingling from the wild-abandon giggle fit, Susannah gathered her thoughts.

"Perhaps we ought to try and locate Beagle Gate, after all."

"Where is it?"

"My guess was Magna, but with being knee-deep in the hoopla,

I haven't even been by to inspect." She fumbled in her purse. "Here's the key envelope. Let's see." She shook the key free. Along with it fell a small card with a typed address. "Oh, look. Not Magna."

"Where is it?"

"D Street. Oh! Right near my fixer-upper. Home, Jeeves."

"Right-o."

Eventually they made their way back to the familiar Capitol Hill area. They drove up A Street where her little shell of a house sat vacant and dilapidated in the searing moonlight.

"It's not much, but it's home," she lamented. Its sagging porch framed its big, sad, empty, dark windows. "Do you think I'll ever get it finished?"

He laughed in sympathy. "What do you say we bulldoze it and plant a forest glade?"

"You mean, let it be gathered home to its fathers?"

"Put it out of its misery." He shrugged, and she couldn't disagree. They rounded the corner toward D Street, home of Beagle Park.

"What was the number again? 615. Look—wait. Is that it?" A huge stone-and-brick mansion peeped out from behind an iron gate flanked by huge oaks. The gate was open to the circular drive, which was lit with low-voltage lanterns, but all the windows were dark. John bravely soldiered into the property. "I hope we don't trip any alarms by driving in." He brought the Cherokee to a halt where they could see the address numbers visible by the light of the lamppost near the porch. 615. This was it. Beneath the house numbers hung the name "Harville." Susannah sucked in her breath.

Vines of ivy obscured much of the front of the house, but even in the dark, Susannah could make out the deep, teak-stained half timbers crisscrossing the white stucco and the texture of the stones that made up the east wing of the house. A carport topped by a weathervane opened a passageway into the tree-filled backyard.

"It's—it's—"

"It's everything you ever dreamed of in a tortoise palace."

"And more." Eyes a-goggling, they climbed out and wandered through the bright moonlight under the carport to amble around the grounds. Susannah felt like an intruder. She kept looking over her shoulder to see if some guard was going to come and accost them for trespassing. Fingering the key in her coat pocket, she reminded herself she was no stranger on these premises. She was the mistress of the house—true and legal owner of a non-condemned property in the Avenues of Salt Lake City.

A fountain nearly tripped her as she came around the corner into the back yard.

"Oh, look!" Beside the fountain a great glass greenhouse loomed above her. She tried the door. "John, tell me this isn't what I think it is."

Swinging the great glass door wide and flicking on the lights, the two saw what could only be termed "Beagle Gate:" huge slabs of rock, an Olympic-sized pool with natural edge and a sand beach, tropical shrubs and trees, every equatorial plant Susannah could identify (and many, many more), a garden filled with lettuce and other greens set up on a complex drip system, and a large, grassy area with a dirt-bottomed pit. The name Beagle was spelled out in smooth, round stones beside the pit, and a lawn chair stood sentinel over the empty nest. At the sight of the home, vacant of occupant and caring keeper, Susannah felt a lump form in her constricting throat.

"It's so sad."

"Yeah, a little." John's voice showed pathos, too. "But, I'll tell you what, Suzie." He rested his strong, rough, kind hands on both of her shoulders.

"I guess it's suspicious for me to bring this up right now, what with the day being one of major inheritances." He turned her to face him, and at long last Susannah could read John's eyes. She finally understood what Trevor meant about knowing when a proposal is impending.

"The thought does occur to me." Her eyebrow arched and she cocked her chin.

"But, you must know, Suzie, it's been coming on for some time now."

"Longer than most people are in medical school." She inched

closer to him. "Longer than it takes for a human to cut and lose and cut two sets of teeth."

"Five times as long as my mission."

"Six and two-thirds times as long as mine," she quickly calculated. "But—only a tenth as long as the average lifespan of a Galapagos tortoise." She smiled, sighed and looked over the miniature tropical world, sheltered from this cold winter's night. Waves from the blue sea lapped up on the shore. John touched her chin and turned it toward him.

"In spite of any suspicious timing, Susannah, and all the time we've both wasted, I think it's due time I gave you this." From his coat pocket he pulled a square velvet box in which sat a round cut diamond solitaire, shiny and new, on a platinum band. He knelt beside her. "Longer than there've been stars up in the heavens, I've been in love with you, Susannah. Will you marry me?" He placed the ring on her finger and kissed her well.

"I tell you what. We won't leave this wonderland vacant for long. I'm sure the children will love playing here."

Susannah melted into John's arms where she felt his cool breath on her cheek and inhaled his peppermint fresh scent. No doubt or confusion hindered her thoughts. The next step for her life was as brightly illuminated as a ray of sunshine glinting off a gold-plated angel. Suppressing a giggle she kissed him again. Ah. Susannah loved love, especially when he was her own.

CHOCOLATE CARAMEL TURTLES

Freshly shelled pecan halves
1 package milk chocolate morsels, melted
1 recipe microwave caramels (follows)

Place a 1/2" square of caramel (the shell) atop the centers of four pecan halves (the legs). Pour enough milk chocolate over so it covers and flows down the sides of the caramel and pecans. Chill until set.

MICROWAVE CARAMELS
(which will simplify your Christmas seasons forevermore)

½ cup of each of the following:
melted butter
brown sugar
white sugar
light corn syrup
sweetened condensed milk

Combine all ingredients and stir well, making sure there are no lumps of brown sugar. Microwave on high 5-6 minutes (all microwaves vary), do not stir. Pour into greased 8"x8" dish. Cool and serve. Use for making turtles or slice and wrap individually in waxed paper.

About the Author

Jennifer Griffith spent a year working in downtown Salt Lake City, and she ate chocolate pretty much every day during that time, just as she does today.

Her favorite recipe from this book is the Chocolate Mousse Filling for Crêpes. Her husband Gary likes the Chocolate Caramel Turtles, and her four kids will eat Grandma Stewart's Never Fail Chocolate Chip Cookies at record speed.

They live in Safford, Arizona. This is Jennifer's third novel.